THE ASSET

A PETE MADDOX THRILLER
BOOK 1

ALAN PETERSEN

17th
STREET
BOOKS

STAY CONNECTED

Sign up for my mailing list to receive a FREE copy of my Shaw-Maddox thriller, RED NOTICE. This exclusive download link is only available to my newsletter subscribers and is not for sale or available anywhere else but through my website.

AlanPetersen.com/join

CHAPTER ONE

COMANDANTE ZOLTAN

Colombia. Nariño Department.

IN THE WORLD OF BLACK OPS, PETE MADDOX MADE HIS bones in the mountains of Colombia near the border with Ecuador. It was FARC territory, and a Cessna aircraft carrying three DEA agents had just gone down.

Miraculously, the DEA agents survived the crash landing only to be kidnapped by FARC guerrillas who were demanding a five million dollar ransom for the agent's release.

The FARC had been battling the Colombian government for decades, with little to show for it. But to Maddox, a seasoned black ops specialist with the CIA, they were nothing more than a criminal organization masquerading as Marxist revolutionaries. They were nothing but ruthless gangsters, abetting the powerful drug cartels and terrorizing the local population.

The three DEA agents were a big score for the ragtag FARC squadron led by Comandante Zoltan, who was already in the DEA's most wanted list for that region. Holding its agents for ransom moved him to the top of the list.

Zoltan was already holding two American and three British citizens that worked for the mining companies in the area. The DEA agents upped the ante.

While the American, British, and Colombian governments pussyfooted with FARC, the Special Operations Group sent in Maddox.

The Bogotá CIA Station had a paid informant in Commander Zolton's group. For a price much cheaper than the five million dollar ransom demand, he would activate a tracking device at Zolton's makeshift mountainous camp and walk away.

They embedded Maddox with an extraction team from the 75th Ranger Regiment and a DEA Rapid Response unit. For Maddox, seeing the Rangers brought back memories. He had been an Army Ranger before joining the CIA.

But that felt like a previous lifetime to Maddox. He had to focus on his mission. His job on paper was to assist the Rangers rescuing the hostages. His actual job was to terminate Comandante Zoltan during the chaos of the extraction mission.

The staging area teemed with Rangers working with Colombian Special Forces soldiers along with the DEA's Rapid Response members. Then there were the spooks. Maddox along with intelligence officers from DAS–Colombia's intelligence agency.

Maddox was going over the dossier he had on Comandante Zoltan when he heard a familiar voice with its distinctive North East England accent.

"How are you doing, mate?"

Maddox smiled, seeing Tom Rose standing there in front of him.

"Nice to see you again, Tom," Maddox said. The two friends shook hands.

"I'm surprised to see you here," Maddox said.

"Well, those bastards are holding some of my countrymen, so they sent me down here to see if I can be of any help," Rose said.

"Absolutely. It will be nice to have someone around that knows my piece of the puzzle," Maddox said.

Tom Rose was with MI6, the British Secret Intelligence Service, which was the CIA counterpart in the United Kingdom. Rose had followed a career path similar to Maddox. Having served in the British military as a member of the SAS—Britain's elite and secretive Special Forces unit.

They had first met in Bosnia when working on a hostage rescue mission there.

"So what's the plan?" Rose asked.

Maddox filled him in with his assignment. Rose smiled and said, "taking out that piece of shit Zoltan is on MI6's wish list as well."

EARLY THE NEXT MORNING, while still dark, the extraction team mobilized to where the GPS tracking device had been planted by the informant.

A two person Ranger team comprising a sniper and spotter had been dispatched to scout the area where the GPS tracker planted by the informant was pinging. They had to make sure the informant had delivered the goods. Word got back to the staging area from the two Rangers that the information was good. They had found a camp deep in the mountainous jungle. And they had made visual confirmation. Comandante Zoltan was there. The scouts had also visually confirmed the small wooden structure with a thatch roof about half a mile from the campsite. It resembled a chicken coop. This is where the hostages were held, according to the informant.

The mission was green lit. The team prepared to strike while most of the guerrillas were sleeping and to take advantage of the cover of darkness. They used night vision goggles to make their way toward the camp in the pitch blackness of the jungle.

Maddox and Rose were equipped with MOPP protective gear provided by the Army Rangers and armed with Colt M4 carbine assault rifles. They stayed back as the extraction team went in full force, unleashing a series of deafening concussion grenade blasts and tear gas from shoulder-fired rocket-propelled grenade launchers.

Maddox watched the action going down with his night vision binoculars. He saw some guerillas crouched down as they covered their ears from the concussion grenades. Others ran off deeper into the jungle. The Rangers quickly put the ones who reached for their weapons down. A smaller unit of Rangers and DEA Rapid Response Team members made their way toward the small structure where the hostages were supposed to be held.

"Let's boogie," Maddox said. Rose nodded, and the two men began running toward the action. The guerrillas they encountered didn't want to fight as they scattered like roaches. Maddox let the Rangers handle them. He was after Zoltan. It would be a miracle finding the commander in the jungle's blackness amongst the chaos.

Minutes after the raid began, three choppers landed. Reinforcement Colombian Special Forces troops spilled out and began rushing the campsite, like angry ants streaming from a kicked out nest.

The screaming and sounds of gunfire soon subsided, and things quieted down. It had taken less than ten minutes to take down and secure the rebel encampment.

Maddox saw the hostages flanked by Rangers and Colombian soldiers as they were quickly led toward the waiting choppers and freedom.

The Colombian forces began zip tying the guerillas that had given up. Maddox saw several bodies laying on the forest floor dead or dying.

Maddox and Rose made it to the bell shaped tent platform the informant had said served as Comandante Zoltan's quarters.

Maddox was sweating profusely inside his gas mask, making it hard to see. Maddox and Rose cleared the commander's quarters. It was empty. Rose pointed to a trail of blood leading toward the back. They followed the trail that led off the tent platform onto the jungle floor. They had made a clearing leading away from the camp down an embankment. The wily veteran of guerrilla warfare had made an escape route. Maddox was crestfallen. He figured Comandante Zoltan had gotten away.

They followed the blood trail for a few feet and then they saw a body rolling on the ground like a turtle on its back. Rose shined a flashlight on the man with the scraggly beard laying there bleeding from several gunshot wounds. It was Comandante Zoltan in a t-shirt and underwear.

Maddox and Rose stood over him. "Ayúdame–help me–" the comandante pleaded as he writhed on the ground.

Maddox and Rose looked around. They could hear voices and action a couple hundred feet from them, but out there, it was just the three of them.

Maddox removed the gas mask. The cool subtropical mountain air felt good against his sweaty face. He switched the rifle from fully automatic to burst mode, then he hit the mounted light on his M4 with the back of his thumb, further illuminating the narco terrorist as he tried to drag himself away.

Maddox pulled the trigger, killing him.

CHAPTER TWO

THE NEXT ASSIGNMENT

CIA Headquarters. Langley, Virginia

Winter 1999

MADDOX STARED OUT OF THE FROST-COVERED WINDOW, trying to see beyond the leafless trees of the national park next to CIA headquarters in Langley, Virginia.

The Claude Moore Colonial Farm was down there somewhere. A long-time history buff, Maddox had always wanted to visit the park—a recreation of an eighteenth-century American tenant farm—but he'd never gotten around to going. It was only during boring meetings like these that his mind wandered to the park across the way.

Amazing, Maddox thought to himself as another CIA bureaucrat spewed out more drivel disguised as an important update. *One day you're in the jungle putting a bullet into the head of a narco-terrorist pseudo revolutionary leader, the next you're in a suit and tie in a bland, fluorescent-lit conference room. That's life in the game.*

It was a side of espionage rarely seen in the movies. James

Bond never filled out paperwork or sat in boring meetings. His office time was spent flirting with Moneypenny and playing with Q's latest gadgets.

It was a doozy of a meeting, one of those two-hour marathons of boredom that kept getting more boring with each passing minute. To an outsider, it would have looked like any other meeting in corporate America—the only difference was that it was a conference room full of spooks instead of businessmen. Some were like Maddox, operatives who had gotten their hands dirty working in paramilitary black ops. But most of those in attendance were pencil-pushing bureaucrats.

Careerwise, things were going good for Maddox. The success of the Colombia operation and his willingness to terminate a high value target had given him a large boost within the agency's special project power players.

After the meeting, Maddox headed back to his desk, which was located among a sea of fading grey cubicles in the Western Hemisphere's Latin America section. Until he received his next international assignment, he was stuck analyzing data from the collectors out in the field, then after work going back to his dull condo in the Northern Virginia suburbs. Life in the Beltway was too dull for Maddox.

———

THE NEXT DAY, Maddox had an early-morning meeting with his boss, Dick Philips. Philips was an old-school CIA legend closing in on his thirtieth year with the agency, and he had become Maddox's mentor. Philips kept his thinning gray hair short and combed to the left. He had a thin mustache which as gray as his hair. He wore black-rimmed, Clark Kent style glasses. He tended to dress in a brown tweed jacket and one of his ever-present bow ties, looking more like a professor than a master spy.

Phillips was born into a wealthy family and was a Yale legacy student. Although he had earned his PhD from there he didn't use the doctor title and didn't allow anyone to address him as such. Maddox liked that even though Philips bled blue he carried himself more as blue collar than Ivy League as most of the other scholarly spooks that permeated the agency.

Maddox walked up to the desk of Lois Gold, Philips's long-time secretary.

"Good morning, Lois," Maddox said as he approached the feared gatekeeper.

"Hi, Pete. He's ready for you; go on in." The gatekeeper had spoken, and Maddox was allowed to walk into Philips's office.

"Morning, Dick," Maddox greeted his boss as he walked into the spacious office.

"Pete," Dick said fondly, rising from his chair and extending his hand across his desk to shake hands. "Please, son, sit down."

Dick picked up a folder from his desk, smiled, and said, "Your new assignment came through. I wanted to let you know we appreciate the great work you've done for the agency over the years."

Maddox had known this was coming. A few months before leading the special operation and hostage rescue in Colombia, he had gone through advanced leadership training at Langley and graduated near the top of the class. That combined with the success of the Colombia mission had pretty much guaranteed him a promotion to running his own station.

"Congratulations, Pete, you're the new station chief for Venezuela." Philips walked around his huge wooden desk toward Maddox.

"Thank you, Dick," Maddox said as he rose from his chair to meet him. Philips shook his hand again and gave him the warm embrace of a proud father.

Maddox's mind raced. *Venezuela,* he thought, *not bad.* He had indicated to Dick that he preferred to remain in the Western Hemisphere division, since he'd worked most of his career in Latin America, and he was grateful his preference had been considered.

Maddox had been born in Panama, but at six three and with fair skin, brown hair, and piercing blue eyes, he looked more like his Minnesotan, farm-born father than his Panamanian mother. Maddox's father was a military man who had been stationed in Panama when he met and married Maddox's mother, a local from Colón.

Maddox had grown up an army brat in Panama, South Korea, the Philippines, and Italy. He was fluent in Spanish and understood the Latin American culture well, which had helped him rise through the ranks of the agency's Western Hemisphere division.

"You take over in January," Philips said.

Maddox was excited. It was a plum assignment for a first time station chief. The usual career track started with assignment to a smaller, backwater type post and then working one's way to larger, higher visibility posts. Landing Venezuela as his first station must have taken Philips a lot of backroom dealing. Maddox hoped he wouldn't disappoint him.

The intelligence community was still abuzz over the recent election of the self-described Bolivarian Socialist Revolutionary, Hugo Chávez, as president. Chávez was a career military man who had formed a secret socialist movement in the 1980s. He had actively sought to overthrow the government while serving as a top-ranking military officer. Chávez, along with a few fellow soldiers, had founded and led the very secretive

ELVP—Ejército de Liberación del Pueblo de Venezuela—the Venezuelan People's Liberation Army.

Chávez had first made it onto the CIA's radar in the early 1980s when he was an instructor at the Venezuelan military academy and began teaching his Marxist-Leninist socialist ideology to military cadets. There, he had planted the seeds of what he would one day call the Revolutionary Bolívarian Movement. His role as a military academy instructor had been perfect setup for Chávez to indoctrinate and recruit young future officers who would remain loyal to him as he rose in power.

After a failed coup attempt and serving a few years in prison, Chávez had been set free. He went from being an unknown revolutionary wannabe to a favorite of the country's poorest citizens, who supported his socialist, wealth redistribution, anti-rich rhetoric. Hugo Chávez spent four years running for president, traveling the country like a big-tent preacher and crusading against capitalism while pushing his Bolivarianism agenda.

Chávez worried the agency. The Langley bureaucrats had watched him closely on the campaign trail as he ratcheted up the anti-American rhetoric that become part of his shtick. Chávez seemingly came out of nowhere to win the Venezuelan presidency.

———

A FEW MONTHS LATER, in January 2000, while Hugo Chávez was about to celebrate his first year in office with a military parade and lots of planned celebrations, Maddox arrived in Caracas, Venezuela, too much less fanfare.

CHAPTER THREE

THE SONIA COLLINS FILE

Caracas, Venezuela. March 2000.

MADDOX HAD BEEN SETTLING INTO HIS NEW JOB. HE HAD been too busy to find an actual place to live, having been holed up in temporary housing at the embassy. It was time to get his own place.

The beautiful brunette who approached Maddox with a big, friendly smile and wide eyes stupefied him. "Mr. Maddox?" she asked, making full-on eye contact with him. It took a few seconds for the befuddled Maddox to get his bearings back.

"Yes, hello. You must be Sonia Collins?" Maddox asked as he felt his face reddening.

"Yes, Sonia Collins with Bolívar Realty. It's a pleasure to meet you." Her handshake was as firm as her eye contact, and it exuded a confidence he found appealing. Maddox was the first to break eye contact as he glanced behind her and focused on the parked Nissan Maxima, desperately hoping she didn't notice his flushed face.

Maddox knew of the country's reputation for being home to some of the world's most beautiful women. Between 1979 and 1996, a Miss Venezuela had become Miss Universe four times.

Sonia Collins had an athletic build and was dressed to the nines in fashionable couture. A white silk blouse was tucked neatly into a black skirt that stopped at her knees. She wore thigh high black leather boots that perfectly gloved her endlessly long legs. Maddox was reminded of a line from *Working Girl*, something about having a head for business and a body for sin. *Indeed*, Maddox thought. *Damn it*. His face was flushing again.

Maddox and Sonia had already spoken several times over the phone, mostly because he'd had to cancel a couple appointments at the last minute. She had never revealed even a hint of annoyance, assuring him that cancellations and reschedules were par for the course in her line of work.

"Are you ready for the first showing?" Sonia asked with a smile. She spoke fluent English with just a trace of an accent. Her voice was flinty and warm.

"Yes, ready to go," Maddox replied.

Maddox like that he and Sonia shared a similar background. Both their fathers were American expats that had married local women. And she too had grown up speaking both languages and straddling two different cultures.

Sonia planned to show Maddox three homes. He wasn't too concerned about the actual house he was going to rent; what mattered most was the location. He wanted a place in Baruta, which was a municipality within the Metropolitan District of Caracas in Venezuela, that was popular with the American expat community that was close to the embassy.

Sonia had already emailed him pictures and descriptions of available homes for rent in that area beforehand. All of them were centrally located in the quaint Baruta neighborhood known as Prados del Este.

Maddox looked at the property brochures Sonia had prepared while she drove through heavy traffic. She laid on her horn as someone cut her off. She smiled apologetically.

"The traffic here makes New York City traffic seem tame in comparison, don't you think?"

Maddox smiled. "It' a mess," he said, looking back down at the brochures.

He wasn't too concerned though. He had bought a red and river Ducati Super Sport motorcycle and even though the Diplomatic Security Service wasn't keen on him riding a motorcycle he wanted to be able to weave in out of traffic. It would save time being stuck in gridlock in one of stock white Ford Explorer SUV's from the embassy motor pool.

———

SONIA COLLINS STOLE another glance at the embassy man. He was good looking, but way too reserved for her taste. She regretted losing her cool with that idiot driver that cut her off since she needed to be as professional as possible with clients from the American embassy. The last thing she wanted was for word to get back to the embassy that she was road raging, getting herself booted from the embassy's recommended real estate agent list. She was excited to have another American Embassy employee as a client, especially a single one, and not just because she was single, single men were better clients since Embassy wives could be a pain in the rear, especially when their husbands were giggling like teenagers around her. The bachelors were great clients. They just wanted a nice place that was geographically convenient. Not much fuss and not likely that she would have to show them a dozen homes, like sometimes was the case with a bored spouse.

Pete Maddox was her fifth embassy client. Two of the previous ones had been bachelors. She had showed one of them three houses before he picked one, and the other single guy went with house number two. By contrast, she'd had to show twenty-one houses to a married couple with six children. *And in the end, they picked the first one they saw.* Sonia remembered. But she never complained, and she hid her annoyance because even the worse embassy clients were still better than non-embassy people. The embassy picked up the tab and made the process nice and easy for her. Embassy clients were money in the bank.

Real estate in Venezuela was not like in the United States. The Real Estate Association was just for show, with little bite to rein in bad behaving real estate agents. There were no real estate classes or tests to take, and agents weren't licensed, so it was a bit of a Wild West out in the market. It seemed every expat and taxi driver was a real estate agent. There was no such thing as an exclusive listing. Houses usually had multiple brokers carrying the listing. It wasn't unusual to see three different broker signs on a house.

Then there was the cutthroat side of the business. She'd had a few commissions stolen from her, so to land an embassy client was a godsend. She knew there would be no bullshit, and she knew she would get her commission. And since the State Department paid for everything, clients didn't usually care about the price as long as it was in their allotted range. *I wish all my clients were from the embassy,* she thought to herself.

All she knew about her new client, aside from his name, was that he was single and he was a Foreign Service officer in the political section of the US Embassy, whatever that meant.

Sonia had lined up four houses to show Maddox. But he

told her wasn't interested in one of them via email. So she was taking him to the other three.

The first home was nestled in the hillside. It sat back from the road, perched up high enough that it offered a spectacular view of the city down below. She parked in the driveway.

"Stunning view," she said.

"It sure is," Maddox said.

She opened the door, and they made their way inside.

———

MADDOX TOOK IT ALL IN. He liked what he saw. After about twenty minutes, he had seen enough.

"I'll take it."

Sonia looked at him befuddled. "I still have two other houses to show you."

"No need. I want this one," Maddox said.

"You're the boss," Sonia said with a smile. *God, she loved single embassy clients.*

———

IT TOOK a few days for the Diplomatic Security Service people to sign off on the property. Once that was cleared and the contracts signed, and necessary payments made, Maddox had his own place.

He settled into his new home, a two-story, white stucco house with a red slate roof. Its high wall and barred windows offered privacy and security, and the sharp glass embedded in the top of the wall—a standard practice in crime-ridden Caracas—provided an additional break-in deterrent.

It had been a few months since Maddox took over as station chief. At thirty-seven years old, he was much younger than most station chiefs—and most station chiefs did not have his paramilitary/black ops background. Although he had run several covert operations and black op missions, and had served as a deputy station chief for Dick Philips in Mexico, this was his first time being in charge of all CIA operations in a country.

Maddox was still besotted with the beautiful Sonia Collins, but had decided not to act on it. He did, however, have his analysts do a full background workup on her; since he did the same with just about anyone he met on the job—crush or no crush—it was easy to justify to himself. And just like that, the Sonia Collins file was created.

Sonia had been born and raised in Caracas. Her father was an American originally from Chicago and her mother from the Venezuelan state of Aragua, which allowed Sonia to enjoy dual citizenship.

Her father was a successful executive for. a pharmaceutical conglomerate that also sold medical supplies.

Her mother, Luz, was a former beauty queen. In her youth, she had also been a model and had acted in several Venevisión telenovelas soap operas in the fifties and early sixties. Maddox had seen an old picture of Luz and knew where Sonia had gotten her *Vogue* magazine looks from.

Sonia had caught the tail end of her father's corporate globetrotting career. She spent a few years as a child in Chicago, where the company was headquartered, before he retired and moved the family to Venezuela.

She was college educated and had been working in real estate for several years.

There wasn't much to her file, Maddox thought. Which was a good thing. He closed the folder and yawned.

He got up from his desk and looked out the window. It was getting late.

The embassy sprawled across a twenty-seven-acre mountainside site and overlooked the Las Mercedes district of Caracas. It was prime real estate with stunning views of the valley. The structure was a five-story, modern-looking building with a red granite exterior, totaling 95,000 square feet. The building housed all the country's US agencies, and the CIA occupied the entire fifth floor. It could be a funny thing, the spook business. Although they were secretive and there wasn't a "*CIA – Fifth Floor*" listing in the lobby directory, most everyone in the embassy knew the fifth floor was the floor of the spooks.

The CIA officially kept its presence secret, but it was an easy giveaway if you worked inside the embassy. The Marine Security Guard Battalion heavily guarded the embassy. This was true for every US embassy in the world. So it wasn't like you could just waltz into the embassy, but access to the fifth floor was heavily restricted (unlike the other floors), even for other embassy employees.

It was the only entrance inside the embassy that was behind a crypto-code military keypad system with a heavy-duty brute lock. No one was coming in without the access code. There was also a camera protruding from the ceiling hovering over the door. Anyone loitering by the entrance for more than a few seconds would hear a monotone voice from the intercom suddenly ask, "May I help you?" which, on more than one occasion, had scared the shit out of employees who might have gotten lost or were curious about the mysterious fifth floor.

Each CIA staff member had his or her own access key, which changed every month. Each agent had to key in their unique code in order to enter the fifth-floor offices – no piggybacking allowed, the eye in the sky was watching.

The fifth floor seemed louder than the other floors in the embassy building. Perhaps it was the radios that were always on in the background – loud noises were a great way to interfere with listening devices. There were more than a hundred employees at the embassy and just about half were CIA operatives, much to the chagrin of the real diplomats.

To keep the diplomatic mission pure in the eyes of the State Department, they insisted that CIA operatives were not to be placed as covers within the Foreign Service Officer core. The CIA agreed on principle and didn't usually place CIA operatives within the FSO branch, but sometimes an operative needed to be buried deep, and the FSO was a great place to hide in plain sight.

For now, Maddox was honoring this long-standing request, and the Caracas FSO branch was spook free. More often, CIA operatives went by the official job title of Foreign Service Staff (FSS). All the political officers were CIA agents. About a dozen other CIA operatives were planted as military personnel with titles like political attaché or military advisor.

For such a secret agency, the spooks were easy for other embassy employees to spot because CIA personnel stuck together. When they went to lunch, met for happy hour, or went on routine embassy business, they usually went with each other and didn't really mingle with non-CIA embassy personnel. Therefore, once you had pegged one from the fifth floor, you could quickly figure out the rest of the spooks. This was an ongoing game for the other embassy staff, playing pick out the spook.

The situation in Venezuela was causing concerns with Langley. At first, the new Venezuelan president had been just a nuisance. As a military commander, his left-wing rhetoric had been more of an annoyance than a threat, and he had been jailed after his failed coup d'état. But then the Venezuelan government had released him from prison in an appeasement attempt, since his Robin Hood image made him a popular figure with the poor. Once free, Chávez had begun to amp up the rhetoric, this time not as a revolutionary soldier, but as a revolutionary politician.

The CIA had provided financial resources to the opposition candidate, but Hugo Chávez had had the poor population firmly on his side and, with almost forty percent of the population below the poverty line, his candidacy received a huge boost.

To the United States, his socialist agenda and cheerleading was annoying, but it didn't rise to the level of action. Still, his anti-Western—and especially his anti-American—rhetoric was making enough people in DC worried that the boys at Langley were keeping a closer eye on what was going on politically in Venezuela.

That Venezuela sat on a lot of oil and many American companies did business there made the US government even more nervous when Chávez talked about nationalization and socialism; his burgeoning friendship with the beard in Cuba and the colonel in Libya didn't do anything to ease the increasing concerns growing in DC.

Forty years ago, the CIA probably would have taken Chávez out. As Dick Philips often said, "If history has taught us anything, it's that we need to take care of problems before they become big problems." As long as it was just talk, two presidential administrations were fine with looking the other way.

Philips had sensed things were probably going to get worse and not better with Chávez, which is was why he had wanted someone like Maddox from the black ops core as station chief.

Maddox yawned again. *Time to go home.* Finally he could say that.

CHAPTER FOUR

EL HELICOIDE

It's always a bit of a dance when spooks meet in person, especially when they serve different flags. The spy business is just that, a business, and as with any business relationship, sometimes it can be cordial, sometimes friendly, sometimes acrimonious, and sometimes even deadly.

Maddox had struck up a friendship with Lieutenant Henry Calderon, DISIP's attaché to the CIA.

DISIP stood for Dirección Nacional de los Servicios de Inteligencia y Prevención. It was the Venezuelan equivalent of the CIA, and the two organizations often interacted with each other in good ways, and bad ways.

Henry Calderon, age thirty-two, was younger than Maddox. Calderon had started his career as a soldier in the Venezuelan Army and then joined the Caracas Municipal Police. Four years ago, he left the police for DISIP. He was educated at the University of Venezuela, received extensive training from the US military, and even attended a training course run by the DEA at the FBI's training facility in Quantico, Virginia.

Calderon had wavy black hair and brown eyes. At six three, Maddox had always been considered tall, but in Venezuela he was a giant. Calderon was average height for a Venezuelan male at around five seven, so Maddox towered over him, but what the DISIP agent lacked in height, he made up for in spades with a Herculean physique that made men jealous and women swoon.

Maddox's dossier on Calderon was thorough on the personal side as usual. The man loved pop culture and American pop culture in particular—American movies, TV shows, and music. The two men hit it off right away with their love of hard rock bands like Iron Maiden, Scorpions, and AC/DC.

Calderon was one of those guys who was always cracking jokes and putting everyone around him at ease. He was married with two young children, but he also had at least two serious mistresses, one illegitimate son—whom he supported—many one-night flings, and a predilection for prostitutes. "Fewer complications that way," he explained. All in all, Henry Calderon loved women, sex, and partying—all dangerous hobbies for a spy.

Even though Maddox suspected there might be a sex addiction at play with Calderon, he still enjoyed living vicariously through Henry's wild stories. But it wasn't just the good-time stories that Maddox enjoyed; Calderon had become a top asset, and addictions could come in handy when managing assets.

Maddox had first met Calderon when the DISIP agent paid him a visit at the US Embassy; he had won Maddox over with his Tony Montana impression.

In between the jokes, stories, and backslapping, Maddox

had sized up Henry and knew Henry was doing the same with him.

Eventually, a true friendship developed between the two men. They even hung out together, drinking Cerveza Zulia and having a good time. Each time they met, Henry tried to get Maddox laid by a Venezuelan beauty queen. Maddox believed it was a misplaced genuine gesture of friendship, but he would never allow himself to be compromised in that way so, to Calderon's dismay, Maddox turned down not only Calderon's attempted hookups, but the other women who would throw themselves at him as well.

Although Calderon and Maddox were getting along well, the relationship between the CIA and DISIP which ran hot and cold depending who was president. Since Chávez became president the American-Venezuelan relationship had deteriorated drastically.

Hugo Chávez had become more and more eccentric, and his anti-American rhetoric was getting worse. The president had also begun putting his most loyal people—known as Chávistas—in power. Maddox thought it gave Chávez a Jim Jones vibe, but at least Calderon had refused to drink the Kool-Aid.

Unfortunately for Maddox, the head of DISIP was one of the most loyal Chávistas in the military. Antonio Dos Santos, a two-star general who went way back with Chávez to when both men were young Army officers. Dos Santos had attended the Venezuelan Military Academy with Chávez and rose through the ranks at the same time.

Dos Santos was political and careful, so he had Johann Brull—Calderon's boss and the chief of the DISIP's secret police—do the heavy lifting when it came to laying down the party line and punishing those who didn't toe it.

Brull was one of the most feared men in Venezuela. He'd

made his terrible reputation in the border skirmishes with Colombia and had earned the nickname "el Sadista del Helicoide" *the Sadist of Helicoide* through his strong-arm tactics and his use of torture deep in the catacombs of the Helicoide building.

Brull's brutality had earned him a feared reputation among not only his enemies, but his own troops as well, and the generals viewed him as someone they could count on to get the dirty work done. He had been quickly promoted through the ranks until he became a counterintelligence commander for the army, where his specialty was ensuring the military remained loyal to the president. He had proven himself as a loyal, skull-cracking Chávista.

———

JOHAN BRULL HAD GROWN up dirt-poor on the streets in the Venezuelan rural state of Mérida. He was of Guajiro indigenous and African ancestry. During his impoverished childhood, he developed a hatred for the elite upper class of Venezuela. Had winning a coveted scholarship to the military academy not saved him, he would have probably become a street mobster. But even though he was a highly decorated military officer, he was just as ruthless and corrupt as a mobster—it was just government mob now.

Because of his pockmarked dark skin and Guajiro ethnic features, he had encountered a lot of prejudice and endured much torment growing up, especially at the hands of the Venezuelan elite class, who were fair skinned and mostly descendent from Spain. Brull's early nickname had been "Indio" *Indian*, and he had hated it. As his power grew and his penchant for brutality became known, however, no one dared to call him Indio anymore. Brull had grown to hate what he perceived as the elite white oppressors of the indigenous people, so it was no surprise that he took an immediate disliking to the fair-skinned Maddox, even though Maddox had been born in Panama, was raised throughout Latin America, and spoke Spanish fluently.

———

MADDOX DROVE through the San Agustin Municipality of Caracas in an embassy-issued white SUV. As usual, the Caracas freeway was jammed with cars, trucks, and buses. There were motorcycles as well, but they buzzed around like mosquitos, zigzagging between traffic and splitting lanes in order to maneuver around the gridlock. Maddox wished he were riding his Ducati. It would have been much less frustrating.

The traffic seemed to get worse as he made way through the concrete landscape of contradictions. Bustling office buildings full of lawyers, bankers, and other business types stood next to all but abandoned decrepit structures populated only by the occasional dregs seen mulling around.

Finally, traffic loosened up as Maddox exited the freeway and began spiraling onto Calle Helicoide, making his way up the steep road toward the huge DISIP compound that overlooked the city below. In the middle of the compound sat the large, cone-shaped building that housed the DISIP headquarters. It was perched on the hilltop like an ominous gargoyle, casting a shadow of fear over the city.

El Helicoide had been built in the late fifties, and it showed. It's weathered, gray concrete slab exterior facade looked like something out of Orwell's 1984. The citizens down below knew this was a building where people went to be tortured and made to disappear, so there was always an uneasy feeling entering that building, even for someone like Maddox.

Henry seemed ashamed as he escorted Maddox down the long winding corridors of El Helicoide to meet with Brull. Twenty minutes passed as they went deeper and deeper inside. The men finally arrived at a windowless, dark and dreary section of the building. Steel doors on both sides lined the corridor like a prison.

Henry stopped at one of the doors and knocked. After a couple of minutes, another DISIP agent opened it, and Maddox could see a young man tied by his wrists to a steel bar fastened to the ceiling. The man's feet dangled about five feet from the floor. He was covered in sweat and blood. A small medical table littered with torture devices—including many rust-covered tools and a car battery—was visible off to the side.

Brull walked out to greet Maddox as he wiped his hand with a dirty rag. "Ah, Mr. Castro," Brull said, addressing Maddox by his pseudonym, Rick Castro. "Dejalo ginando" *Leave him hanging*, he ordered to the other man inside, tossing the rag onto the concrete floor. The other DISIP agent closed the door behind him.

Brull wiped the sweat from his brow on the sleeve of his olive green uniform and then tugged at the rest of the garment in an attempt to look more presentable. He had a thin, cheesy mustache; his jet-black hair was combed back and held in place by some god-awful smelling gel.

Finally satisfied with his appearance, he extended his hand and offered Maddox a dead fish handshake as he gave him a quick, indifferent glance.

"Walk with me," he ordered condescendingly as he began to lead Maddox and Calderon back up to the main part of the building. Even though it was Brull who had asked for the meeting, he acted as if Maddox's visit was an inconvenience.

Maddox knew his witnessing the torture scene in the cell was no accident. Brull had wanted to give him a glimpse of their interrogation methods and show his true colors without saying a word.

Ever the pragmatist, Maddox thought to himself, *Who knows? Maybe the dude hanging from the rafter had it coming.* Maybe he was a terrorist. Or a drug kingpin—though that was unlikely since the government and the drug cartels had a cozy working relationship. Regardless, Brull's pathetic display of power and arrogance and the thinly veiled threat it implied made Maddox dislike him even more than before.

Twenty-five minutes later, they all sat in Brull's scantly decorated office. The man himself sat behind a large steel desk, still acting as if Maddox were inconveniencing him. *Hey, this is your meeting, asshole*, Maddox thought to himself as he stared back without saying anything. *Let's see who blinks by talking first*, Maddox said to himself, still staring down Brull in silence.

"Mr. Castro," Brull said, placing a cigarillo between his lips, "what can you tell me about our two soldiers killed near the Colombian border last week?" Maddox smiled at the broken silence as Brull focused on lighting the cigarillo. When the secret police chief finished his task, he looked at Maddox, who sat opposite him. Plumes of smoke trailed up from his mouth and quickly filled the small, windowless office.

"Absolutely nothing," Maddox replied in his most offended tone. "You guys have been at it for years. Don't try to pin this on us." Maddox returned to playing the stare down game with Brull.

Though he was intentionally egging Brull on, Maddox wasn't bullshitting. Colombia and Venezuela shared more than the same liberator from Spanish colonialism; they had a long antagonistic history in the same vein as India and Pakistan. When the two countries gained their independence from Spain they became one nation—Gran Colombia. That union quickly dissolved due to infighting, and two separate countries were formed. Since the nineteenth century, diplomatic relations had been strong, severed, back on, strong, severed, and back on. Sometimes there was peace and friendly cooperation, other times there were border conflicts and bilateral struggles. This had gone on for over a hundred years, so for Brull to take a pot shot at the United States for this latest brouhaha annoyed Maddox.

"What about DEA?" Brull said in his broken English.

"I don't know, Colonel Brull. Ask them. We're not involved here, and I have no information for you," Maddox replied curtly.

Brull's infamous temper flared, and he became furious. "I know CIA and DEA are all the same, and you American, are all spying!" he shouted as he banged his fist on his steel desk.

"I can assure you that is not the case," Maddox said calmly.

Brull stewed and threatened to kick the CIA and DEA out of Venezuela for spying. Maddox let Brull blow off the steam over his two dead soldiers. Maddox wasn't being coy. This was not a CIA operation, and the DEA did not spy for the CIA. The two agencies did work together fighting drug trafficking into the US, as a lot of the drug money went to terrorist groups like the FARC in Colombia, but that wasn't the case here. Venezuela had long been a stop on the illegal drug path from Colombia to the United States.

The Venezuelan military was corrupt, and they worked with the Colombian drug cartels with impunity. More than likely, what had happened was a drug deal gone bad, and Brull wanted to know what had happened to his drugs.

The meeting abruptly came to an end as Brull continued threatening to expel Maddox from the country in between drags from his cigarillo.

As Henry escorted Maddox out to his vehicle, he apologized for Brull.

"Your boss is a real asshole," Maddox said when they made it to the visitors' parking lot.

Henry took a quick glance around to make sure he wouldn't end up hanging from the rafters. "Yeah, man, sorry about that. We're good?" he asked as he put out his arms toward Maddox.

"Yeah, man, we're chevere cambur," Maddox said, using the Venezuelan slang expression for "excellent."

Henry grinned at Maddox's use of the Venezuelan colloquialism and waved as the CIA agent got into his SUV and drove off.

Things are chevere indeed, Maddox thought to himself. Maddox had recruited Calderon a few months ago as a paid asset, and the attaché was passing him valuable information as to what was going on inside El Helicoide. As US-Venezuelan diplomatic relations continued to worsen, Calderon was proving to be more and more valuable.

Little did Maddox know whatCalderon was working on.

As Maddox drove off El Helicoide and back down the hill, Calderon remained outside, smoking a cigarette as he watched his friend depart. Calderon felt he could trust Maddox, and he knew the time was just about right to bring him in on the deal; he just had to wait for the okay to do so.

Maddox had also grown to trust Calderon. It was he who had confirmed Chávez making Gaddafi's *The Green Book* required reading for all his military officers and school-age kids in rural Venezuelan public schools. Chávez had long been one of Colonel Gaddafi's biggest supporters and, while in the army, he had studied *The Green Book*, a short text that laid out Gaddafi's political philosophy—namely the rejection of democracy, free press, and capitalism. That alone was enough to get Langley's attention.

CHAPTER FIVE

RECRUITMENT

Caracas, Venezuela.

AFTER SIX MONTHS IN THE COUNTRY, MADDOX FELT HE had a good grasp at the lay of the land as station chief.. For all the Chavezism rhetoric against the United States, the job was of a desk job than he thought it would or that he liked. He was a man of action, not one to ride a desk.

His social life had been nonexistent and couldn't stop thinking about Sonia Collins, so he called her.

At first, they met for coffee a couple times, Then lunch. They had gotten along well. Although he tried to minimize political talk she had made it clear she wasn't happy in the direction the country was headed.

The Chávez regime had made Venezuela a more dangerous country—one with increased murder, kidnapping, and violent crime rates—which had led the US State Department to recommend Americans not travel there; this recommendation had decimated the lucrative tourist business. Additionally, the nationalization of many of the principle business sectors had forced expats out of the country in droves, directly impacting Sonia's real estate business.

Maddox thought she would make a good asset for the agency, so he invited her out for dinner.

He had always played it professionally with her, not wanting to mislead her, but when she showed up at the bar dressed to the nines, Maddox felt like he had indeed sent the wrong message. And he felt like an idiot about it. But he had already decided to recruit her as a potential asset to the agency. Nothing more.

They ordered drinks, a Zulia beer for Maddox and a Smirnoff Vodka Lemon Drop Martini for Sonia, and then even though it made Maddox feel like an asshole, he immediately got to the point of why he had asked her out as to minimize the mixed signals he must have been sending.

"Sonia, I have a business opportunity I want to discuss with you tonight."

The disappointment in her eyes was palpable, and the reaction took Maddox aback. Before, he had dismissed the idea that Sonia had feelings for him, but that look told him he had been wrong.

Push through it, he said to himself.

"The embassy would like to retain your services as our exclusive real estate broker," he said. "We'll offer you a monthly salary and an operational budget for a new office so you can bring on new agents to handle embassy business. Your real estate commissions would stay the same, so these other benefits would be on top of your sale commissions."

"You're offering me a job?" she asked, annoyed.

"You would be an independent contractor for the US government, but basically, yes, I'm offering you a job," Maddox said. He shifted uncomfortably, then thankfully the waiter arrived just then with their drinks, and Sonia broke her steely glare and sipped on her Martini.

The tension and awkwardness was palpable. Maddox could see her mulling the events of the evening thus far. She took anther sip of her drink. Then she looked at Maddox and smiled. She raised her glass in the air.

"To new business opportunities," she said. A chill to her voice.

Maddox clinked her glass.

"Cheers," he said.

Sonia pressed Maddox for more details, but he was evasive. He couldn't talk freely in a public restraint like this, so asked her to meet with him at the embassy in the morning.

She seemed annoyed, but agreed. Dinner arrived, and Maddox felt like a heel having ruined the evening. At first they ate in silence, but not for long. Soon they began to smile and laugh as they ate. He felt at ease with her.

———

THE NEXT DAY, Maddox welcomed Sonia to the embassy. She was now in business mode.

"Cut the shit, Pete, You're with the CIA, right?" Sonia said.

Maddox loved her spunk and directness. "Not directly. I'm a liaison." Lying was part of the job for spooks like Maddox.

"I'm no spook. I don't know any secret government secrets that I can pass along to your government. So what do you want with me?" Sonia said.

"I'm not asking you to spy. As I mentioned to you last night, you would be the exclusive real estate broker for the American embassy. That means all embassy employees and contractors would go through you for all real estate needs."

"I can't drop my other clients."

"Not asking you to do that. It's not as if this would be a full time job for you," Maddox said. "Continue doing what you're doing, just that now you would handle our real estate needs. Sometimes it will be for embassy personnel, sometimes, we'll just a place that you can find for us and get us in there without making it official that's it's for the US government and without you knowing what we need it for."

Sonia eye's got big. "Liaison my ass."

Maddox shrugged. "That all I am, sorry to disappoint."

She looked at him suspiciously.

"Honestly, that part of the job will be a tiny part of you'll do for us. Ninety percent is just like what you've been doing for the embassy already. Finding homes for our people. Just like you did for me."

"That's it?"

"Scout's honor," Maddox said flashing the scout salute which made Sonia laugh.

———

ON THE DRIVE HOME, Sonia wasn't sure what she had gotten herself into. The previous night, she thought she was meeting Maddox out for a date. Only to find out it was a business dinner. And how he wants her to be the exclusive real estate agent for the embassy. At first she was disappointed. She liked him. But then the businesswoman took over. This could be a boon for her business. There was all the weird talk about providing houses on the download. She'd seen enough movies to know these were probably CIA safe houses. But in typical spook talk he wouldn't confirm or deny it. But he reassured her that most of the business needs would be on the up and up. Finding homes for embassy people.

Not only would her commissions increase but they would

also pay for office space and offer her a monthly salary for her troubles.

It seemed like a great opportunity. There was a concern and fear that niggled at her. What would the Bolivarian Secret Police to do her if they found out about this arrangement?

And for all the denials and who me looks Maddox gave her, she knew, deep down, who he was, and it wasn't just a simple liaison. He was CIA. And that could be dangerous.

CHAPTER SIX

ASSETS

Six Months Later.

BOLÍVAR REALTY BOOMED. IT HAD BECOME A PREMIERE real estate company. Sonia had leased office space in a modern business commercial center in Caracas with the agency picking up the tab.

Sonia added three full-time real estate agents. One agent, Graciela Kohl, had grown up with Sonia and was one of her best friends. Graciela excelled in sales and marketing and was fluent in English, German, and her native Spanish. There was also Eddy Rocamora and en American expat, Jerry Low. The new agents allowed Sonia to take on more of a manager and allowed her to become the unofficial property manager for Maddox. She was the only one at Bolívar Realty that deal with that part of the business.

They had dropped the veneer of her role as she began working directly with Maddox, who was very pleased at what a valuable asset Sonia had become.

He trusted her and when he wanted to put surveillance on

the Russian and Libyan embassies; he relied on her to find the properties and handle the transaction that shielded that the agency was the actual owner or tenant.

Once the property was under CIA control, Maddox would send in a team from the Special Surveillance Group to wire up the house with state-of-the-art surveillance to keep tabs on the comings and going via audio and video day and night.

Sonia had also proved to be an invaluable and trustworthy asset in the field. She had handled the transactions on several properties along the Colombian border, which served as safe houses for Colombian cartel informants and undercover agents, and she had made sure the residents were taken care of and the homes stocked with supplies.

She had kept her finger on the pulse of the neighborhoods. On more than one occasion, wounded men had been treated in these safe houses. Sonia's company had so many listings and properties under management that she could easily switch safe houses without raising the suspicions of the neighbors or, even worse, the DISIP.

As Sonia's role as an asset had grown, so did the danger. Maddox was trained to handle it, and if he were exposed, they would expel him from the country; it would be a different situation for Sonia. For all intents and purposes, she was a traitor to the Chávez government. Assets like Sonia, who were on the CIA payroll but weren't official employees, did not have diplomatic protection, so they were subject to arrest, torture, and death.

Professional spies know the risks, but civilians like Sonia were more naïve about what they were getting into, and Maddox had felt the old Catholic guilt for bringing her into his world.

To make sure the connection between Bolívar Realty and the CIA wouldn't be exposed—that there were no financial trails leading from Bolivar Realty to Langley — Maddox had handpicked the best CIA attorney and accountant to set up the business entities for each transaction that would hide where the money was coming from. On several occasions, he'd had one of the top CIA forensic accountants look into the documents to see if they were leaving a paper trail that could expose Sonia. The audits checked out. And she was safe.

The more time he spent with Sonia, the more feelings he had developed for her, which was just the situation he had tried to avoid since they had met. The timing was made worse now that he had involved her deeply into the agency business.

As the Hugo Chávez problem became bigger, Maddox's need for safe houses increased. There were many phantom renters and homeowners around Venezuela who only existed on paper. Maddox relied on Sonia to manage the safe houses more and more. He needed someone who knew the country and real estate market well and who he could trust. Sonia was that person on the ground that he could trust.

* * *

Sonia Collins wasn't Maddox's only important asset. Henry Calderon, the Intelligence officer with DISIP, had provided Maddox with worthwhile intelligence that became more important as Chávez amped up his ant-American policies while getting closer as political allies to the likes of Muammar Gaddafi and Fidel Castro.

For assets like Henry Calderon, who were professional intelligence officers, death was a certainty if caught, but he knew this and risked it willingly. Most assets usually did it just for the money, but for Calderon, there was more to it, though the money was an enormous factor; it was expensive having a wife and three kids, two mistresses, and another illegitimate child on the way, especially on a DISIP salary.

Corruption in the government was the norm, but although

Calderon had his fingers in many pies, he wasn't as corrupt as his colleagues; he avoided drug cartel payouts, so the extra income stream from the CIA was welcomed.

———

BEYOND THE GOOD money he was making from the Americans, Calderon had other non financial reasons. He had become disillusioned with Hugo Chávez Bolivarian Revolution. It seemed they had swapped one corrupt entity with another one to run the country into the ground.

For all the president's talk of helping the poor and changing the dire economic situation of Venezuela, nothing had yet come to fruition.

Venezuela was an oil rich country. Calderon believed it should be the Kuwait of Latin America; instead, over fifty percent of Venezuelans lived below the poverty line, and the percentage had gotten worse, not better, since Chávez became president. Crime and violence were becoming national epidemics, and Chávez's buffoonery embarrassed Calderon. While other countries largely saw the president as a joke, Calderon knew well how brutal this buffoon could be and how he led with an iron fist, stifling dissent and opposition. And Calderon wasn't alone in thinking that way. A group of disillusioned government official had began to meet, including Calderon.

But if they were to succeed they needed help from the Americans. Calderon had been tasked with reaching out to Maddox.

CHAPTER SEVEN

RAID

WHAT THE HELL AM I DOING BRINGING HER ALONG? Maddox thought to himself as he flew a Cessna airplane from Caracas to San Cristobal. Sonia sat next to him looking out the window bewildered and feeling airsick.

"I don't like this puddle jumper," she said as the small aircraft took off from Caracas.

San Cristobal was the capital city of Tachira which was located high up in a beautiful, mountainous region of Western Venezuela; it was also only thirty miles from the Colombian border, making it a hotspot for drug activity and FARC.

The mountain winds effortlessly whipped the small aircraft around, causing it to bounce up and down in a nauseating and nerve-wracking dance. The turbulent skies gave everyone aboard the corporate jet an uneasy feeling that they were about to tumble from the sky.

Sharing the flight with Maddox and Sonia were Ron Bateman, a twelve-year CIA Officer and Maddox's second in command in Venezuela; Troy Sennight, a technical analyst and Maddox's go-to tech guy; Ruben Guzman, an intelligence officer with Colombia's DAS.

Guzman had reached out to Maddox for help. A small group of Colombian FARC guerrillas had hijacked a bus in the Colombian-Venezuelan border town of Ragonvalia.

This was the same cell that had kidnapped an American, Brian Hart, over a year ago. Hart had been a former member of the Peace Corps who moved to Colombia to work as a math teacher for one of the English-language schools in Bogotá. He had been exploring the countryside when he drove into an ELN checkpoint near Ragonvalia. The rebels had kidnapped him and demanded a million dollars in ransom—money his family did not have. He was now presumed dead.

The groups latest attempt at kidnapping had spiraled out of control, resulting in the massacring of several civilians.

The rebels had stopped a public bus carrying thirty-two passengers who were headed from Ragonvalia to Medellín. They had already killed the bus driver and were unloading the passengers when a Colombian Army platoon stumbled upon the scene. A firefight erupted and the guerrillas had opened fire on the bus passengers, killing eleven innocent riders, and then engaged in a short but fierce battle with the Colombian Army before retreating back into the mountains, using the remaining hostages on the bus as human shields.

The Colombian military had killed six of the FARC terrorists before the rest of the group were able to escape. The Colombian Army had lost one man in the fight and several others were wounded.

Although it faced intense pressure from the Colombian government and the press, the Venezuelan government was dragging its feet, refusing to investigate and make arrests in order to extradite the guilty men back to Colombia.

The DAS feared Venezuelan officials would tip off the FARC terrorists hiding in Venezuela that they were on to them, so it was time to take action. While the negotiations continued between the Colombian and Venezuelan governments, Ruben Guzman had reached out to his old friend, Pete Maddox.

Venezuela would never allow the Colombian military to cross the border to get the men responsible for the massacre, so they needed to get in and out quickly, which was Maddox's specialty.

Sonia had located a house for rent near the FARC safe house in San Cristobal, so they were en route to set up a command center there. Within hours of landing, Sonia had the keys to the property. An explanation involving the need to prep the house for its impending occupant and paying six months' rent in advance had worked like a charm.

Sonia was waiting to let Maddox and his team inside when they arrived at the house. Within a few hours, Guzman and a team of six Colombian Special Forces soldiers had arrived as well, and Troy Sennight had set up his eavesdropping and surveillance gadgets in the house.

The plan was to keep an eye on the guerrillas, who were hiding in a safe house a few houses down from the CIA house Sonia had set up. It was small, low-income neighborhood where most people kept to themselves.

Although Sonia had secured many such properties for Maddox and the CIA, this was the first time she had seen this type of action up front in that way.

The Colombian Rapid Deployment Force and the DAS agents were armed with their Heckler & Koch MP5 machine guns, the same weapons used by the American Special Forces.

Maddox carried his SIG Sauer at his side and Walther PPK .380 compact pistol strapped into an ankle holster, but since this was especially dangerous mission, he had also brought an FN P90 submachine gun with a fifty-round, double-stack magazine. Sennight also carried a P226 SIG Sauer. Bateman was armed with a 9mm Glock.

This display of firepower was Sonia's first glimpse of the dangerous side of the work Maddox did. The cutesy flirting she had engaged in with the good-looking CIA officer seemed silly to her now that she was seeing this side of him.

Maddox caught her staring at him as he armed himself and checked the other weapons. He flashed a reassuring smile, as if to say, *Hey, it's still just me.*

She looked down nervously. Sonia wasn't used to this world. It scared her.

While Sennight set up the gadget, Maddox walked down the block to an arepa luncheon he had seen. He bought cheese and ham arepas for everyone and brought them back to the house. Sonia made a pot of coffee.

Sennight scarfed down the arepa as he worked setting up his monitors and computer equipment. He wore a wrinkled Captain America t-shirt and dirty blue jeans. He looked like a cross between John Belushi and Jack Black—save for having dirty blond hair. He might have looked like a shrub but he was also a highly skilled MIT educated CIA tech expert.

"You don't like a spy," Sonia said.

Sennight and Maddox laughed. "That's because I'm not. Think of me as his IT support," Sennight said pointing at Maddox.

Ron Bateman was all business. Sonia got the feeling that he didn't care much for her. She didn't know why, nor did she ask him, but she just got a vibe from him.

Bateman looked like an actuary, not a CIA agent. He had

thinning black hair that was always neatly combed to the side. He wasn't totally bald yet, but was dangerously close to sporting a comb-over.

Since Sonia got the feeling that Bateman did not like her, she didn't care much for him either. Perhaps Bateman wasn't thrilled with having a female real estate broker who dressed in the latest fashion and always had perfect makeup coming along on CIA business. They never said anything bad to each other; they simply kept their interactions limited. But she had overheard Bateman telling Maddox:

"A trained operator should be managing our safe houses, not a civilian."

"First, I trust her. Second, she manages the procurement of the safe houses, not what goes on inside," Maddox had replied.

Two hours after arriving at the house, the command center was up and running and the joint Colombian-American operation on Venezuelan soil was in motion.

The plan was for the Colombian team to enter Venezuela, illegally and rendezvous with Maddox at the San Cristobal house. They would then all hit the cell down the street.

They would take them out and collect intelligence. Maddox wanted to find out what happened to Hart. Once the mission was complete they would cross back into Colombia — its border was thirty miles away.

Maddox had set up Sonia in a hotel room where she would wait for his return. As nerve-wracking as all this was to her, it was also exhilarating. To be in the middle of an operation involving the CIA, the DAS and FARC. It was something she had never imagined to be privy to and as twisted as it seemed, she had also enjoyed getting to spend time with Maddox, even though he was only here to hunt down terrorists.

"Lay low. I'll be back for you as soon as possible," Maddox said.

"I'm going to crazy here waiting and wondering," Sonia said.

"I won't be long."

Maddox left her in the hotel and he walked back to the command center.

CHAPTER EIGHT

AN AMBUSH

San Cristobal, Venezuela.

"I GOT VISUAL!" SENNIGHT SAID. MADDOX, BATEMAN, AND Ruben Guzman gathered around Sennight and his monitors. The heat-sensing infrared camera had picked up nine bodies.

"Do you have audio?" Maddox asked.

"Give me a minute," Sennight said, putting on headphones and furiously tapping away on a keyboard. The temperature was perfect, a clear night with a gentle crosswind.

After about a minute, Sennight yelled out, "Got audio, dude!" and flipped a switch on the console of his radio equipment.

As if by magic, they could now hear all the FARC conversation going on in their no-longer-safe house.

Guzman smiled as he patted Sennight on the back. "Muy bien, Troy. You did it."

Sennight smiled ear to ear and proudly replied, "Like taking candy from a baby."

"Are you recording this?" Bateman asked him.

"Of course," Sennight replied with a hint of annoyance.

It didn't take long to figure out this was the cell responsible for the bus massacre. They were in panic mode. There were seven FARC rebels and two Venezuelan nationals who owned the house.

It could turn into a hairy political mess if the Venezuelan citizens were killed, therefore, the decision was made to hit the house at 3 a.m. when everyone would be asleep.

The Venezuelan citizens slept in the upstairs bedrooms of the house, while the guerrillas were holed up in a room off the side of the house near the laundry room and patio. It was a perfect setup. One team would hit the area where the rebels were staying while the second team rushed to the bedrooms upstairs to keep the Venezuelan nationals from fleeing and safe from gunfire.

Maddox, Bateman, and Guzman were going over the plans one more time when Sennight interrupted.

"Pete, they're moving out in the morning," he warned.

Maddox expected that. Highly sought after terrorists like these didn't stick around too long in one spot. He assumed they would itching to get back into the jungle where they would feel safer.

"Perfect," Maddox said.

"What do you mean?" a confused Guzman asked.

"We hit them while they're on the move, away from the safe house and away from the locals."

"An ambush?" Guzman asked.

"Yes. We nail the bastards while they're en route; they won't know what hit them."

———

GUZMAN GATHERED his men for the evening ambush. Thanks to Sennight's work, they knew the exact time the rebels were moving out and that they were heading south to another safe house, one closer to the Colombian border.

"They are preparing to jump over the border back into Colombia soon," Maddox warned.

"Then they'll vanish into FARC territory," Guzman said.

The rebels planned to move out at 9:30 p.m., which pleased Maddox since the teams would have cover of darkness to carry out their assault.

Guzman and his men got into position once sunset hit, around 6:00 p.m. By 7:00 p.m., it was pitch dark outside.

They all had their weapons suppressed and wore protective gear and patchless and unidentifiable black battle dress uniforms with black face masks.

Bateman remained back in the command center with Sennight, preparing everything they would need to interrogate one of the rebels for information on Brian Hart—at least they hoped they would get the chance.

The death of the Colombian soldier during the firefight at the bus had left Guzman's men with a thirst for revenge rather than justice. That was one of the reasons Maddox wanted to be there, to ensure he could at least snag one of the rebels alive.

At 9:49 p.m., a beat-up late seventies Datsun pickup with a camper top on the back pulled up to the ELN safe house. The rebels had been made complacent by the unofficial support of the Chávez government, and they seemed unconcerned as they loaded up the pickup with their gear. One by one, they climbed into the pickup bed through the open tailgate until the six targets were crammed inside.

Once the pickup gate slammed shut, the green Datsun pulled out of the driveway and began heading south—as expected—leaving the local Venezuelans behind in their home. The trap was set two miles down the road.

———

As the Datsun pickup truck made its way down a quiet street, it pulled up behind an old gold-colored Toyota Camry and right into the ambush.

A few seconds later, the Camry, stopped short. The pickup truck's driver didn't have time to react. He saw the Camry's taillights switch from braking to reversing, and then the gold-colored car backed up right onto the Datsun's front bumper. At the exact same time, a second car came out of nowhere with its lights off.

"Ojo, ojo, ojo, algo está pasando!" the Datsun driver shouted through the pickup's small rear window.

The second vehicle in the assault team sped toward the truck full of rebels. It switched its headlights on. The ELN rebels scrambled for their weapons as the red Toyota Land Cruiser came at them full speed. It slowed just a bit before plowing into them from behind.

The impact tossed the rebels around like rag dolls inside the Datsun, and their vehicle was now sandwiched between the Camry and the Land Cruiser. A white van screeched up beside them, and Colombian Special Forces commandos jumped out with their suppressed MP5 weapons drawn before the vehicle had a chance to come to a complete stop.

Another Colombian soldier, who had jumped out of the backseat of the Camry, met them there. He fired a short burst from his MP5 into the front seat, instantly killing the driver and the passenger.

The team from the van shoved their weapons into the small side windows of the pickup cab while three other soldiers jumped out of the Land Rover and shoved their weapons into the back of the pickup truck, using the headlights of their car to view inside.

"No se muevan!" *Do not move!* the assault team screamed as the FARC troops scrambled like trapped sardines in the pickup truck bed.

Inside the pickup truck, utter confusion and panic ruled. The men were already dazed from the rear and front-end collisions, and then they saw machine guns with silencers pointed in their direction. They began to pull out their weapons, old AK-47s courtesy of Cuba, but they didn't stand a chance and were quickly shot dead. This prompted the three still living rebels at the rear of the pickup truck to scream that they were surrendering. They held up their arms in defeat and yelled, "No me maten!" *Do not kill me!* over and over.

Guzman's men dragged the three surviving rebels from the pickup truck and into their van, where DAS agents and Maddox waited.

The DAS agents duct-taped their new prisoners' mouths, hands and feet before pulling white cloth bags over the rebels' heads and securing those with duct tape as well. They then cut a slit in each sack so as to prevent suffocation.

Before the first piece of duct tape had even been applied, the van had already peeled off into the night. The lead vehicle peeled off south, and the rear vehicle made a sharp U-turn and sped off north.

In mere seconds they were gone, leaving the Datsun pickup truck idling on the street, as if it were waiting on a light to turn green. A faint cloud of smoke from the recent gunfire lingered near the bullet-riddled truck and four dead ELN rebels littered the inside of the bloody vehicle. The entire assault had taken only a few minutes.

Maddox wondered how the Venezuelan government would

handle the potentially embarrassing situation in which FARC guerrillas were killed inside Venezuela. His money was on them spinning this as another violent drug cartel street battle.

The van holding the three prisoners pulled into the driveway of the secured safe house. Sennight had made it surveillance-proof with an array of jammers that would block out any listening devices or attempts to eavesdrop on cell phone calls and gad also set up some tech that would block infrared detectors unlike the rebel's safe house, Sennight's was impenetrable from gadgetry.

This was why Sennight was Maddox's go-to tech guy; he knew his stuff and loved the job, especially the thrill of it all. He looked forward to the challenge of locking a safe house down tight, hacking into a secure website, and bugging the hell out of a target.

Not only was Sennight a whiz at what he did, he was also a team player. CIA techs could sometimes get a bit squeamish when faced with some of the more visceral data collection methods officers used, but not Sennight.

In the past, he'd wolfed down a sandwich while a target was being interrogated. He was also a good shot, scoring forty-seven out of fifty targets when qualifying with his weapon— outstanding for any CIA officer, but for a tech guy, it was downright impressive.

Maddox had Sennight there for his tech skills, but it was nice to know that he could back him up with his weapon if needed.

Because Maddox had helped him and his men capture their targets, Ruben Guzman was allowing him an hour to interrogate the prisoners before they were to be sneaked back across into Colombia.

CHAPTER NINE

COBIJA

San Cristobal, Venezuela.

WHEN MADDOX HAD ARRIVED AT THE SAFE HOUSE HE'D
noticed the DAS agents had slapped the prisoners around a
little, but nothing that would affect his interrogation. He only
had an hour though, so he would have to focus on just one man
and do without properly preparing the prisoner for interrogation like sleep deprivation.

Maddox had already devised his angle; he would use fear—
not fear of anything Maddox was going to do to the prisoner,
but fear of what the DAS was going to do to the rebel. The
Colombian military and FARC had been going after each other
for decades. And this cell had killed one of their own.

Maddox had no idea what was in store for these guys, but
more than likely they wouldn't be killed since the Colombian
government wanted them alive and on trial in Colombia for
killing all those civilians on the bus—but the prisoner he would
be interrogating didn't know that.

As Maddox made his way to the interrogation room,

Guzman pulled him aside and reminded him, "Do not leave any marks; we're going to parade these malparidos in front of the media."

"No worries," Maddox said smiling.

Maddox walked in and introduced himself in Spanish to the man with an old rice sack over his head. "I'm with the CIA, and I need to talk to you," he said, emphasizing CIA.

Maddox removed the rice sack from the man's head. He was in his mid-twenties with brown hair and eyes and a patchy beard that announced to everyone he was unable to grow a full one. He was drenched in sweat and blinking profusely.

Even though the safe house was just a family home and hadn't been built to interrogate or torture people, it was still amazing what you could do with a room stripped of everything but two chairs and a couple of Coleman 500-watt work lamps.

Maddox gave the prisoner a few minutes to adjust to the blinding lights shining toward him and the heat searing his face. Even then, the brightness of the lights hid Maddox from view, so the prisoner was startled when his interrogator tore the duct tape from his mouth. Spit and blood drooled down his chin and he began to breathe harder.

Maddox spoke again in Spanish, "Keep quiet or I will shoot you in the head, okay?" Maddox put the tip of his Sig's silencer onto the man's forehead.

The prisoner nodded in agreement.

"Okay, muy bien," Maddox said in a more pleasant tone as he finished tearing off the duct tape from the man's face. The young terrorist squirmed in pain as the duct tape tore off more chunks of hair from his patchy beard.

After a few more seconds of breathing heavily, the prisoner squinted at the shadow in front of him.

"See-ah?" *CIA?* the rebel asked.

Maddox responded in Spanish. "Yes. What's your name?"

"Jose," the man answered softly, his head slung low.

Maddox figured it was a fake name, but it was a good sign, better than the, *"Go fuck yourself, gringo,"* Maddox had thought would be coming.

"Jose, you have two choices here. One, you tell me the condition and the location of your American hostage, the guy you snatched near Ragonville last year. You help me with that, and you'll stay in my custody. The DAS has already agreed to this if you cooperate.

That was pure bullshit. As soon as Maddox had the information he needed, he would turn the youngster over to the DAS.

Maddox let choice number one sink in for a few seconds and then continued, "Or, if you want to be a pendejo and not help me, I'll just turn you over to the DAS. I don't have to play games. I know they'll get you or one of your comrades to talk about the location of your camp. You dumbasses killed a busload of civilians and a Colombian soldier. They won't stop until you're all rounded up. And you know what that means, right?" Maddox asked.

Jose stayed quiet as he processed the information and calculated his options.

Maddox continued, "You know the drill. A bucket of cold water is poured over you, your balls or tongue hooked up to a car battery. Nice little jolt to make you shit, puke, and talk. And that's just for starters. If that doesn't loosen your tongue, they'll pull out your fingernails one by one. Or maybe they'll first shove pins in your fingernails before pulling them off. They're so pissed off that perhaps they'll break out the blanket."

Maddox stopped to give "Jose" time to think on what he had just said.

The *cobija*, Spanish for blanket, was a brutal method of getting someone to talk. The interrogators would strip a prisoner naked and force him to lie down on the floor or on a table. They would then place a cotton blanket that had been doused in gasoline on the victim's back. The blanket was set on fire and allowed to burn for a few seconds. Then, like a magician revealing the big finale, they would quickly remove the flaming blanket from the victim's back, as well as his skin.

"Jose, are you going to help me or not?" Maddox asked.

"Yes, yes," Jose said, his voice trembling.

For the next forty-five minutes, Jose told Maddox what he wanted to know. The American hostage was alive in a camp in the mountains of Colombia about fifty miles from the Venezuelan border. But accessing the controlled area would be a suicide mission, the prisoner warned Maddox.

Maddox smiled. *Special Forces loves a challenge,* he thought. Then, Jose dropped a bombshell. He wanted to make sure he wasn't going to be turned over to the DAS. He wanted to be transferred to CIA custody and released.

"If you provide me with valuable information, I can arrange that," Maddox said.

"I can tell you about the secret training camp," the prisoner said.

———

TEN MINUTES LATER, Maddox burst out of the interrogation room looking pale and pissed off; he looked at Guzman who had been listening to the interrogation.

"Have you heard about this training camp?" an incredulous Maddox asked.

"Yes," Guzman answered. "We've passed this information up the chain of command and to your government already. That camp is on Venezuelan soil," he explained and then leaned in so they were almost nose to nose, "deep inside Venezuela. We can't get to it without starting a war."

Maddox was shocked by the revelation. He couldn't believe it. According to Guzman, Chávez had allowed the creation of a Libyan terrorist training camp on Venezuelan soil.

Recruits from the FARC, the ELN, Peru's Shining Path, and jihadists trained in Venezuela under the auspices and support of Libya.

Maddox was furious—furious that this was the first he was hearing about the camp located in his station. Furious that Chávez was so bold as to allow the Libyans to set up a camp, and furious that Guzman was relatively blasé about it—that he had already known about it and hadn't told him about it.

"What do you mean, you can't touch it? You guys are the ones who have been going at it with Venezuela in that little hundred-year-old border conflict. If there is a terrorist training camp in Venezuela, your country will be first on the hit list, my friend."

Guzman smiled. "I know this. Believe me, we want to take action, but my hands are tied. That's why we passed it on to your people. After 9/11 we figured your government would be eager to take care of it, but nothing has been done."

After he calmed down — these were decisions outside both of their pay grades — Maddox thanked Guzman for his help and support. Guzman did the same. They both relished that Colombia and the United States had just violated Venezuela's sovereignty. The FARC terrorist known as "Jose" was left in the hands of Guzman and his men, much to his outrage and screaming that he wanted to be in American custody.

Despite the operation's success, Maddox seethed on his drive back to the command center safe house. *Why didn't I know about the camp? Did his predecessor as station chief know?* he wondered. *It was just a rumor, but if Guzman and*

DAS knew, for Christ's sake, I should have known. Maddox kept thinking as he drove into town.

———

BACK IN THE COMMAND CENTER, Maddox used the secure line Sennight had set up with an Inmarsat satellite phone. He punched in the numbers to Dick Philips's direct line.

"Identification, please," a monotone voice on the other end of call answered.

"Polar, access code ninety-four, Zebra, eighty-five," Maddox responded.

"Is the line secure?" the operator asked.

"Yes."

"One moment, Polar."

The line clicked several times, and a few seconds later, Philips came on: "Polar, this is Duke."

After quickly briefing Philips on the whereabouts of Brian Hart including the GPS data where he was being held so he could be extracted. Then Maddox moved on to more pressing matters. He relayed the intelligence he had gathered from the captive about the Libyan terrorist training camp in Venezuela.

"Have you heard about this?"

"This is new to me, Polar. Stand down for now while I look into it."

Maddox hung up. He didn't want to believe it. *Could Chávez be so brazen as to let the Libyans build a terrorist training camp in Venezuela?*

———

Back at Langley, Dick Philips was seething. He picked up his secure line. "Operator, get Rodan on the line immediately. Red priority."

Rodan was the codename for Dennis Cameron, the new station chief in Colombia. Cameron wasn't one of Philips's handpicked men, so he couldn't really trust him like he could Maddox. Cameron had made a name for himself working in the narco wars of Colombia and Bolivia. He had a good relationship with the DEA, which was why he had been the appointed station chief in Bolivia for the past year.

Perhaps having someone with a strict background in law enforcement instead of espionage might have affected his judgment, Philips thought, but he was about to find out what possible reason there could be for not red flagging the camp. Within a minute, Rodan was on the other end of the secure line from Bogotá.

Philips's worst-case scenario fears were true; Maddox's information was correct. Dennis Cameron confirmed that his DAS contact had passed on information that the Libyans were in Venezuela building a training camp with the full support of the Chávez government. But since there had been no visual or hard evidence, Cameron had perceived it as just hearsay—not much more than a rumor. He had filed the requisite report and uploaded it to the CIA's threat-assessment database at Langley, but he hadn't marked it as red alert priority, so the information had been buried deep in the database, waiting for whenever an analyst got around to it.

Since 9/11, analysts had been too preoccupied with the Middle East to pay attention to database threats in Latin America that field agents hadn't marked as a top priority.

Even more infuriating to Philips was that Cameron didn't bother to follow up nor did he copy Philips, so the report just sat there, taking up bytes in the database. As head of the

Western Hemisphere for the CIA, Philips should have been at least made aware of the report, but Cameron had made no effort to inform him. Philips ordered the Colombia station chief to Langley for an in-person dressing-down.

Maddox read the secure email communication from Dick Philips, which included Cameron's report filed months ago. It corroborated what the ELN prisoner had stated: Libyan intelligence agents and commandos were setting up an Afghanistan-style training camp right in America's own backyard.

Maddox was furious at Cameron's incompetence and decision to not follow up on the issue. Even though there was no hard proof and it had been just rumor, it still should have been looked into, not just filed and forgotten.

CHAPTER TEN

SPLIT SECOND DECISIONS

San Cristobal, Venezuela.

Maddox didn't want to think about the training camp. What the CIA knew or did not know about it. He just wanted to see Sonia.

Around 7:30 p.m., Maddox pulled up to the Buena Vista Hotel on Avenida Central in San Cristobal. Sonia had been on her own in the hotel room for almost forty-eight hours. Maddox had had Bateman check up on her and let her know everything was okay, so he didn't feel too bad for dropping her off at the hotel and disappearing for almost two days, but he wondered if she would feel differently.

Maddox's adrenaline was still pumping from the mission and the supposed camp, but as he approached Sonia's door, a different type of rush took over; he felt like a goddamn teenager going to the house of the girl he liked. Pete Maddox, trained killer and CIA station chief, was giddy about seeing Sonia Collins. The plan was to fly back to Caracas in the morning.

Why not dinner with Sonia tonight? he had thought to himself. *The Libyans and Chávistas will be there tomorrow anyway.*

He had called her to let her know he was coming over. Sonia's face lit up when she saw Maddox, and that expression turned him on more than how beautiful she looked wearing a tight-fitting white shirt tucked into artfully faded blue jeans, knee-high black leather boots, big silver hoops earrings, and her brown hair pulled back in a ponytail. She also smelled amazing.

He doubted she had been lounging around like this at almost 8:00 p.m., and Maddox smiled at the thought that she had gotten ready for him.

"Is everything okay?" she asked.

"Yes, everything is fine. Thank you for everything. We're headed back to Caracas at seven tomorrow morning, so please be ready to leave the hotel by six thirty."

A look of disappointment washed across Sonia's face, and it hit him like a kick in the balls. Her look said it all: *Is that the only reason you wanted to see me tonight?* Then he saw anger begin to percolate in her expression. "You could have just told me that over the phone," she said.

Maddox was used to having to make split-second decisions while doing his job, and now he needed to make one concerning his personal life. He was certain Sonia liked him, and he sure as hell had fallen for her.

For over a year, they'd been flirting with each other, and Maddox had refused to cross the line. Why now?

Split-second decision time, Maddox thought.

"We have a few hours, and I'm starving. Do you want to get something to eat?" Maddox asked.

The look of frustration, confusion, and anger left immediately, and she was once again beaming. "I'd love to," Sonia said.

Maddox and Sonia drove a rented Toyota Corolla south on the Pan American Highway to San Pedro Del Rio, a beautiful and charming colonial town nearby that was a popular tourist attraction.

At 8:30 p.m. on a Tuesday, they didn't have any problems getting a table at the popular restaurant, El Balcon. Although they had gone to eat out together before, this time it had the feel of a date. Maddox felt silly thing that.

They ordered arroz de mariscos with fried plantains and yuca. and A heart of palm and avocado salad. They also shared a bottle of red wine from Chile.

They ate, laughed, and enjoyed each other company.

———

BACK AT THE HOTEL, Maddox walked Sonia to her room. She walked inside and smiled. "Want to come in?"

Maddox followed into her room and closed the door. His heart felt like it was going to burst from his chest. They didn't speak. She turned to face him as he slowly closed the distance between them. Neither broke the silence. Their lips touched gently at first, but then months of pent-up passion took over.

———

IN THREE HOURS, Maddox would be flying back to Caracas, where one of the most challenging missions of his career waited for him—to confirm whether the Libyans were setting up terrorist training camps on Venezuelan soil—and here he was, lying in bed naked next to an asset he had recruited. But the guilt he should feel about getting intimately involved with her was not there.

Lying in bed next to her felt right. Maddox knew that he'd had feelings for her from the time they met, but he had kept his emotions in check, making him feel miserable. And worse, Maddox had seen that it made Sonia feel miserable.

Sonia opened her eyes as Maddox sat up on the side of the bed and started getting dressed. He looked back at her and leaned over to gently kiss her on her forehead. They exchanged smiles as he got out of bed.

If they were going to continue to see each other romantically, Sonia agreed that it was best to keep it a secret. *Easy for CIA man Maddox,* Sonia thought. It would be a bit harder for her.

———

BATEMAN, Sennight, Sonia, and Maddox rendezvoused at the small municipal airport in San Cristobal, where Maddox would be flying them back to Caracas.

Bateman was business as usual, going over intelligence reports, and he didn't seem to pick up on anything different between Maddox and Sonia. Sennight, however, could tell something had changed by the way they now looked at and talked to each other. *Hmm, too many smiles,* he thought, smiling widely at the new lovers as they got settled for their flight.

"Everyone get a good night's sleep?" Sennight asked in the best smart ass voice he could muster as he grinned at Sonia.

Sonia smiled right back at Sennight; without saying a word, she was able to tell someone how happy she was. Maddox just rolled his eyes and told Sennight to get his ass in gear for the flight back to Caracas.

"Yes, sir," Sennight said, still smiling.

CHAPTER ELEVEN

BARRIO RENDEZVOUS

Caracas, Venezuela

When Maddox needed to meet with Henry Calderon, he left a simple mark in one of their predetermined spots around the city. It was an old-school spy tactic that was still effective.

Maddox or one of Maddox's agents, Jack Duffy or Mary Dent, checked the different spots daily. This prevented Henry Calderon from developing routines that could be easily detected.

Mary Dent was on her daily morning jog through Parque Morichal in the Prados Del Este neighborhood of Caracas. It was early and damp; the cool air of the morning would keep the coming heat at bay for another few hours. As Dent approached the spot she checked daily for messages, she almost tripped over herself when she actually saw one. She quickly regained her bearings and continued her run, slowing down to stretch right next to the tree with the white mark.

Mary Dent was a five-five foot redhead from Boston with

the Southie accent to prove it. She looked like actress Julianne Moore, but she spoke with a JFK-like accent that drove Maddox nuts. "Like nails on chalkboard," he would tease her. "Basten foreva," she would reply laying the accent even thicker with a shit-eating grin.

Mary Dent was a triathlete, and her body showed it. She had just turned forty-two a few weeks before and had joined the CIA ten years ago after spending eight years with the Boston Police Department and four years in the Marines.

She was tough and good-looking, so Calderon would hit on her relentlessly, but he was always shot down.

Mary Dent was doing her stretching in order to confirm that Calderon had left a mark and there it was, at the bottom of the tree trunk, letting her know that he needed to meet with Maddox that night.

The single mark had been made using agricultural chalk, which was resistant to whatever the weather could dish out, and could easily be used to mark trees. But this wasn't the type of agricultural chalk used by arborists or farmers. It was custom-made, CIA. Dent reached into her iPod armband case and removed a small packet designed to look like a supplement powder for hardcore runners. She removed the lid from her water bottle, ripped open the packet, and poured in the contents. She screwed the lid back onto the water bottle, shook it for a few seconds, and then squirted the chalk mark. It took just seconds for the liquid to erase the white from the tree. She had no idea what was in the packet. A special chemical cooked up at the CIA labs that caused a reaction with the water to do what a hard rain couldn't do, get rid of the mark. Dent got back on her feet and continued on her run.

Maddox knew what that specific mark on that specific tree meant. They were to meet at a safe houses in the Jose Felix

Ribas barrio—one of the most infamous and dangerous barrios in Caracas.

The barrio was one of the many sprawling shantytown slums that littered the mountain hilltops surrounding Caracas in stunning contrast to the bustling, modern neighborhoods with their many malls, restaurants, and office buildings down below.

The Jose Felix Ribas barrio of Caracas wasn't found in any Lonely Planet travel guide, and a person would have been hard-pressed to find a taxi driver willing to drive there, but Calderon had a loyal informant who controlled one of the blocks. He allowed his informant to run an illegal businesses in exchange for information and the use of one of his homes—a simple stone house known as "El Rancho" that stood on the higher end of the poverty scale in the slum hierarchy.

This was not the type of safe house Sonia Collins would procure—Maddox would never have her go up into the barrios, neither would Sonia want to—but Calderon had several safe houses stashed within the barrios. The people living in the barrios were Chávez's most ardent supporters, so the locations wouldn't be compromised or bugged by Brull's secret police and neither the Venezuelan army nor the police would dare go into the barrios without a battalion backing them up. Those facts combined with the blessing of the block jefe meant the houses were safe, secure spots at which to meet for Calderon.

In the barrios, the jefe ruled, and the jefe of El Rancho's block was a thirty-year-old gangster by the name of Elvis Presley Jimenez.

"Elvis Presley, are you shitting me?" Maddox had asked Calderon the first time he had heard about Rancho Elvis Presley at the top of the barrio's hillside. Maddox couldn't believe that was really the barrio jefe's name.

Venezuelans, especially the working class, were known for

giving their children wild names—names that would make even Hollywood stars do a double take. Infamous terrorist and native Venezuelan Carlos the Jackal had been born Ilich Ramirez, named after Soviet leader Vladimir Ilyich Lenin by his Marxist-Leninist father.

Elvis Presley Jimenez's father had been a fan of the King of Rock and Roll, and now Elvis Presley Jimenez was the king of his block—several blocks in fact.

Maddox and Jack Duffy pulled up and parked next to the steep stairs that led to the otherwise inaccessible parts of the barrio. Maddox had brought the six one former West Point quarter back and army captain to drive him and then stay with the vehicle.

"Wait for me here," Maddox told him as he prepared to climb the stairs.

"No problem, sir," Duffy replied. Maddox sighed. He had long since stopped trying to remind the young CIA agent that he was no longer in the army and didn't have to address him as "sir."

Maddox looked up at the crumbling concrete stairwell. The stairs in front of him, as with most of the homes in the barrio, had been handmade by the residents. They were uneven, and the weather and years without maintenance had left them in precarious condition. Maddox smiled and began huffing up the stairs, armed with his stainless steel SIG and his Walther PPK.

Elvis might control the block, but Maddox wasn't about to take any chances.

Elvis' rancho was at the very top of the steps, where it sat like an old medieval castle, overlooking the affluent neighborhoods down below. The jefe was the king of the hill, but just like in the children's game of the same name, there were plenty of competitors trying to knock him off and take his place, so there were always lookouts on the roof; the men kept watch for enemies and the rare police raids that were more for show than anything else.

"Hola pana," Elvis greeted Maddox at the door, with his ever-present cigarette dangling from his mouth. "Come in, come in. I was just leaving." Maddox looked over Elvis' shoulder and saw Calderon smiling inside.

"Hey, Elvis, como estas?" Maddox asked in Venezuelan slang. He shook hands and gave Elvis a friendly embrace.

"Todo bien. I'll let you two be," Elvis said before the jefe walked outside. Maddox watched Elvis disappear down the street.

Elvis didn't look like a feared barrio jefe. He was short and scrawny—Maddox doubted he weighed more than one hundred fifty pounds—with dark skin, hair, and eyes. He dressed like a pimp, wearing a big gold Rolex watch and several gold necklaces, including a prominently displayed diamond-encrusted crucifix; each finger sported a gold or silver ring. But the bling wasn't just about showing that he had money; it was about showing that he could walk around in the slums with it and no one would dare jack him. The bling showed he had power.

Everybody knew Elvis, and he treated the residents of his barrio like they were his children, paying for medicine, helping with school supplies, and providing baseball gear. This kept the block residents happy and on his side.

But they weren't loyal just because Elvis gave them things once in a while; they knew that although the jefe was short and skinny, he was also tough and ruthless. He was also a bit of celebrity from his glory days as a welterweight pro boxer; he could fight and pummel men who towered over him and outweighed him by a hundred pounds.

Calderon and Maddox sat at a table, alone in the two-bedroom house. The power was off, a common occurrence in the barrios where electricity and running water were spotty at best. Although Elvis had a generator, Calderon had shut it off. There was no need to draw attention at 2:00 a.m., even though Elvis had assured them that no one would dare gawk at the house, much less complain.

Calderon slid a folder across the table. Maddox looked at it, and his worst fear materialized before his eyes.

Maddox was looking at ten photographs of bulldozers and other construction equipment; the quality was excellent. In one, it looked like they were building a landing strip. Other pictures featured heavily armed Venezuelan secret police and intelligence paramilitary soldiers milling about the camp.

As Maddox flipped through them, he saw that Calderon had saved the best picture for last. There, in the black-and-white photograph, stood Abdullah Zlitini, the Libyan intelligence chief for special operations in the west, a known supporter and trainer of terrorists who had run training camps in Libya and abroad for years.

"Where did you get this?" Maddox asked.

"Brull," Calderon replied. He then slid a piece of paper over to Maddox.

"You can see for yourself," Calderon said as Maddox looked at the paper; it had a set of coordinates, presumably those of the camp. Maddox knew that Calderon hated his sadistic boss Brull and had been disillusioned for years with Hugo Chávez and his empty promises for a better Venezuela. Calderon had been an invaluable asset, but this was information he was passing on because there was more. And Maddox was right.

"Let's say there is a group of powerful men from all branches of this government—military, intelligence, and congressional—who feel it is time for a change." Henry

Calderon spoke in a serious manner, something he almost never did.

"Chávez?" Maddox asked.

"Yes. We believe he might be mentally unstable, as are his policies. He keeps taking us more and more to the left, beyond the beard in Cuba. He admires Pol Pot, for Christ's sake! He believes he can succeed in Venezuela where Pol Pot failed . . ." Calderon took a deep breath, "and now this." Calderon pointed at the pictures on the table.

"Venezuela will not be the next Afghanistan, providing safe passage to terrorists," Calderon said with a steely resolve Maddox had never heard from him before.

"What's in it for Chávez? It's not like he's an Islamic fundamentalist."

"No, but his hatred for the United States and capitalism is deeply rooted. He believes the US to be on its way out, and that by teaming up with the Libyans, he can help with that final push so that Libya's style of socialist government can flourish. You've read *The Green Book*, yes?"

"Yes," Maddox said as he continued to stare at the pictures.

Calderon whipped out his pocketsize, government-issued Spanish version of Gaddafi's book. "This is what he wants, and he won't stop. He will destroy our great country if we don't stop him." He said it with such seriousness that Maddox found it surprising coming from the usually joke-cracking, sex-obsessed Calderon.

"We?" Maddox asked.

"There is a special council; it has been meeting for over a year. I'm a member. We're moving forward with or without the United States, but we would like your help," Calderon said looking at Maddox. "Material help, Pete," he added, "We're not asking for, nor do we want, boots on the ground from your country."

"Understood," Maddox said without looking up from the photographs. "I need to do my own fact-checking, then we can talk about the future," he said and looked up at Calderon, finally breaking free from the trance of the photographs.

"I know that," Calderon said as the usual sly grin returned to his face. "That's why I gave you the coordinates of the camp, so you can see it for yourself."

"I appreciate that, Henry; you've been a good friend. Let's meet in three days."

"Good. We'll meet in three days. I also want you to meet the council."

BY 3:15 A.M., Duffy and Maddox had driven out of the shantytown, down the hillside east of Caracas, and onto the freeway.

"How did it go?" Duffy finally asked. He knew all about "need to know," but it didn't hurt to ask.

Maddox was looking out the window as the city lights passed by in a blur. "It's big. I'll fill you in with the rest of the team during our morning briefing," he said.

"Sounds good," Duffy replied as he continued driving down the freeway.

Maddox tore his gaze away from the window and looked out the window. It was nice to sit back and see it in action when someone else was driving.

Maddox had finally ditched the embassy-standard Ford Explorer he was issued when he first arrived. His new silver Jeep was the perfect low-profile vehicle. It looked just like any other Jeep of the same make and model, except it had been special ordered and equipped by the CIA's science and technology department.

The car had several hidden compartments where he could stash his two FN P90 submachine guns, each with a fifty-round double stock magazine, as well as surveillance and tracking equipment. It also boasted bulletproof protection against small-arms fire and high-power armor-piercing assault rifles: The entire passenger compartment was protected from top-to-bottom, and the tires, fuel tank, and major engine components had been upgraded as well.

They drove to Duffy's house in Prados del Este, and Maddox slid over to the driver's side as the other agent exited.

"See you in a few hours, Jack," Maddox said to him.

"Sure thing, Pete," Duffy replied as the condo complex's security guard buzzed him in.

Hey, the kid is learning. None of that "sir" shit this time, Maddox thought to himself as he floored the gas pedal and zoomed down Calle Morichal toward Avenida El Paseo to his house for some much needed sleep. That early in the morning and without any traffic, he would be home and in bed in about twenty minutes.

CHAPTER TWELVE

1,300 MILES FROM MIAMI

Caracas, Venezuela.

MADDOX AND HIS TEAM—RON BATEMAN, MARY DENT, Jack Duffy, and Troy Sennight—sat in the CIA's secure communications conference room inside the CIA's floor at the embassy.

There wasn't much to the room but it was secure against bugs, satellites, and any type of off-site listening devices. The room was swept for bugs before each use.

Sennight had also set up multiple additional anti-eavesdropping devices for added security. Even if someone were able to breach the building's DMZ—the demilitarized zone—they wouldn't be able to listen in thanks to his gadgets and scramblers.

The walls surrounding a US Embassy formed the de facto international border between the United States and the foreign country which was supposed to be respected and off limits, but intelligence communities, Maddox's included, didn't often respect the imaginary DMZ of the embassy so additional precautions had to be taken to ensure that anyone trying to listen in through the DMZ would be rebuffed.

Even if they were good enough to breach the DMZ, then they still had to get through the vault-like perimeter Sennight had set up inside. Maddox knew Sennight had bricked them in and they were secure to communicate freely.

Inside the room there was a large conference table that sat twelve people comfortably. Several telephones were on the dark wood-colored table. The entire back wall was a whiteboard for notes and strategizing. There was an overhead 46" projector for presentations and to web conference via a secure line directly with Langley. From Langley, they could instantly be patched through to the White House, State Department, or the Pentagon.

Maddox, Bateman, Dent, and Duffy sat around the table with their laptops. Sennight sat in what he called the cockpit. It didn't seem much, just a computer with four twenty-one-inch monitors all networked together, but from the cockpit, Sennight could control the secure connection with Langley, instantly send and receive files regardless of megabytes, and monitor inside and outside the DMZ.

Dick Philips and his deputy Dave Lucas were on the large, TV-like monitor.

"The sat team has zeroed in on the coordinates you provided," Philips said, staring into the webcam.

"Visual has been confirmed. Sennight, we're patching you through the sat team signal," an offscreen voice said.

"I see it; I'll have it up in a few seconds," Sennight replied.

The sat team was the nickname for the CIA's elite satellite team. From hundreds of miles in the air, they could zero in close enough to see the tiny hairs on a person's small mole.

"Got it!" Sennight confirmed. It was difficult for Sennight to keep the geek inside of him in check when he was in action behind the cockpit. As tense as this meeting was, Maddox couldn't help crack a smile about Sennight's geeky passion for his job.

A few seconds after Sennight's declaration, the Zulia Team, which Maddox had named after his favorite Venezuelan beer, watched the satellite images download onto their monitor. Calderon's coordinates had been right on the money.

The images Maddox had seen in the grainy black-and-white pictures Calderon gave him were now clear, in full-color, and live; the landing strip and training camp had been completed. Though they had been built deep in the jungles of Venezuela, there were only fifty miles from Puerto Ayacucho, the capital and largest city of the Venezuelan state of Amazonas.

As Puerto Ayacucho was located across the Orinoco River from the Colombian village of Casuarito, Maddox now understood why Colombia was just as worried as the US about the rumors of a terrorist training camp so near its own border. Venezuela and Colombia had a long history of border disputes, and Maddox couldn't help but wonder if that was one of the reasons why Chávez wanted this camp so near the Colombian border.

The Venezuelan Army and Navy were also based in Puerto Ayacucho, adding credence to the government's involvement with the camp. Their presence was explained as conducting low-level campaigns against incursions from the military and drug runners from nearby Colombia.

The clearing for the camp would have been difficult to detect from satellite surveillance; the surrounding rainforests were some of the world's most untouched areas and the clearing itself was strategically located in the heavily forested Tepuis Mountains. It was also in an area CIA satellites weren't that interested in anyway, so it was no surprise that the camp had gone undetected, even by the DEA who normally had their eyes peeled for drug routes. But thanks to Henry Calderon's coordinates, Langley and Team Zulia were now looking at live images of the terrorist training camp, a first in the region.

The purpose of these types of training camps was to teach extremists their methods of terrorism, including how to launch attacks, ranging from suicide bombings to field combat. But they were often located in areas known for extremism, like Pakistan, Afghanistan, Iraq, and Somalia. Now they were looking at the first confirmed terrorist training camp in the Americas, about thirteen hundred miles from Miami.

———

BACK IN HIS OFFICE, Maddox reached out Calderon. They spoke in code. If anyone was listening to them they wouldn't be able to know that Maddox was letting Calderon know that he would meet the Council that evening.

After hanging up the phone, Maddox sat back in his chair. The weight of what taking places felt stifling.

He got up and looked out the window. It was a nice calm day out there. *Not an inkling of the coming political storm out there*, he thought.

He went home. He would try to get a couple hours of sleep. He needed it. He set his alarm for 9:30 p.m. That would give some needed rest before heading out to meet Calderon's people.

He had no idea who was part of the Council, or even how many members it had since Calderon wouldn't divulge any of that information. He just told them these were important people with the ways and means of changing the political make up of the current country.

CHAPTER THIRTEEN

THE ALTAMIRA

Caracas, Venezuela.

MADDOX SET OUT ALONE AT AROUND 10:00 P.M. HE DROVE for thirty minutes to make sure he wasn't followed before going to the address Calderon had given him. Unlike their meet ups in the Caracas slums this time he was heading toward the posh Altamira neighborhood.

The Altamira neighborhood was located in the Chacao Municipality of Caracas and known for having great restaurants and shopping centers as well as housing many members of Caracas's upper class. It was quite the contrast to Elvis' Ranch in shantytown.

Maddox drove up to the gated community where a security guard greeted him with an Israeli Uzi submachine gun slung over his chest.

"Que se le ofrece, Señor?" he asked.

Maddox replied in Spanish, "I'm Rick Castro, visiting Quinta Jasmine."

The guard looked at his list and waved Maddox through as

he nodded to the second security guard stationed in the control booth. The gate opened and Maddox drove in.

Inside the gated community protected by Uzi-carrying private security guards, the houses had large fences and high walls. Those measures had been the first taken to protect the homes, and when they weren't enough, the community had built walls and gates around the entire neighborhood. When even that hadn't been enough to keep the criminals out, the armed guards had been hired. Such was life in Caracas.

Upon arriving at the address, Maddox was greeted by a large metal gate that automatically opened for him as he pulled up. The guard must have relayed that he was on his way. Maddox drove up the long driveway to an imposing Mediterranean-style home on a large piece of land. Although the home still exuded wealth, it did appear to have seen better days, most likely because Hugo Chávez's nationalism didn't extend only to business and industry.

The Chávez government had nationalized prime urban real estate, including the homes of wealthy Venezuelan families who wouldn't kowtow to Chávez. For that reason, many refused to spend money keeping up their large homes since there was a real risk that the government would take them away from them. Their homes remained frozen in better times, long gone.

Henry Calderon greeted Maddox at the long roundabout where he had parked. There were several other cars parked there too. There was a man standing next to him.

"Rick, how are you?" Calderon greeted Maddox, using his pseudonym.

"Hola, Henry. Pleasure to see you again," Maddox said as he shook Calderon's hand.

"This is Francisco Chacon, the council president," Calderon said, introducing him to Maddox.

Chacon was about five-nine and light-skinned with brown wavy hair. He wore a grey, shiny Hugo Boss power-suit.

Then Calderon turned toward Chacon. "This is Rick Castro, political attaché to the US Embassy." The two men shook hands.

"Please, call me Frank," Chacon said in perfect English.

Although Maddox didn't know who he was meeting with he knew who Frank Chacon was. He was a powerful, and rich man that came from old Venezuela money those who the Chavistas hated the most.

The Chacon family had made its fortune in the Venezuelan oil industry before it was nationalized by the Chávez government. They had lost billions since Chávez came to power, which drove Frank's father to commit suicide. Frank ran the business with his brother, Johnny.

It didn't surprise Maddox that the Chacon Brothers were involved in the Council.

Calderon and Chacon led Maddox inside, where about a dozen bon-vivants dressed to the nines gathered inside the large family room. The men and women all stood facing Maddox as he entered the room. Most of the guests wore civilian clothes, though Maddox could see an army colonel and major in uniform, as well as a police captain. Many had drinks in their hands. They greeted him cautiously.

It felt like he was the guest of honor at a party no one wanted to be at.

Chacon introduced Maddox to his wife, Aurora. She offered him a drink, which he politely declined.

"Please, come in and we'll get started," Francisco Chacon said as he sipped his Scotch and led Maddox to the dining room, offering him a seat at a large table that could easily sit fifteen.

Maddox sat, and everyone took his or her seat. Five of the

guests sat across from Maddox, the other six or so guests, including Henry Calderon, sat in chairs along the wall. Maddox figured it was safe to assume he was sitting across from the leaders of the council.

"Mr. Castro," Chacon addressed Maddox, making it obvious that he was leading this meeting. "Please, allow me to introduce you to everyone. This is Colonel Maximo Coronado representing the Army, Captain Rogelio Nieto representing the Navy, Commander Ramiro Navarro representing the metropolitan police, Deputy Minister of Defense Julio Wilson, and I'm representing the local business community."

Maddox stood and shook each man's hand when introduced.

"We also have the support of DISIP with Mr. Calderon, whom you already know, as well other important community leaders," Chacon continued. He then turned to a man Maddox already recognized, Carlos Rafael Espinoza, a member of Venezuela's National Assembly—the Venezuelan equivalent of the US Congress.

Assemblyman Espinoza was a member of the Unidad Democrática, a coalition of several political parties united in their opposition to Chávez and his powerful United Socialist Party of Venezuela, which controlled the Assembly.

Unbeknownst to Chacon, the Assemblyman, along with Colonel Carmona and Captain Navarro, was already on the CIA payroll. Though the three men's involvement was minimal, limited to passing along intelligence of low to medium value, it was good to see them now in this position. *That is why it pays to keep even low-grade assets around*, Maddox thought, *you never knew when it might really pay off.*

For the next two hours, Maddox and the Council discussed its goal, to overthrow Chávez in a military coup led by Colonel Carmona and Major Nieto. Once in power, the council would suspend the Chávez constitution and establish martial law until the entire country was under their command. Chacon's role would be to assure the people that they did not intended to establish either a military dictatorship—like the ones Venezuela had previously been subjected to—or a junta.

As president of the council, Chacon would take temporary control of the country. Once the situation stabilized, he would appoint Assemblyman Espinoza as the interim Venezuelan president until a special democratic election could be held, hopefully within six months of the coup.

What the Council wanted from Maddox and the United States was material support for a coup against Chávez. A tall order.

Although the coup had been in planning for months, Maddox had an intelligence collection relationship with half the Council leaders and with Henry Calderon. Maddox's presence there, backed by Dick Philips, was upping the ante. The Council was asking the CIA to provide tear gas, weapons, and ammunition for the coup as well as money to quickly stabilize the country and move it to democratic elections. The debt would easily be repaid from Venezuela's deep oil coffers.

It was now obvious why Calderon had provided the information about the Libyan terrorist training camp. The Council knew that was chum in the water against Chávez.

The Council left the disposal of the camp up to the US government to do as they saw with it. They wouldn't interfere.

The plan of the coup was to kidnap General Andres Zurita, commander of the powerful and Chávez-loyal national guard, then battle the Venezuelan Army and National Guard units.

They did not want to assassinate Chávez since doing so would make him a martyr in the eyes of the country's large poor population. The poor supported the populist president, who bought their loyalty with government-subsidized grocery stores and health care provided by Cuban doctors in an oil-for-doctors program Fidel Castro and Chávez had cooked up.

"We'll put him on trial," Chacon said.

———

AFTER THE COUNCIL MEETING, Maddox drove straight to the embassy where his waited for a debrief.

Maddox exited the Fajardo freeway onto Avenida Casanova to Avenida Del Country Club, making his way down to Calle F where the embassy was located. The embassy guard —a US marine—waved Maddox into the underground parking lot. From there he took an elevator into the embassy and was waved in again by another guard. In five minutes, Maddox was double-timing it down the hallway towards the conference room.

Jack Duffy had apparently been the first to arrive and had brewed coffee for everyone, Mary Dent was already enjoying her second cup, and Troy Sennight was performing his customary bug sweep of the room, using a piece of equipment that resembled a metal detector. Since this was an emergency meeting, Ron Bateman would also be attending. Maddox was an anomaly among station chiefs—who tended to be administrators. Maddox was hands-on and had delegated his administrative and political dealings to Bateman, which suited both men fine. Bateman was an administrator, and their arrangement would ensure he would soon lead his own station.

"Good, everyone is here," Maddox said, pouring himself a cup of coffee and splashing some fat-free milk into his cup for his cafe con leche before proceeding to fill everyone in on the events of his meeting with the Council.

The briefing left Team Zulia stunned. The implications ran the gamut. They were on the cusp of a history-making event.

Maddox knew Dent and Sennight would be ready to rock and roll; they were both seasoned field agents who'd had not trouble getting their hands dirty so far. Jack Duffy was the rookie, on his first foreign assignment. Ron Bateman understood the threat to America's national security with those Libyan terrorist training camps, but he was by the book, and Maddox knew he could only count on Bateman if they had the backing of the White House.

The meeting remained high-level since the details and their roles were still undetermined, so they wrapped it up and the team headed home fro some much needed sleep.

Maddox hit the sack at 4:20 a.m.; he was headed to an emergency at Langley in the afternoon, so this was his only chance to catch a few hours of sleep.

CHAPTER FOURTEEN

RETURN TO LANGLEY

CIA Headquarters. Langley, Virginia.

IT HAD BEEN ALMOST A YEAR SINCE THE LAST TIME Maddox was in the states. He pulled into CIA headquarters at Langley and successfully maneuvered through the security checkpoints into the compound. The CIA Office of Security manned these – heavily armed men and women CIA officers wearing black and grey jumpsuits. Their only job was to provide security at the Langley campus.

Fifteen minutes later, he walked into the Western Hemisphere section. It was a sea of cubicles in where analysts worked through the reams of intelligence data collected by field agents. Maddox stopped at a two-person cubicle where Mary Dent, who had just arrived from Venezuela, and Pat Mendoza, Maddox's staff operations officer, were meeting. Mendoza was based out of CIA headquarters and he was the link between the Venezuela station and Washington, DC. Mary Dent had flown in to assist Maddox with the scheduled briefings he had to give.

After a brief chat with Dent and Mendoza, Maddox headed for Philips's office.

"Hi, Lois," Maddox said as he greeted the secretary with a smile.

"Pete, welcome back. You can go right in," Lois said, flashing him a rare smile in return.

Philips had a large office with a large double pane window overlooking the CIA's wooded campus below. Maddox could make out the Berlin Wall Monument off in the distance. The monument included a graffiti clad piece of the former wall taken from Checkpoint Charlie, the former border crossing point that divided Germany into the communist East and the democratic West during the Cold War.

Seeing Maddox step through his door, Dick stood up, walked around his desk, and greeted him with a warm hand-shake and a fatherly pat on the back.

"Pete, so nice to see you again," the grizzled CIA warrior said warmly.

"Hi, Dick, glad to be back," Maddox replied, returning the handshake.

"Bullshit," Philips said with a sly grin, referring to Maddox's love of being in the field and distaste for the politics required to survive at Langley.

The election of Hugo Chávez had already put Venezuela into red alert notice at Langley and the White House years ago. As far as Philips was concerned, Chávez was a nut, but a very popular nut who had the military behind him. His social programs were popular with the poorest population in the country making him popular with them further solidifying his power. Paying for those programs would bankrupt the country if oil prices were too drop.

Chávez had been playing a dangerous game and the writing was on the wall. Him cozying up to Fidel Castro had been a rather embarrassing thing for the United States and the never-ending embargo, but it was pretty harmless in comparison to cozying up to Muammar Gaddafi, a long-time sponsor of terrorism; that relationship had much more serious repercussions, especially in a post-9/11 world.

When he was younger, Dick Philips had served as station chief in Chile, where he was the point man in the overthrow of communist president Salvador Allende. He had known in his gut that Hugo Chávez was going to be a problem, posing a threat that Salvador Allende hadn't even come close to matching in the early seventies.

Back then, the Cold War was in full swing, and having a Communist government like Cuba a mere ninety miles away from Miami was already a slap in the face. Latin America was considered the United States' backyard. To have a Communist-sympathetic regime in Chile as well would be too much and, on mere principle, Allende had to be overthrown. The mistake in Chile had been letting Pinochet and the military stay in power, and that was something Philips feared about this council Maddox spoke of.

The political climate had changed dramatically since the carefree, government-overthrowing free days of the agency. The Soviet Union had collapsed and no longer threatened to spread Communism throughout the Western Hemisphere. Latin America was all but ignored by the White House. Hunting Jihadist was now the mission du jour.

Philips and Maddox went over their notes during their pre-meeting, preparing to brief the CIA Deputy Director and his senior staff on the growing threat brewing in Venezuela.

"Pete, I really appreciate the work you've been doing down there in Venezuela," Philips said to Maddox as they prepared to walk out of his office.

"Thanks, Dick." Maddox knew Philips meant it, but he also

knew he was also prepping him, giving him a little pick-me-up before the senior staff put him through the wringer.

The two men swung by the cubicle farm to pick up Mary Dent, and then all three headed to the DI's secure conference room.

Doug Van Loon, Ben Rouget, Max Hoban and their staffs were already in the conference room when Maddox's group arrived.

Retired General Ben Rouget was the Deputy Director of the CIA. He'd spent thirty-two years in the US Army, including four years as commander of the elite Delta Force, and six years commanding the US Army Military Intelligence Division, before serving the last two years as the Joint Chief of Staff's point man on Intelligence and Special Forces operations. Although he was sixty-two years old, Rouget didn't look it. He was Army fit, and not only did he look like Chuck Norris sans the mustache, he could fight like Norris, too, having just won his age-group karate championship.

Rounding out the senior leadership of the CIA was Executive Director Max Hoban, the number three man in charge and a career CIA man who had been appointed Executive Director by Van Loon's predecessor, a man widely disliked by the CIA agents.

The former DCI, like Van Loon, was a politician, but unlike Van Loon, he was a man who disliked the role of the CIA and shared the former president's vision of minimizing its role. During the last eight years, the CIA had been gutted and morale was at its worst.

The new administration had been a shot in the arm for the CIA community, and Van Loon and Rouget's appointments had boosted morale. Still, there was disappointment surrounding the holdover from the previous leadership in the number three role at the CIA, especially a weasel like Max Hoban.

Hoban had been with the CIA for twenty-eight years, mostly served as an administrator, and he was known for kissing up and kicking down—and for not making any decisions that might harm his career. He had very little field experience, preferring to run operations from the safety of a control center in Langley.

Another Yale man, he was short with thick, greying hair and even thicker glasses. He was a chain-smoker who always reeked like a stale ashtray and his nicotine stained yellow fingernails and fingertips gave him a jaundice look. He exuded a paranoid aura to those he met. As to why he was left as executive director, the train of thought had been that bringing in two new leaders from outside the agency would be too much change. Max Hoban could be sold to the Democrats to get their support for confirming Van Loon and Rouget quickly. Plus, at fifty-eight years old, they figured Max would only stick around for a couple more years anyway.

The popular version around the water cooler as to why Max Hoban remained as Executive Director was that he might have some incriminating pictures of congressmen in his office safe, which had helped him extend his CIA career.

Hoban's paranoia and nasty disposition were infamous around the CIA campus. Serving as chief of the counterintelligence and later as the internal affairs chief could bring that out in someone.

Just about all his peers already disliked Max Hoban, but running the Office of Professional Conduct for ten years had sealed his fate, a hard-ass fate he embraced. Just as cops didn't like internal affairs digging around in their business and second-guessing their actions, neither did agents like the OPC doing the same thing. While Hoban was busy trying to rein in so-called "rogue agents," he somehow let double agents like Aldrich Ames slip undetected for years. Yet he was able to survive all these setbacks to become the Executive Director. *He must have some interesting pictures safely tucked away in that private safe of his,* Maddox thought.

Hoban and Philips were like oil and water, and there was no love lost between the two older CIA men. They saw the role the CIA should play on the world stage very differently. Hoban believed that the agency should focus solely on analysis, without direct action or involvement in the field. After the agency's spotty track record with direct action operations, Hoban, with the backing of the previous White House administration, had been able to move the agency in that direction. The CIA budget had been slashed, the paramilitary division shut down, and the clandestine branch gutted. Hoban's vision of a CIA, whose role was to observe and report, had come to fruition as the agency became as powerless as a mall security guard.

In Max Hoban's CIA, if actual trouble brewed, the agency passed the buck on to the White House and, if action was needed, then the military could take it. He viewed old spymasters like Dick Philips as relics from the past, and Dick viewed pencil pushers like Hoban as gutless.

Hoban had seen and heard about the work of the legendary CIA operative throughout his career and harbored a deep resentment that had been festering for years. Field operatives like Dick Philips got the respect and the glory within the CIA and at the White House while his work labeled him as a bureaucrat and a rat. His heading the CIA Internal Affairs office hadn't exactly won him any favors within the agency rank and file, but it did with the politicians who liked having an inside person who shared their distrust of the CIA—even though Max Hoban was a career CIA man himself.

President Carlson's administration believed in the need for direct action by the CIA and, to Hoban's dismay, it began rolling back Hoban's vision for the CIA. Director Van Loon had long been lobbying for the creation of a paramilitary wing of the CIA. In the last few years, the CIA's Special Operations Group, or SOG, had grown in size and influence. Maddox was cut from the same fabric as his mentor, so Hoban despised Dick Philips's protégé.

Philips immediately began the meeting. "Thank you for attending this briefing on the escalating situation in Venezuela. Station Chief Peter Maddox, with the assistance of Mary Dent —one of his operations officers—will be showing us some of the evidence he's collected from the field."

Philips spent fifteen minutes on general information and background about the rise of Hugo Chávez and why the increased threat level now warranted action before turning the meeting over to Maddox.

Maddox bluntly laid out the current threat brewing in Venezuela. "It's common knowledge that Chávez has long been a follower and admirer of Colonel Muammar Gaddafi," Maddox began, "and now he has made Gaddafi's *Green Book* required reading for his intelligence officers and all members of the military."

Dent slid him Calderon's copy of the infamous book, which Maddox grabbed and held up for everyone to see. "This copy belongs to a high-ranking DISIP agent who is also an asset," Maddox said and handed the book to the DI.

"Sir, as you can see, it's well-worn and heavily highlighted. It's been the bible for the entire DISIP community, the military, and the Chávistas. It's also now being used to indoctrinate Venezuelan children, just like it has been used to indoctrinate Libyan children for over twenty-five years."

Maddox directed the group's attention to the large television monitor. The photograph on the screen showed a small, rural Venezuelan classroom full of children holding their copies of *The Green Book*.

Maddox nodded at Dent and the image changed. "This is a hidden landing strip in the Amazonas state of Venezuela. It's being used to set up a terrorist training camp."

"How do you know this?" interrupted an incredulous Hoban.

Maddox nodded to Dent again and the room went silent as the photographs Calderon had provided and the images taken by the CIA satellites filled the screen, one after another.

While everyone stared, Maddox leaned over and tapped the key for the next slide himself. A photograph of the fallen towers and rubble that used to be the World Trade Center filled the screen.

"This was conceived and planned from Afghanistan with the blessing of the Taliban government. Before Al-Qaeda, there was Gaddafi, and now no one is watching his ass," Maddox explained, as Dick Philips cringed over Maddox's direct manner and the use of the fallen towers only four months after the attacks.

"We have gathered information that Libyan intelligence officers are in Venezuela, including Abdullah Zlitini, a senior officer with Mukhabarat el-Jamahiriya." Maddox let that sink in for a few seconds before moving to the next slide.

"We believe these are crates of weapons that have arrived via this airstrip," Maddox said, pointing to the image on the screen.

"This is a remote area of Venezuela; I can see no other reason for this activity except conducting some sort of training here. All our efforts are currently focused on Afghanistan, Iraq, the Middle East, and some of the African countries like Somalia. So even though Venezuela is right in our own backyard, they're so under the radar that it's easy to set up a training camp there."

"Chávez wouldn't be that stupid," Hoban growled.

"No, sir, but he could easily be manipulated and duped by Gaddafi, who could seize this opportunity to plan an attack while we're busy in Afghanistan and Iraq," Maddox replied.

"Abdullah Zlitini set up and commanded terrorist training camps in Afghanistan and Pakistan back when Osama Bin Laden was just another bored rich Saudi," Philips added. "And now Zlitini is doing the same in Venezuela," he leaned forward, "in our own hemisphere." He tapped his index finger on the table with each word for added emphasis.

"I also have a high-value asset inside the DISIP who tells me they're ramping up their crackdown on political dissension by illegally detaining and torturing members of the opposition," Maddox warned.

Doug Van Loon had sat in silence during this whole presentation, taking it all in. He appeared deep in thought as his hand rubbed his chin. Then, he leaned forward and spoke.

"Dick, do you agree with this assessment?"

"I do, sir," replied Philips.

Inside, Maddox smiled. He had known Philips would have his back, but not just out of blind faith. Philips had devoured all the intelligence Maddox had sent to Langley, and he was alarmed.

"Pete, tell us about Operation Puma," Philips said, ready to drop the bombshell.

Maddox laid out the operational plan. It would consist of two teams. Team Alpha would include Maddox and Delta Task Force 77, the elite direct-action, anti-terrorism unit known as the hunter-killers.

They would take advantage of the planned coup by the council. Caracas would be in chaos during the coup. The

Chávez and his military would have their hands full fighting to stay in power. During the bedlam of the coup, Operation Puma would strike taking out the terrorist training camp, landing strip, and Abdullah Zlitini.

Team Bravo would be led by Bill Anderson's CIA Special Operations Group, commonly referred to as SOG.

SOG would provide the council with the material support it needed, but their role during the actual coup would be more observational, giving Team Alpha the opportunity to strike the camp while keeping an eye on what was happening in Caracas during the same time.

Maddox continued with the briefing.

Team Alpha's base of operations would be near Casuarito, Colombia, which was separated from Puerto Ayacucho by the Orinoco River. The coup in Caracas would be the perfect cover, as Maddox and the Delta Force squadron would take care of the camp some three hundred and thirty miles from the fracas that would consume Caracas.

"Are you nuts?" Max Hoban grunted under his breath.

"No, sir. Doing nothing would be nuts," Maddox responded pointedly.

"Care to elaborate, Max?" Van Loon asked.

"Is this the seventies?" Hoban asked. He glared at Phillips for his role in overthrowing Allende in Chile. Phillips sat there stoically. He didn't even flinch. Hoban then glanced around the room looking for support. None came so he chided the room, "We can't overthrow a democratically elected government."

"This operation is to deal with the terrorist training camp, using the already planned coup against Chávez as cover. This coup will happen with or without us. Our main objective is annihilating that camp. If the coup is successful and Chávez is overthrown, well, that's just gravy, sir," Maddox smiled.

"Bullshit. If the camp is the target, we can use drones to take care of it," Hoban countered. "You want Chávez out."

"Using drones is like leaving our business card," Maddox said. "This isn't Afghanistan. We want to get in and out while everyone is preoccupied in Caracas. They won't know what hit them until we're gone. We have no room for error. We can't have an errant drone hit Puerto Ayacucho. Up close and personal, that's how we can nip this in the bud quickly."

"And the Colombian government is onboard with this?" DI Van Loon asked.

"Yes, sir. They'll let us launch from their soil into Venezuela and return back there once the camp is destroyed. They're every bit as unnerved about the existence of this camp as we are," Maddox replied.

"Okay, then. Thank you, Mr. Maddox," Van Loon said before Hoban could retort.

That was Maddox's cue to leave. He gathered his things while motioning to Mary Dent that it was time to go. They thanked the gathered group for their attention and left the sit room.

———

MADDOX and his team regroup in small conference near the Western Hemisphere section. Once inside, Maddox breathed out loudly.

"That Hoban is an asshole," Dent said. Then she asked, "What now?"

"We wait. It's politics time," Maddox answered, his disdain for that part of the business evident in his voice.

Maddox, Dent, and Pat Mendoza were going over some new intelligence data in the Western Hemisphere bullpen. To an outsider, it would look like a bunch of stock traders analyzing data, staring at computer monitors and scrolling ticker bars. But these weren't stockbrokers gambling away their clients' 401Ks; these were analysts who were sorting through raw intelligence data collected by the field agents. Maddox and Dent hadn't yet found any new information that would affect the operation when Maddox received the call from Dick Philips he had been waiting for—he and Anderson were waiting for Maddox in Philips's office.

"Hoban, what a prick, right?" was how Dick Philips greeted Maddox. Bill Anderson sat quietly with a grin on his face.

"Typical bureaucrat pond scum," Maddox replied.

"Pete, DI Van Loon is behind us, but we need to move quickly. The director doesn't think he can rein in Hoban. He's going to more than likely leak this to Congress, and then Operation Puma will be dead in the water."

"The sooner the better, Dick; the Council is ready to move on this in April. I have a good working relationship with and complete trust in Major David Lucas and his men of B Squadron."

Maddox had worked with Lucas's team on two other separate occasions; he was impressed with their skills, and he and the men got along great, a rarity for CIA and Delta Force personnel.

"Good. I'll call the joint special operations commander and have them on the ground posthaste. But Pete, Van Loon wants plausible deniability for the president, so SOG is riding shotgun on this one. This won't get tied to the White House. You hear what I'm saying, right?"

"Loud and clear," Maddox responded without hesitation.

CHAPTER FIFTEEN

S-RACK

Langley, Virginia. Western Hemisphere Command Center.

"HOBAN WILL FIGHT IT TOOTH AND NAIL, BUT I THINK we'll get the green light for Operation Puma," Philips announced as he walked into his command center.

"Will he go to Congress or the White House with this?" Maddox asked.

"Max Hoban is more of a political animal than anything else. He won't risk his hide right now; he'll be watching from the sidelines to see how this plays out politically for him before he does anything one way or another. But if things go bad, he'll sell us all up the river in a New York minute," Philips explained.

Maddox detested people playing politics with America's security more than anything, and the prevalence of that practice in the city was one of the reasons he hated working in DC.

Too many politicians polluting the air, he would think to himself over and over during his trips to the nation's capital.

The Hugo Chávez training camp problem wasn't going

away, and Maddox had just handed them solution to this problem on a silver platter. He wondered what there was to think about. He wanted the green light to proceed with Operation Puma by the time he went back to Venezuela in three days, but he had to let the bureaucrats to do their thing.

"I know how much you hate this part, Pete," Philips said consolingly. "Trust me, I do as well. I've just been doing this a lot longer than you," he said grinning.

Maddox knew that was the truth. Especially for an old spy warrior like Dick Philips, who operated in years gone by when the CIA was much more active in taking care of problem regimes. The new breed of timid CIA operative that rose from the cutback-happy nineties was one of the reasons the Special Risk Assessment Commission had been established.

The SRAC was a secret organization within the already secretive Central Intelligence Agency. Its creation had been deemed crucial in an era when Congress openly questioned whether the CIA's existence was even necessary, and it had one goal: to act when the politicians refused to do so.

The commission's existence was but a rumor; its members were unknown and they met in secret. Even the president was kept in the dark about the SRAC.

Some presidential administrations welcomed the commission and its secrecy. It provided them with the real plausible deniability they craved when the shit hit the fan.

The creation of the CIA's Special Operations Group brought back black ops in full force and gave the commission an actual paramilitary arm it could use. With SOG now in existence, Hoban knew the commission would proceed with Operation Puma, regardless of the official directive from the White House and Director Van Loon.

Hoban had tasked himself with exposing and destroying the commission, even though he had no proof, no leverage. But he wasn't going to let it go, especially since Dick Philips, a man he had despised for years, was overseeing the operation.

———

On Maddox's flight back to Venezuela, the last meeting he'd attended still played in his head.

Dick Philips called him in just hours before his flight back to Caracas, and when Maddox arrived at his boss' office, a man he didn't know was sitting there with Philips.

"Mr. Maddox, it's a real pleasure," the man said to Maddox, extending his hand and offering a firm shake. "Do you go by Pete or Peter?"

The man whose hand he was shaking looked to be in his late forties, had a shaved head, and spoke with a Southern drawl, *possibly Texan*, Maddox thought.

"Pete is fine, sir, and you are?" Maddox replied.

"My name is Bill Anderson. Dick has told me a lot about you. Your briefs on Operation Puma are very impressive. Excellent briefs, Pete."

"Thank you, Mr. Anderson," Maddox said.

"Please, Pete, call me Bill; we're all friends here," Anderson said, gesturing toward the room.

"Okay, Bill, what's going on here?" Maddox said. He loathed inane chitchat.

"You're right, Dick, he doesn't beat around the bush," Anderson said smiling.

"I have a flight to catch," Maddox responded with a tinge of annoyance.

"Right, right. Pete, Operation Puma has been green-lit by the SRAC," Anderson said, pronouncing it S-RACK.

"What about the chain of command?" Maddox asked.

"I'm here, which means you don't have to worry about the

chain of command," Anderson said, the smile now gone from his face.

"Pete," Dick said calmly and coolly, "Director Van Loon is behind you, but the official line from the White House is that you're to continue your surveillance and intelligence gathering —especially on the air strip—for more concrete proof that a terrorist training camp is being built. As for the planned coup, the official command is we're not to be involved, nor are we supposed to provide aid. Van Loon wants to ensure the president is cocooned from it."

"Therefore, Operation Puma will be funded by the SRAC, off the books," Anderson added.

"The money is from the SRAC's budget, and support will be coming from Bill's SOG team, not from the Western Hemisphere desk," Philips explained.

"Do you know what that means, Pete?" Anderson asked.

"Yes, that we're going Ollie North on this operation," Maddox said grinning. Maddox said that to get a rise out of Philips and Anderson, but it also made the point that he knew exactly what he was getting into.

During the Iran-Contra scandal of the eighties, Oliver North had paid the price, as well as several CIA operatives who their own agency and the White House labeled as rogue agents and booted out of the CIA.

If the shit were to hit the fan, it was Maddox who would get splattered, not the president. The commander in chief would be able to say he'd had no knowledge of the operation and to blame it all on those damn pesky rouge CIA types.

Maddox had no idea if the president actually knew about this operation or not. Perhaps Van Loon was insulating him so he could look reporters in the eye and deny knowing about any covert operations to oust a foreign government. Or perhaps the president knew exactly what was about to happen.

Bill Anderson and his team didn't officially exist. Sure, the man was standing there in Dick Philips's office talking to Maddox, but he didn't exist on paper. The man and his SOG team were ghosts, and as station chief, Maddox was the bagman —if need be, he would be left holding the bag.

"That's right. If this mission fails, if the operation is exposed, the agency will not have your back. Once we're done here, there is no turning back," Anderson confirmed. "And for every Oliver North that becomes a book-writing celebrity, there are twice as many anonymous stars on the wall, and some don't even make it on the wall," he warned ominously.

Maddox knew the wall he spoke of—the CIA's memorial wall. Located in the north side of the lobby of the agency's headquarters, it honored the men and women who gave their lives in the service of the agency and their country. Most entries were marked with only a single gold star; their names, deaths, and missions would remain secrets never to be revealed.

Maddox had grown tired of the Beltway political maneuvering. He was ready to get back to Venezuela for Operation Puma and for Sonia Collins.

"I understand and am eager to kick some Libyan ass," Maddox replied with a smile.

Anderson and Philips both shook Maddox's hand.

"Bill and his team will be in Caracas in seventy-two hours," Philips said as he returned to his desk.

"We'll be operational in twenty-four hours once on the ground; because of your thorough brief, we'll already have the tools needed to aid the mission," Anderson informed him.

"What about Hoban?" Maddox asked.

"He's my problem," Philips said.

"I think you got the short end of the stick," Maddox said to Philips as he got out of his chair. "Gentlemen, I have a flight to catch. Bill, see you in Caracas."

CHAPTER SIXTEEN

LA ORDEN PARA LIBERACION

Caracas, Venezuela

MADDOX'S MIND RACED AS HE MADE IT BACK TO CARACAS. Excited and nervous that his operation was approved. He chucked reading tits name, Operation Puma.

Naming it Puma was a Venezuela inside joke. A tongue-in-cheek reference to Jose Luis "El Puma" Rodriguez, one of the most popular entertainers in Venezuela. He was a well-known superstar, a singer and star actor of popular Venezuelan TV soaps. He was a heartthrob who looked very much like a Latin George Hamilton. Dick Philips got it, but advised Maddox to leave that tidbit out of his presentation and let them think he named it after the large, secretive cats found hunting in the Venezuelan mountains.

Coup d'états had a long and storied past in Venezuela. Chávez himself had tried to overthrow the elected president back in 1992, but his coup had failed and he spent three years in prison. Such a fate would not be an option for these new plotters if Chávez got his hands on them; they would be tortured and killed by the merciless Chávistas. Things would be particularly brutal for Calderon who would meet a slow and excruciating death at the hands of his boss, Johan Brull.

But this group was intent on not failing. It had formed a secret organization known as La Orden Para Liberacion, the Order for Liberation. The Order had been planning the coup for five months when Calderon approached Maddox for assistance. Maddox remembered the night well.

Calderon had scheduled another meeting but not an official DISIP-CIA meeting; Johan Brull had forbidden any DISIP cooperation with the CIA months before. Mary Dent saw Calderon's chalk mark during her daily run through the park.

Maddox met Henry Calderon at the predetermined location. Every month, the meeting location changed: public libraries, parks, bars, safe houses—they used them all. But arranging the meetings was getting tougher and tougher as Johan Brull had Chávistas on every corner, and they could be anyone. Times were so tough that you couldn't really rely on your neighbors, friends, or even family members to not rat you out to Brull's internal security force for a few Bolivars.

Calderon arrived first, bringing with him a prostitute he had hired as cover. As par for the course for Calderon, she was quiet the looker, which made her a perfectly believable decoy. If Calderon were being followed, the DISIP counter-intelligence agents would pack it in once they saw Calderon show up at a friend's house with his new girlfriend and a bottle of wine.

Calderon rang the doorbell. His friend and co-conspirator, Juan Carlos "Juanca" Castilla, greeted them at the door. Inside, a dinner party was in full swing. Maddox had already been at the house for two hours, lying low in the maid's room, waiting for their meeting.

"Pete, how are you?" When it was just him and Maddox, Calderon used his friend's real name; he was one of the only people in the Order who knew it. Everyone else continued to call him Rick Castro.

"Good, Henry. One of these days we'll have to meet without all the maneuvering," Maddox said with a smile and quick embrace.

"Yes, and that's what I want to talk to you about tonight. Perhaps we can expedite things so that day comes sooner than later," Calderon said, punctuation the second statement with a grin.

Maddox returned the grin and took a look at Calderon's girl before shutting the bedroom door.

"Hot date you got there," Maddox said.

"She's a pro," Calderon informed Maddox with proud smile.

"DISIP?" Maddox asked, thinking she was an intelligence agent.

Calderon burst out laughing. "No, no, my friend. 'Pro' as in a working girl. You know, like the movie *Pretty Woman*? I pay her to be my date and decoy and after our business," he motioned to Maddox and himself, "we get down to the business of the oldest profession," Calderon finished with lustful chuckle.

"Hey, I can have one of her friends come over for you. Good looking, just like her," Calderon offered.

"Thanks, but I'm okay," Maddox said with his hands held out in surrender as he steered the conversation back to work. "So how are you planning on expediting things?"

Calderon filled Maddox in on the activities of the council these past few months. The coup was all planned and they had just been waiting for the perfect time, which seemed to be now. Chávez had recently passed a number of laws in his attempt to strengthen government control over the state oil company, PDVSA. Many organizations condemned this action, and the council now had the support of the union leaders in beginning a general strike to protest the strong-arm tactics.

The power struggle between the Chávez government and PDVSA would be the perfect distraction. Frank Chacon and the commission were ready. Chacon had been waiting for this moment for years. He was one of the few who dared to speak out against Chávez. Chacon planned to run for president against Chávez in the next election, but the chances of a fair election were slim. As the council's chairman, Chacon would be the primary leader until Assemblyman Espinoza was installed as interim president after the overthrow of Chávez, with the elections planned within six months of the coup. Francisco Chacon planned to run for president then, but until that time, he would be the man running the country from behind the scenes. The strikes and protests were the perfect opportunity to make that happen.

As the Chávistas were out cracking skulls to break up the strike, the council's military action would begin to oust Chávez from power. The coup would also be the perfect cover for Operation Puma, which would destroy the terrorist training camp in the Amazon.

Maddox thought the overthrow of Chávez would be a bonus. Maddox believed getting rid of Chávez was in the best interest of the United States, but while the days of having CIA-planned coups might be over, the backing of a US-friendly coup was the next best thing.

CHAPTER SEVENTEEN

SATURDAYS

Caracas, Venezuela

SATURDAY HAD QUICKLY BECOME MADDOX'S FAVORITE DAY of the week because usually got to spend it with Sonia. They would go for a run around Parque del Este, play tennis, run errands, go to dinner, and later make love. Maddox really enjoyed spending time with her.

A few times, on a whim, Maddox had whisked her away on his Cessna airplane for a thirty-minute flight to the beautiful white sandy beaches of Playa Puerto Cruz.

There were also days like today, where they would just spend time with each other at her house in Prados del Este. Maddox's job prevented a normal courtship, but their relationship had flourished in the months since they had first become romantically involved in San Cristobal.

This was a scenario he had intentionally avoided during his CIA career, and even though he was the happiest in his personal life he had been in years, his love for Sonia was causing him to take risks he normally wouldn't.

Although they were not broadcasting their relationship, they weren't exactly hiding it either, and Maddox was very aware of the danger of the situation. Sonia's safety was constantly on his mind. Even though she was on the CIA payroll, she was not an employee, so she didn't have diplomatic immunity.

Maddox was always careful to ensure that someone like Johan Brull couldn't find out how important Sonia was to him, but he was still concerned. He desperately wanted Sonia to go stay for a while with her mother and sister, who had finally had enough of Chávez and moved to Florida. His attempts to do so, however, had been the cause of the few fights they'd had during their short romance. That still didn't stop him from trying again.

"Babe, have you given any thought to what we talked about?" Maddox asked.

"I'm not leaving or hiding, especially when you won't give me any information other than 'Don't be here for all of April.' I can't do that; I have a business to run," Sonia said, giving her standard reply.

"I've told you, there are things about my work that I cannot share with you. You need to understand that and trust me," Maddox pleaded.

"I do trust you, but I'm not leaving."

Maddox hinted that Caracas was not going to be a safe place soon. She scoffed at his statement. "It's safe now?"

She had a point. Crime in Caracas was not only increasing, it was becoming more violent, and kidnappings especially were on the rise.

But Operation Puma was moving forward. In one month, Venezuela was going to be under fire and he would be some 300 miles away from her. Still, Maddox had figured this attempt at convincing her would fail like the previous ones, so he had already initiated plan B.

Plan B had consisted of Maddox calling his good friend Tom Rose, a former British SAS soldier who had retired from MI6 last year and was now doing freelance work. He had told Rose that he wanted him to provide security for Sonia and that the job was of a personal nature. Rose had agreed immediately and promised to be in Caracas in the next forty-eight hours.

Since plan B was already in effect, Maddox—much to Sonia's surprise—let the argument drop and decided to focus on enjoying as much time with her as he could during this calm before the storm.

———

Tom Rose arrived in Caracas as promised. As thrilled as Maddox was to see his friend again, he was even more relieved to have someone he could trust to watch over Sonia. Maddox was going to be fully engaged with Operation Puma and was not going to be around to protect her. He couldn't tell her that a coup was brewing, but he wasn't going to leave her in the middle of that shit storm alone.

Rose had refused to take his money—this was about helping a friend—but Maddox had wanted to make sure that Rose would get paid, so he'd brought him in as an official contractor for Operation Puma. This would allow Maddox to share details about the entire operation with him and run Rose's fifteen-thousand-dollar fee through the agency.

Rose had accepted the standard twenty-one day CIA contract for freelancers. The contract was for providing security and logistics and that's exactly what he would be doing, but for Sonia; he would become her shadow for the next month.

Maddox and Rose indulged in some friendly catching up

on the drive from the airport to the embassy, but when they reached eventually reached the situation room, the conversation switched gears, and Maddox explained what Chávez and the Libyans had been up to.

Maddox showed him the pictures of the Libyan terrorist training camp and the landing strip, and briefed him on the details of Operation Puma, including the upcoming coup attempt.

"My high-value asset inside the DISIP provided me with the coordinates of this place. Our satellites took these pictures," Maddox explained.

"That fucking runt," Rose seethed in his thick, Lancashire accent.

"We have two operations going; my man inside the DISIP brought me in on a planned coup scheduled for April 11," Maddox said, continuing to lay down the groundwork for Rose.

"Bloody hell, the agency planned it?" Rose asked.

"No, we don't do that anymore," Maddox said with a shit-eating grin. "But seriously, it's a local op that they've been planning for over a year. They brought us in for material support; you know the drill: guns and money, shit like that. In exchange, not only do we get that fucking midget Chávez out of power, but they'll let us handle the Libyan camp on our terms."

"Who is working with the locals?" Rose asked.

"SOG. They'll play second fiddle in Caracas, just providing weapons and taking an observe-and-report role during the coup.

"When the military operation in Caracas hits, I'll be with Delta Force in the Amazon jungle taking care of that camp and landing strip. There is an Army and a Navy base in Puerto Ayachucho, so any action up there will be assumed to be part of the coup. Since they'll also be scrambling with what's going on in Caracas, that camp will be the last thing on their minds," Maddox finished with a smile.

"Brilliant, mate," Rose said, impressed with Operation Puma.

"Now, the third operation—our operation, Operation Asset —is just between you and me, Tom," Maddox said tapping his chest and then Rose's.

"Sonia Collins is my most valuable asset because she means a lot to me *personally*," Maddox explained. "I don't want her solo when all hell breaks loose here, and if Johan Brull finds out about her role as an asset, he will have her arrested." Maddox paused for a few seconds, mentally shuddering at the thought.

"If he finds out she's special to me on a personal level, he will skin her alive just for fun," Maddox's voice trembled.

"You don't have to worry about your girl, mate," Rose assured him. Then he asked, "Did you get my shopping list?"

"I sure did," Maddox said, placing a large black weapons suitcase on the table. He spun it around to face Rose and opened it so he could see the contents. "I got it all right here."

The two SIG Sauer P226 9mm handguns, HK MP5 submachine gun with fifty-round magazines, and case of flash-bang stun grenades would easily provide enough firepower to hunker down during a military coup while protecting an asset.

While Rose and Maddox went over how to best protect Sonia, she was having a hard time dealing with Maddox's job. Although she had figured there would be danger getting involved with a CIA agent—hell, she had seen him armed and in action in San Cristobal—she apparently hadn't really had a clue as to what she was getting into when she fell in love with him.

She just didn't understand what was going on. She had refused to leave the country when Maddox begged her to, and now he was assigning her a 24/7 bodyguard.

The danger of her situation was starting to sink in, but it was still infuriating because Maddox wouldn't tell her why this was necessary.

The honeymoon period of a relationship wasn't supposed to last forever, but usually new couple arguments didn't involve life-and-death matters or whether or not someone needed to have an armed personal bodyguard.

"I'm sorry, honey, but this not negotiable," Maddox said. "You have to trust me on this – you do trust me, don't you?" Maddox tilted his head and gently took her hands in his.

The guilt trip attempt backfired and Sonia angrily yanked her hands away, but she still seemed willing to listen.

"Yes, of course," she finally responded in a near whisper. *Backfire averted,* Maddox thought as Sonia continued, her voice full of frustration. "It's just hard. First you want me to leave the country, now you want me to have this bodyguard with me 24/7, but you won't tell me what the hell is going on. You're scaring me, Pete."

Maddox once again took her hands, tenderly interlocking his fingers with hers.

"We've talked about this, honey. There are parts of my job that I can never discuss with you. Ever. You need to understand that. But it's going to become even more dangerous here than usual. I shouldn't even be telling you that," Maddox said as he looked into her tearful green eyes.

"Tom isn't just some bodyguard. He is a friend, and I trust him with my own life, which is why I asked him to watch over you. Just for a week or so."

"Is he with the CIA, too?" Sonia asked.

"No. But he's good at what he does. He's retired MI6, and since I won't be able to be here to protect you, I'll feel better if he is."

"Protect me from what?" Sonia asked anxiously.

"Sonia, you know that Venezuela is a dangerous place if you're not a Chávista; that's why your mother and sister moved to Miami after your dad died." Maddox was now caressing the tops of her hands.

"Not only are you involved with me, you're an asset for the CIA. You're on our payroll, so you could be in danger. "I'm probably overreacting, but I'm going to be gone for the next couple weeks, and I'll feel better knowing you'll be safe with Tom." Maddox gently brushed a strand of hair away from her face and kissed her.

Sonia looked down, allowing a tear to escape. She was experiencing so many emotions. She was worried about Maddox's safety, about her own safety.

Maddox kissed her again, and then they just held each other for a while.

CHAPTER EIGHTEEN

THE AMAZONAS

MADDOX VERY MUCH HAD SONIA ON HIS MIND AS HE landed his Cessna at the one-lane Cacique Aramare Airport in Puerto Ayachucho. The small plane rocked and vibrated as it taxied down the poorly maintained asphalt lane that served as the landing strip.

When Maddox stepped out of his plane, the steamy, hot weather of the Amazonas state hit him across the face like a barber's towel. Caracas was warm, but nothing like the stifling heat he felt now as he glanced to the west, toward the clandestine Libyan terrorist camp hidden only seventy-five miles from the small airport.

Operation Puma was moving into operational mode very quickly. Maddox felt his adrenaline surging. He was worried about Sonia, but felt relatively at ease knowing her safety was in Tom Rose's hands.

Still, Maddox was second-guessing himself again for not forcing Sonia out of the country. The alpha male inside that helped him track down and kill terrorists could have taken hold and ordered her out, but that wasn't the type of man he wanted to be anymore, at least not with her. Plus, Sonia was an independent woman who wouldn't have reacted well to being ordered to do anything. Unfortunately, trying to reason with her hadn't worked either; she was staying in Caracas, but at least Tom Rose was with her now.

Maddox's mind shifted gears when he saw a vehicle approaching. He smiled when he recognized Ruben Guzman behind the wheel of the red Toyota Tundra pickup truck.

Maddox liked and trusted Guzman. Corruption ran rampant in the Colombian military and police force, so it was difficult for Maddox to trust anyone from their ranks, but this man had proven to be a good ally.

Guzman had been the agent in charge of the ELN rebel safe house raid the year before, and his letting Maddox interrogate one of the prisoners had led to the discovery of the training camp. That successful raid had also led to a nice promotion for Guzman; he was now head of the DAS special operations team.

The truck came to a stop and Guzman quickly popped out from the driver side with a smile and a wave.

"How are you, my friend?" Guzman said as he walked toward Maddox. The two men shared a handshake and quick embrace.

Guzman had been critical in making it possible for Maddox and the Delta Force to launch their assault from Colombian soil, giving the operation the critical element of surprise.

The thought of the Colombian drug cartels striking an alliance with Libya and Venezuela to train at the camp had been keeping Colombian president Miguel Angel Perez awake at night. He pledged full support to allow US forces to set up their command center on Colombian soil.

The Delta Force squadron was already bivouacking in the Colombian jungle near Casuarito, just across the Orinoco River from Puerto Ayachucho.

Maddox had the full confidence of Delta Force B Squadron, commanded by Major David Lucas and Command Sergeant Major Mickey Welch. He'd worked with the squad before, and they were also the same Delta Force operators who had successfully rescued Brian Hart based on intelligence from that same safe house raid with Guzman.

The intelligence Maddox had collected led right to the ELN camp where Hart was held. Eight ELN rebels had been killed, and the hostage was rescued unharmed. A damn fine operation, Maddox thought. He held these operators in high regard indeed.

Delta Force was used to having to mobilize quickly, but due to the intelligence Maddox had collected, they'd had the luxury of prepping this time. They had left their headquarters in Ft. Bragg, North Carolina, and had spent a week in the Panamanian jungle training before setting up their bivouac camp in the Colombian jungle, where they could easily cross into Venezuela to conduct surveillance before the assault. Now, they were ready and eager to strike.

Guzman and Maddox took one of the frequently departing ferries from Puerto Ayachucho to the small village of Casuarito. They paid the ferry operator the equivalent of two dollars for the quick trip across the Orinoco River. It was a beautiful part of the world, and Maddox allowed himself to enjoy quiet ride across the river for a while.

"How are things looking, Ruben?" Maddox finally asked after spending what felt like an hour staring at the soothing waters.

"Your boys have set up camp not far from Casuarito. It's only about a thirty-minute drive, but it's a world of difference;

we're headed into the thick jungle," Ruben warned with a friendly smile.

"I love camping," Maddox replied with his own smile.

The conversation turned serious. "Those bastards are here in full force," Ruben said, referring to the Libyans at the camp.

"We'll get those fuckers," Maddox replied, his adrenaline surging a bit before the waters calmed him back down.

CHAPTER NINETEEN

SONIA'S BODYGUARD

Caracas, Venezuela

SONIA WAS ON EDGE. WHEN TOM ROSE ARRIVED, THE seriousness of the situation had finally hit her full force, and her worry for herself and for Maddox had gone through the roof. *Maybe I should have left the country*, she'd kept thinking.

Fortunately, Rose had put her at ease. She quite liked the tall, funny Brit; he was like a character out of *Wild Geese*. But while Rose was funny and a bit silly, he was also very meticulous and professional about her security—so much so that his over-cautious, at least to her, way of doing things could get on her nerves. Everything from running errands to hanging out at home required its own strict security routine, which seemed a bit much. Nevertheless, she followed along since she felt safe under his care.

Sonia wasn't sure what she being kept safe from, but she knew something big was going to happen. Maddox had warned her that he would be unable to communicate with her for the next week or two, and that was the type of thing that was causing her to cast serious doubt on her relationship with him.

Sonia was in love with Maddox, but it was hard carrying on with a spy. There were a lot of secrets, of course, and at first she had thought that wouldn't be a problem for her, but she was finding it more difficult to deal with than she had imagined.

She hated the not knowing—not knowing what was going on or if he was okay. There was also the fact that Maddox was on year three of his four-year assignment, and the future seemed uncertain.

Sonia had already gone through a similar situation when she had dated a young diplomat. The man had moved away to Italy, breaking her heart. She had ended up recovering rather quickly from that when she'd realized she hadn't truly been in love with him, but with Maddox it was different—her heart very much belonged to him.

But she was also thirty-one years old now; how much time was she willing to devote to a man with a job like that? A job that required secrecy and deception, that often put him in dangerous situations and now appeared to have done the same to her?

At first, being a paid asset had been exhilarating, and the money was great. Sonia looked around her beautiful office. She would still be in the old family place if it hadn't been for Maddox.

Sonia couldn't be mad at Maddox for her involvement as an asset. She could have said no.

It was driving her mad having no idea where he was or what he was doing. Or what was going on that required a 24/7 bodyguard. And, to top it off, she wouldn't hear from him for a couple weeks. No phone calls. No emails. No text messages. Nada.

Thoughts of ending the relationship occasionally crept into

her mind, but they were just that, thoughts—thoughts she would never act on. For better or worse, she was in love with Maddox, and she wasn't able or willing to just walk away from what they had together.

Sonia needed to get her mind on other things, so she decided to get some work done by going to the office with her bodyguard in tow.

Graciela Kohl walked into the realty office to find Tom Rose sitting in the lobby. She lit up when he stood up and introduced himself as Sonia's new client from London. Graciela introduced herself and flirted with him for a moment before she made a beeline into Sonia's office and begged to be allowed to show him properties.

"You can keep the commission; he's just so handsome! Come on, Sonia, I'm tired of being single," Graciela pleaded.

If Graciela only knew, Sonia thought, that this client was really an ex-Special Forces soldier and spy who was now basically a mercenary sent here to protect her from who knew what.

"Ay, Graciela, this isn't a dating service. Don't you have work to do?" Sonia replied in exasperation.

Graciela looked like a scolded puppy for a moment before throwing an irritated, "Fine" at Sonia and stomping out of her office. She did, however, manage to regain her composure quickly enough to flash another flirty smile and bat her eyes at Rose before she disappeared into her cube.

Sonia felt a little bad; she had never been so short with her friend before, but she had too much going on in her head to deal with Graciela's desperate need for a man. *I need to get out of here. This isn't working to clear my head,* she thought.

Sonia walked out of her office and asked, "Mr. Rose, are you ready to look at those properties?"

CHAPTER TWENTY

FORWARD BASE CAMP

Near Casuarito, Colombia

THE COLOMBIAN MILITARY HUMVEE DRIVER EXPERTLY navigated the rough road from Casuarito up into the jungle, but it was still a bumpy ride that tossed Maddox around the back-seat like a rag doll. As the vehicle crossed a rather deep seeming river, water seeped inside. *A little deeper and we'll need a fucking boat,* Maddox thought to himself as he looked out the window at the water lapping against the middle of the doors. Finally, at the end of the long, winding, unpaved road, they arrived at their destination.

The command center was only thirty miles from the village, but it was deep within the jungle at a camp the Colombian military had built a few years before to house their troops fighting the cartels and rebels in the area.

The setup consisted of three stand-alone structures—a meeting room and two sets of barracks. They were all small, low-framed buildings made completely out of wood, with rusted tin roofs and creaky slabs of wood serving as a floor, which surprised Maddox. Dirt floors were usually the norm in these types of settings. The upper halves of the buildings were wide open to take advantage of Mother Nature's air conditioning but screened in with mesh to keep out the vicious mosquitoes and other Amazon critters.

"Fancy," Maddox said to Guzman as he pointed to the floor and the mesh of the barrack they stood in.

"Only the best. The real Four Seasons hotel," he said with his arms pointing toward the open air. Guzman then extended his hand out to Maddox.

"Get those cabrones."

"We will. Thanks for everything you've done, Ruben."

"Goddamn, if it isn't Mad Max," a voice brayed from inside the other barrack. Although Maddox couldn't make out the figure behind the mesh, he recognized the booming voice of Sergeant First Class Hermes Ramos.

Ramos was a gregarious, loudmouthed, pain in the ass and former Ranger buddy from Maddox's army days. He was from Ponce, Puerto Rico. Maddox had been shocked when he'd first run into Ramos again during an operation a few years back. He'd thought for sure the man would have worn out his welcome with the army, but Ramos had found his niche and become a skilled Special Forces soldier, and now he was with the best of the best, Delta Force.

"Good God, man, don't you have your twenty in yet?" Maddox teased as Ramos walked into the barracks where he was setting up his gear. The two embraced.

"Good to see you, Mad Max," Ramos said, using the nickname he'd hung around Maddox's neck years ago.

The other members of the squad began addressing Maddox as Mad Max. There was a deep respect for secrecy within these troops. Everyone operated on a need-to-know basis, and no one needed to know their CIA contact's real name.

During a past operation in Europe, Maddox had dyed his hair blond and slicked it back. When he'd put on a pair of dark shades, Ramos had quipped, "Goddamn, it's Max Headroom," and the name had stuck.

Maddox always tried to tell a different story, that his nickname came because he reminded people of Mel Gibson's Mad Max character, but that version hadn't stuck.

"I thought Delta Force only accepted the best," Maddox teased as he gave Ramos a friendly shove.

The relationship between the CIA and Delta Force had become strained the past few years. In the late eighties and through the nineties, the bureaucrats had stripped the CIA's role as a direct participant in operations due to past scandals, successfully turning the agency's role into one of observing and reporting.

But during the last few years, things had changed and President Carlson had authorized Van Loon to create SOG, which its detractors coined the CIA's army.

SOG became more and more involved in direct paramilitary action, which stirred up a turf war between the military and the CIA. The military didn't want SOG involved in direct action—that role belonged to Special Forces. They also weren't too keen that the CIA kept recruiting Delta Force troops into SOG.

But Squadron B got along well with Maddox. He was at least a former Ranger, and he stayed out of their way, letting them do their jobs. Even before the recent formation of SOG, Maddox had enjoyed a good working relationship with Delta Force. He was not one to micromanage from Langley or his office in Caracas. He was out here in the field alone. He didn't bring any other CIA operatives. That was the reason why Maddox wanted Bill Anderson and his SOG troops in Caracas assisting with the coup, while he worked with Delta Force in taking out the Libyan terrorist training camp.

Maddox had confidence in these Special Forces operators. He rather missed being in a tight unit like Delta Force. These men would probably be shocked to learn that Maddox was a station chief since he preferred to be out in the field.

The Delta Force came in, did their job, and got out; there were no politics to deal with. And, in the highly structured world of the military, Delta Force was given a lot of leeway. They wore their hair in civilian styles, not telltale military haircuts, and many had beards and mustaches so they could blend into the real world.

They mostly wore civilian clothes, and in operations like this one where they did wear fatigues, they were bereft of any of the usual military uniform markings: no ranks, patches, name tags, dog tags, or anything like that. They looked like mercenaries, not regular military.

Delta Force was a soldier's unit, made of sergeants. The commanders were officers, but they mostly played more support-based roles, ensuring the unit had everything it needed as well as coordinating the missions. The officers also dealt with the bureaucratic and political headaches so the actual unit of noncommissioned officers could just do their jobs.

The unit commander, Major Dave Lucas, would man the command center from the jungle on the Colombian side, in direct contact with Squadron Commander, Colonel Nathan Coolidge, who would be monitoring the strike team from the Pentagon.

In the field and during the assault, Command Sergeant Major Mickey Welch would run the show, with his direct strike and sniper units reporting up to him. He would report to Major Lucas.

Maddox entered the impromptu command center in one of

the open-air buildings for CSM Welch's intel briefing. After he and Maddox greeted each other and took a couple minutes to catch up, Welch was ready to start the briefing.

Mickey Welch was a farm boy from Iowa, big and country strong. His daily briefing was based on intelligence gathered by the sniper team, who had taken up observation posts near the training camp for the past three days.

The Libyan and Venezuelan forces had no idea they were being watched by Delta Force snipers, who would radio back the data collected to the command center.

"Gentlemen, listen up," CSM Mickey Welch boomed. "No new targets today. We have twenty-one targets to clear from the camp, both Libyan and Venezuelan, including the big fish, Abdullah Zlitini." Welch inserted a jump drive into the laptop in front of him. "I've uploaded the pictures taken by the sniper team this afternoon. They match perfectly with the pictures the CIA snapped from the sky." Welch nodded in appreciation toward Maddox.

"There are four structures already built: a guardhouse that they're also using for weapons storage and two barracks—all concrete from floor to ceiling—as well as a prefab structure used for training purposes." CSM Welch swatted a fly away before continuing, "There is also a four-lane firing range and an obstacle course with five obstacles. There is also what appears to be a helipad. Construction is ongoing, so the plan here must be 3 for a rather large, permanent facility. We'll make sure that won't happen," he said with a smile.

"The camp is located in the nearby forested mountains, twenty-six kilometers from Puerto Ayachucho. But don't let that proximity fool you; this is remote as shit terrain we're talking about. The landing strip is three kilometers from the main structures. We'll be taking that out as well."

Welch paused for effect and then continued with his briefing. "It's going to be a coordinated assault. We're going to strike once the local military action is in effect down in Caracas. Max will be giving us a briefing about that momentarily." Welch gestured towards Maddox.

"The sniper team will take out the guard detail, and then the direct action team will storm the guardhouse under sniper cover. At this time, we'll C-4 the fuck out of the two barracks, the obstacle course, helipad, and landing strip. We'll hit them hard and fast."

"Fuck yeah," Hermes Ramos called out, interrupting Welch who simply smiled and shook his head.

Maddox then briefed the unit on the details of the coup. It was the cornerstone of Operation Puma. The entire Venezuelan military, including the army and naval bases in Puerto Ayachucho, would be focusing their attention on the ongoing coup while the assault on the camp was under way. The official date, which had been confirmed by Henry Calderon, was April 11.

Maddox made his way through the barracks. It was quiet as the men prepared for the assault. Master Sergeant Wes Palokangas was the explosive and demolition expert, and he and his team were busy prepping the C-4 packs. These were highly explosive bombs made from materials found in any hardware store.

The plan was to go low-tech, nothing too fancy. These would be simple but highly destructive explosives that could have originated from a rival terrorist group, like the ELN or the FARC, or the drug cartels. Langley was adamant that the unit not leave any calling cards pointing to the United States, especially since the Langley analysts gave the coup only a 30 percent chance of being successful; the agency didn't want its illegal presence in Venezuela to be known.

MSG Palokangas and crew had created twenty-five home-made claymore mines, enough firepower to level the camp and destroy the landing strip. Under the cover of sniper fire and the C-4 explosions, the direct action team would assault the buildings, killing anyone left standing.

It was a beautiful, quiet, and calm night in the jungle. There were so many stars in the sky, more than he had ever seen in the smog-glutted skies of Caracas. Maddox laid on his army cot wondering how Sonia was holding out and thinking how this would be the last night of calm for at least several days. *I love the calm before the storm*, Maddox thought as he drifted into sleep.

CHAPTER TWENTY-ONE

LOCK DOWN

Caracas, Venezuela

TOM ROSE AND SONIA COLLINS WERE ON LOCKDOWN AT her house in Prados Del Este. Caracas was paralyzed from one of the biggest strikes the country had ever seen. The strikes started to protest the Chávez hard line, but they came to fruition when Pedro Carmona, head of the unions, led his members in a strike to show their support of the other strikers.

There had been two hundred thousand people on strike, protesting on the streets with signs, whistles, flags, and drums and chanting in unison—a massive sea of people that clogged the streets and brought the city to a standstill. The Chávista thugs were unleashed onto the streets. They had beat protesters back and then begun firing upon them, all on national television while a panicked nation watched. It had been the catalyst the council needed to implement its coup.

At first, Sonia had been dismissive of the dangers.

"A strike? This is what Peter was so worried about?" she asked. "These are normal in my country, Tom."

Rose just smiled, not about to confirm or deny anything.

"I should be out there protesting against Chávez," Sonia stated defiantly as she stared at the television.

He couldn't keep quiet about that comment. "Absolutely not, my dear; we just need to stay put. Please, listen to me. I gave Pete my word that I would keep you safe. Going out into that zoo is not keeping you safe."

Sonia had felt like she was being held hostage in her own home when Frank Chacon had appeared on television, announcing to the nation that a coup was in place to oust Hugo Chávez.

"Our only objective is to restore true liberty to Venezuela," he said in front of a bank of microphones.

A shocked Sonia alternated between staring at the TV and looking at Rose. As the serious events unfolded right before her eyes on national television, she began to realize why Maddox hadn't wanted her in Caracas.

"Is this really happening?" Sonia asked Rose without looking at him, her eyes fixed on the television as it broadcast Frank Chacon's press conference.

"It appears so," Rose replied neutrally.

"Cut the shit, Tom. Is this what Peter is mixed up with, overthrowing Chávez?" Sonia demanded as she finally broke away from the television screen and turned her gaze toward Rose.

"No. Believe me, Sonia, Pete had nothing to do with this coup. He's not even in Caracas at the moment, which is why I'm here. But the next few days are crucial for your country and for your safety, so you need to listen to me now, okay?"

Rose wasn't really lying. Maddox had not been involved in planning the coup, and he wasn't even in Caracas providing support or advice to the coup members; that's what Bill

Anderson was doing. Apart from encouraging the coup and knowing the date of it, he really wasn't involved in the action currently engulfing Caracas. He was off somewhere in the jungles of Venezuela, where Operation Puma would soon begin.

CHAPTER TWENTY-TWO

PUMA

Near Casuarito, Colombia

Maddox gathered with the Delta Force team in their war room, an open-air wooden frame that was had been used as a mess hall in the Colombian encampment. A communication device that resembled an oversized briefcase sat on one of the tables.

Troy Sennight had set up a direct line with the situation room at the Pentagon where Dick Philips; a dozen other individuals from the White House, the military, and the CIA; Delta Force Commander Colonel William Chase; and other high-ranking personnel were gathered. He had also patched in Bill Anderson, who was giving the briefing from one of Sonia's safe houses in Caracas.

"Gentlemen, the military action against Chávez is now in full force," Anderson said calmly. "We'll know in the next forty-eight hours which way it will break."

There were a few seconds of silence before another voice jumped in.

"We're at critical mass here, people," cautioned General Marcus Wade, the joint chief of staff commander, from the Pentagon's situation room. "Polar," he addressed Maddox, "are you seeing any problems with moving forward?"

"No, sir," Maddox replied confidently, having learned long ago that it was best to keep answers short in these types of situations, when generals and politicians were in decision mode.

"Good to hear your say that," General Wade responded. "Major Lucas, are your men ready?"

"Yes, sir. The unit is ready and in position," Lucas confirmed.

"Colonel Chase, are you good with this?" General Wade asked the Delta Force commander sitting to his right.

"Yes, sir. We're ready. This is the cover we've been waiting for," Colonel Chase responded to Maddox and the Delta Force team's delight.

After a brief pause, General Wade spoke again. "Okay, then we have a go. Good luck, men, and God bless."

And just like that, Operation Puma was operational.

————

Caracas, Venezuela

Caracas was in complete turmoil, and Council member Colonel Maximo Carmona had mobilized his men toward Miraflores Presidential Palace. Inside, Deputy Minister of Defense Julio Wilson—one of the Council leaders—and his small cadre of soldiers loyal to the council ensured Colonel Carmona's men could storm into the palace unopposed in order to reach Chávez, who was holed up inside.

Nearby, Bill Anderson was stationed in a safe house with Troy Sennight. The tech whiz manned communications, ensuring Anderson was in constant contact with the SOG operatives on the ground serving as advisors to the council's armed forces, the Pentagon, and with Forward Base Camp Puma. Anderson was also keeping Maddox in the loop with the situation in Caracas via satellite phone.

Near the Colombia-Venezuela Border

While flames from burning cars and gunfire between coup troops and government forces lit up the night sky of Caracas, four MH-6 Helicopters took off from the Operation Puma base camp near Causarito, Colombia, en route to the terrorist encampment in the Venezuelan jungle. They were using the cover of night to strike the camp across the Orinoco River.

The choppers flew low to avoid radar detection even though it was probably common to see them in the area due to the Puerto Ayachucho military bases. Helicopters often patrolled the border, on the lookout for Colombian drug cartel incursions onto Venezuelan soil.

The MH-6 choppers flew so close to the ground that if Maddox let his feet hang over the side, he was sure they would scrape the ground below. It only took minutes for the MH-6s to cross the Orinoco River and cross illegally into Venezuelan airspace.

"Puma one, Team A is in position," sniper team leader Sergeant Major Ted Blanco's voice cracked over Maddox's radio. The Delta Force sniper team had been in surveillance mode for several days, and now they were ready to rock and roll.

"Puma one, Team B is in position, too. The packages have been delivered," Master Sergeant Wes Palokangas, informed them over the radio.

Palokangas and his team had dropped into the area near the

terrorist camp two days earlier clad in ghillie suits and covered in local foliage, making them nearly invisible, even in broad daylight.

For two hours they had methodically and quietly inched their way toward the camp undetected and then placed enough C-4 explosives to reduce the place to rubble and turn the landing strip into a giant sinkhole.

It was a painstaking and intense process that required the patience of Job and the discipline for the men to not move an inch for hours, sometimes even having to piss right where they lay.

Palokangas and Ramos crawled in, littered the camp with C-4, and crawled back out undetected by the enemy and under the protective cover of their sniper team.

Nightfall had blanketed the entire jungle in an all-encompassing darkness never seen in an urban area. At this hour, there was minimal activity, but the second sniper team had switched on their night vision and continued to provide cover to Palokangas and Ramos as they fell back to a safe distance where they would detonate the explosives and provide additional cover for the strike team.

It was 10:30 p.m. and, as expected, most of the guards and terrorists-in-training were either in their bunks or glued to a small black-and-white television, watching the events unfolding in Caracas. The only movement was the occasional attempt of one of the television watchers to improve the poor signal by moving the rabbit-ears antennae around.

The MH-6 helicopters were heading to the drop zone. Maddox and CSM Mickey Welch and his men exited the little bird clutching their M4A1 carbine assault rifles, each fitted with an under slung M203 40mm grenade launcher, aimed with a Close Combat Optic red dot sight.

By 11:15 p.m., the assault team was ready to strike. The

fourth chopper carried the Army Rangers squad that was attached to Operation Puma; they would serve as the security detail for the choppers on the ground would also be on standby as backup if Delta Force requested it. A second Ranger unit would patrol the outer parameters of the camp, ensuring that any reinforcements heading toward the encampment would be neutralized.

"Team A, are you in position?" Welch asked, speaking into his shoulder-clipped radio.

"Roger that," replied Blanco.

"Team B, are you in position?"

"Roger that," Palokangas confirmed.

"Red Bear, all teams are in position," Welch radioed back to Lucas.

"Roger that, it's a go. You've got your green light," Lucas responded, giving Welch the okay to strike at will.

With that, Welch screamed into his radio, "Execute!" and the sniper team opened fire.

SFC Peavy and Master Sergeant Singleton's rounds found their targets inside the guardhouse with direct shots to the head. Master Sergeant Castro took out the men on the rooftop with precise headshots from his sniper rifle. Clouds of red mist exploded into the air as the men's heads jerked back, and then their bodies collapsed to the ground.

"Execute!" Welch commanded again. Before the bodies hit the floor, Palokangas began detonating the C-4. Ramos laid down cover fire, spraying the buildings with rounds from his M4A1. He then hurled two grenades into the building as the C-4 explosions continued going off one by one.

"Execute, execute, execute!" Welch shouted, commanding Team C, the assault team, to storm the now-smoldering structures. Several men exited the buildings on fire and then dropped and rolled on the ground, trying to put themselves out. Welch and his men quickly put them out of their misery with a short burst of M4A1 fire. The sniper team was still in position, taking out the men who tried to reach the vehicles parked nearby.

Maddox and the Delta Force strike team members entered the wooden building, blasting anyone still moving inside. Palokangas and Ramos joined them from their pre-assault positions right outside of the encampment. In teams of two, back-to-back and hunched down low, the soldiers quickly swept through the building, clearing it of terrorists.

If it moved, it died.

The men inside were stunned at the attack. A few of them returned fire with their Kalashnikovs and pistols, but the concussion grenades had done their jobs; dazed wounded from the initial strike, they were no match for the assault team that came barreling into the building with the element of surprise firm in their grasp.

While Maddox and the other Delta Force operators cleared the buildings, Palokangas detonated the C-4 packets planted on the helipad, leaving a fifteen-foot blackened and smoldering crater in its place.

The well-orchestrated maneuvers continued flawlessly as the MH-6 helicopters landed in the pickup zone; their five-bladed rotors circled over and over as they waited to extract the unit back to the Colombian side of the jungle.

"Clear! Clear!" began to ring out as the unit scoured the destroyed training camp. Maddox, Welch, and Ramos made their way to the back of one of the barracks, which was now just rubble.

Behind it lay a clearing that served as a makeshift parking lot, and six bodies littered the ground, gunned down by the sniper team as they had attempted to enter their vehicles.

Maddox needed to verify that their high value target, Abdullah Zlitini, was among the dead.

The third body turned over proved to be the one he was looking for. A sniper had ended his reign of terror with one bullet to the back of the head from three hundred yards away. *Damn, these guys are good*, Maddox thought to himself as he pulled out a digital camera from his LBE and took several pictures, including two close-ups of Zlitini's face. They would serve as proof that the terrorist leader was indeed dead.

"King Cobra, targets have been taken out, we're now clearing the camp, gathering intelligence," Maddox reported back to the command center in the Pentagon, where the Delta Force Commander, Colonel Wade was waiting for news with a dozen others, including Dick Philips.

"Roger that, Puma. You're in the clear. No bogies in sight, but wrap it up," Lucas instructed from the base camp across the Orinoco River, where they were keeping a close eye out for reinforcements from the military bases in Puerto Ayachucho, but there wasn't any activity.

The action deep in the remote jungle west of Puerto Ayachucho had so far gone unnoticed or, if it was noticed, the events in Caracas prevented anyone from investigating a disturbance deep in the jungle. They'd probably chalked it up as a drug-related skirmish between cartels. Maddox had counted on this, since knowledge of this training camp resided with just a handful of Chávez's most trusted insiders who were now up against the wall in the Miraflores Presidential Palace, five hundred miles away.

CHAPTER TWENTY-THREE

COUP

Miraflores Presidential Palace. Caracas, Venezuela

THE BATTLE FOR THE MIRAFLORES PRESIDENTIAL PALACE hadn't been as fierce as expected. The Chávista paramilitary types had exchanged gunfire with the coup troops, but Miraflores fell rather quickly. However, the roaming gun battles on the streets of Caracas caused many of the two hundred thousand strikers to flee.

The local news media, whose freedom of the press had suffered under Chávez's iron fist, made sure to record every act of violence perpetrated by the still-loyal Chávez military and the fanatical Chávistas.

Dario Gonzales, the chairman of the largest news and media conglomerate in Venezuela, had long been critical of Chávez. He was also a friend with Council chairman Francisco Chacon, so he was making sure the news coverage slanted towards the coup leaders. A little propaganda to win over the populace that was loyal to Chávez.

Francisco Chacon quickly put Assemblyman Espinoza, the

face of the council and soon-to-be interim president, on the airwaves to make a case that the Chávez regime had been overthrown in a carefully planned coup that had been in planning for ten months. While Espinoza battled in front of the cameras, Colonel Carmona and his troops seized Miraflores.

Bill Anderson advised Colonel Carmona to kill Chávez, but the council refused. They didn't want him becoming a martyr, and they felt that having a very public trial where they could air his abuses would win over the poor, who were Chávez's main base of support.

The coup appeared successful. Chávez was placed under arrest and paraded in front of the television cameras, and Francisco Chacon immediately called a press conference from the president's office in the Miraflores compound.

He urged calm. He informed everyone that Chávez was under arrest for crimes against Venezuela. Chacon then suspended the constitution and called for all members of the military and the police to join them in restoring peace to Venezuela.

He promised a democratic elections in six months, insisting the council members were not seeking long-term power, and then announced Assemblyman Carlos Rafael Espinoza was being appointed interim president of Venezuela. Within twenty-four hours of the initial push, Chávez had been ousted and arrested. Interim President Espinoza then introduced the Council leadership to the stunned and confused nation.

"Oh shit, look at all those people. We can't get through," a scared Wagner Barboza warned Henry Calderon. The young DISIP agent and Calderon's protégé sweated profusely even though the tinted windows of their government-issued white 1999 Toyota Land Cruiser were up and the vehicle's AC was on full blast.

Twenty-eight-year-old Barboza had joined the DISIP from

the Venezuelan Army's Special Forces branch, but after two years under the command of Johan Brull, he'd had enough. Barboza had not signed up to watch civilians be tortured in horrific ways by his boss.

General Dos Santos, the director of the DISIP, had served in the army with Chávez and now reported directly to him. He was the muscle behind the people's smiling president, and Brull's penchant for brutality served him well. He had those who opposed Chávez, and whose trial could give them some extra mileage, arrested on trumped up charges. Those who needed to be taken care of discreetly simply vanished into the Helicoide building.

"Take a right here," Calderon ordered Barboza as the younger man nervously attempted to maneuver through the chaotic streets of Caracas. Although they were in an unmarked vehicle, everyone knew the secret police rode around in white Toyota Land Cruisers with dark tinted windows. This allowed them to traverse the volatile streets with a bit more ease. The vehicle alone instilled fear into the strikers and even the Chávistas on the street.

Calderon was concerned. He had expected many DISIP agents to join him once Chávez was arrested, but that hadn't happened. Dos Santos was standing firm with his friend Chávez and had headed out to Miraflores with several units to repulse the coup using their specialty, brutality.

Brull and his men had flooded the streets of Caracas. At first, they clubbed and beat the protesters, but now Brull had the green light to begin firing into the crowds. Colonel Carmona had control of Miraflores, so he was going to go up against Dos Santos and his troops on the steps of the presidential palace.

Calderon and Barboza needed to find and kill Brull to keep the momentum of the successful coup moving. Finally away from the throng of protesters, the white Land Cruiser pulled into the driveway of small home on the outskirts of the Prados del Este neighborhood near the US Embassy. Barboza signaled with the headlights: three quick flashes, wait ten seconds, three more quick flashes.

Calderon couldn't see them, but he knew one or two snipers had their sights trained on him and Barboza as they exited the vehicle. Using the key Bill Anderson had given him, he entered the safe house and stepped inside the SOG base command center for the operation.

"Gentlemen, come in," Anderson called out and waved Calderon and Barboza over. "We've got a tail on Brull. He's in the Petare barrio."

"Shit," Calderon said exchanging a concerned glance with Barboza. "He's reaching out to the community organizers."

"Robin Romero?" Anderson asked, already knowing the answer.

Romero was the leader of the Chávez socialist movement in the crime-ridden and poverty-stricken barrios. He had been waging a gang war with one of the other barrio crime lords as well as Elvis Presley Jimenez, who remained Henry Calderon's ally. Elvis didn't kowtow to the government and thus had lost ground and power to Romero's gang, who now controlled the Petare barrio—the largest and most dangerous of all the barrios. Chávez had set up community centers to provide free medical care and food to the barrios from the expropriation of the oil companies and other industries.

Romero controlled all the government subsidies in Petare— milk, fuel, medical care, all of them. He used that control to keep the barrio loyal to him and Chávez and to stuff his pockets by skimming from the top. He even diverted milk meant for newborn babies into his own warehouse to sell wholesale.

Robin Romero was a wealthy man who chose to continue living in the barrio he controlled.

Romero was known as "Robin Rojo" and his gang the "redshirts" for the red shirts and bandanas they wore to show support for the Chávez revolution. These sorts of alliances were a cornerstone of Chávez's ability to remain in power. Community organizers like Robin Romero were key because they could mobilize the barrios to pour onto the street and pay thugs—like redshirts—to crack some skulls.

"Yes, that's the only reason Brull would go to Petare—he needs Romero's redshirts." Calderon rubbed the back of his neck. He could feel Brull's grip getting stronger, even with Chávez under arrest.

This was exactly what Calderon and Anderson had been trying to avoid. Their objective had been to put a stranglehold around Petare to keep Brull out so he couldn't unleash a coordinated attack. It now appeared that they had failed.

"You need to nip this in the bud, Henry," Anderson lectured. "How many men you got?"

"You're looking at them," Calderon responded calmly.

"Jesus Christ, Henry. You said if Miraflores fell, so would El Helicoide!" Anderson seethed.

"I miscalculated the fear of the DISIP rank and file. They're not ready to turn on Brull and Dos Santos," Calderon explained, "but if I can take Brull out, his men will follow me."

"And you two can do it? He's in a Chávez stronghold, for Christ's sake," Anderson bellowed.

Calderon fixed Anderson with a pleading look and opened his mouth to speak.

"No fucking way, Henry," Anderson interjected before Calderon could get a word in. "We're here to offer material support, remember? I can't send my men in to help. I want to, but I can't. No fucking way." Anderson shook his head and waved his hands as if to physically halt the DISIP agent's idea.

"I understand," Calderon said turning to Barboza. "Let's go."

"Are you nuts? Don't even think of going up there," Anderson warned him.

"We have no choice. I can get close enough to Brull to put a bullet in his head—I know I can," Calderon stated confidently. "He doesn't know I'm part of the coup."

Anderson was still trying to talk Calderon and Barboza out of going up to the Petare barrio as the two men left the SOG safe house, jumped back into the Toyota Land Cruiser, and peeled away toward the east.

"Team C, we have friendlies heading your way, license plate CH920RW. Continue surveillance," Anderson said into his radio, ordering the SOG observation team to keep an eye on the two DISIP agents.

It was late and yet still a balmy eighty-five degrees when Calderon and Barboza pulled into the Petare barrio. The two men began navigating the Land Cruiser through the streets, toward the Simon Bolívar Libertador Community Center; it was Robin Romero's headquarters and the place they were most likely to find Brull.

Calderon's original plan was out the window, but twenty-four hours after the coup, Francisco Chacon had introduced to the nation the interim president of Venezuela, Assemblyman Carlos Rafael Espinoza, so they had to keep the momentum going.

"It's now or never," Calderon said to Barboza as he locked and loaded his AK-103 assault rifle and racked a round in the chamber of his Glock handgun. Barboza did the same and the men continued their suicide mission up the streets of Petare.

Barboza slammed on the brakes as a large crowd of

redshirts began to approach the vehicle. Most were armed with rebar and baseball bats, but Calderon could see some of the men carrying shotguns and handguns, including a few TEC-9s.

"Shit, shit, shit," Barboza said, trembling in fear.

"Keep calm, Wagner; we can't fuck it up now," Calderon said as he eyeballed the situation.

Suddenly, he felt a sharp jab to his ribs. He looked down to see Barboza's Browning Hi-Power 9mm semi-automatic handgun pressed to his side.

"What the fuck are you doing, Wagner?" Calderon asked, shocked.

"I'm sorry, Henry, but I'm not going to die like this or on one of Brull's fish hooks! You said we would be victorious!" he responded nervously as shoved the barrel of his gun deeper into Calderon's side.

"We are winning. Chávez is under arrest, and Espinoza is now president, but we need to make sure Brull is out of the picture," Calderon pleaded. But it was too late. The driver's side window shattered into a million pieces from the strike of a redshirt's rebar.

"Don't shoot! I'm with you; I have captured an enemy of the state!" Barboza yelled as the mob of redshirts pulled both men from the vehicle and began pummeling them.

"Basta!" Robin Romero ordered the mob. They immediately obeyed and stepped back so Romero could see Calderon and Barboza on the ground, bloodied and bruised. Their AK-103's and handguns had vanished into the crowd.

"Well, well, well, what do we have here?" a giddy Brull cooed as he approached behind Romero.

"Comandante," Barboza said catching his breath and looking up from the ground, "Captain Calderon is a traitor. He's part of the coup, and I'm delivering him to you."

Calderon was now sitting up with his knees bent in front of

him, spitting blood, and looking annoyed. He said nothing as he studied the situation.

"And you?" Brull asked Barboza, tilting his head as he surveyed the two battered men on the ground below him.

"No, sir. I've been your double agent," Barboza pleaded. "I can tell you everything that has been going on, including where the gringos are hidden."

Brull's eyes lit up like a kid hearing the ice-cream truck bells ringing at the chance of catching the CIA red-handed, but before he could respond, a shot rang out, causing the crowd to scatter for cover.

A bullet ripped into Barboza's forehead, splattering blood onto Calderon had bolted up into a kneeling position, pulled his P2000 SK sub-compact handgun out of his well-hidden ankle holster, and taken the younger man out. Barboza slumped forward, still on his knees and facing Brull; his dead body looked like it was bowing to Brull.

Calderon quickly swiveled to his right to take a shot at Brull, but there was no time as the mob of redshirts pounced. As he tried to get a shot off in Brull's direction, a redshirt stomped on his hand, shattering his wrist and causing the bullet to stray into the air.

Several redshirts kicked him in the head and others quickly disarmed him. Calderon was dazed and bleeding even more profusely. One of the thugs grabbed him by his hair, holding his head up to face Brull and Romero.

"Feisty pendejo, this one," Romero marveled at Calderon's bold move.

"I trained him," Brull said, annoyed at Barboza being killed before he could get the information he wanted, but proudly taking credit for Calderon's courage.

Brull then knelt down so he could be face-to-face with his former Captain.

"And you? You're not going to help me, are you?" Brull asked Calderon with a smile.

Calderon kept his answer short and to the point. "Fuck you."

"Fine. You shut Barboza up, but you, my friend, you will talk," Brull said with a sadistic grin.

Calderon looked up and sent a bloody stream of spit sailing onto Brull's face.

"Hijo de puta," Brull said shooting back up to standing and wiping his face with his shirt. "Arrest him and get him out of here before I kill this motherfucker right here." Brull's voice trembled in anger.

Brull's DISIP agents made their way through the throng of redshirts and handcuffed Calderon before patting him down for any other hidden weapons. Then they dragged him off to a waiting paddy wagon, threw him in the back, and locked the door. The vehicle drove off toward El Helicoide, where Calderon would eventually find his way to one of Brull's chambers.

"Condor, the friendlies are down, the cub is dead, and the bear is in custody en route to HQ," the SOG Team C leader reported to Bill Anderson over the radio.

"Fuck!" Anderson yelled. "I figured this was a suicide mission; I didn't think they would arrest him." He looked down and then stared at the radio in his hand for what felt like an hour but was just a few seconds.

"Team C, this is Condor; do you have a shot? Over."

"Affirmative, over," the voice crackled on Anderson's radio.

Anderson once again stared at his radio. The entire safe house had fallen silent as they waited for Anderson's order. He slowly brought the radio back to his mouth. "Take it," he said sadly.

Anderson had gotten to know Henry Calderon well the last

few weeks, and he liked him. Calderon was a good operative, but there was no way of knowing what he would say under the torture of a sadist like Brull. Anderson had heard of the horrors that went on in Brull's hidden underground chambers in El Helicoide. It would be difficult for anyone to withstand such torture, and Anderson couldn't risk Calderon talking.

"I'm doing him a favor," Anderson said under his breath, rationalizing his order to himself. A quick bullet to the head would be preferable to a slow death at the hands of Johan Brull.

The Team C vehicle, a black Nissan Pathfinder SUV, maneuvered on the freeway to about three hundred feet ahead of the paddy wagon transporting Calderon. A SOG operator popped out of the Pathfinder's sunroof with an HK69-A1 grenade launcher and pulled the trigger, delivering a well-aimed grenade through the windshield. The vehicle lifted off the ground, landed on its side, and slid down the freeway for fifty feet until a second direct hit struck the undercarriage. The exposed gas tank exploded, causing a huge fireball to shoot thirty feet into the air.

The van was completely destroyed, reduced to a mangled heap of metal engulfed in flames. Knowing that none of the occupants could have survived, the SOG operatives sped off down the highway.

Robin Romero descended from the shantytown barrios perched on the hillsides of Caracas into the fracas and led his thugs in a full-force attack on the protestors and strikers. The redshirts swarmed in an orgy of violence, cracking skulls, crushing bones, and beating the masses until they retreated.

The redshirts, armed with guns and rifles, began firing into the crowd, sending the protesters into mad dashes for their lives.

General Dos Santos struck at the media's coverage of the

crackdown by shutting it down and giving the redshirts the green light to take no prisoners.

Brull's men followed the wave of redshirts, dragging protesters away into already crowded paddy wagons. The metropolitan police tried to intervene, but they were made targets and then soon overrun. Those who were left fled, leaving the citizens to fend for themselves.

Dario Gonzalez was arrested. Now that he had total control of the media, General Dos Santos began appearing on the newly seized national television stations. He informed the country that Chávez had been illegally removed from power, denounced the interim president, and urged the masses from the barrios to flood the streets of Caracas in a march to Miraflores in support of Chávez.

The Council had been in power for less than forty-eight hours, and they were beginning to lose control.

CHAPTER TWENTY-FOUR

FIREBALL

ROSE AND SONIA WATCHED THE TUG OF WAR FOR POWER on the television in disbelief. Less than twenty-four hours before, they had popped open a bottle of champagne to celebrate the arrest of Chávez, the end of his socialist revolution, and the installation of the council and Interim President Espinoza.

Now, the new government appeared to be falling apart on live television, and Rose's gut was telling him that the tables were turning against the coup planners.

If that happened and Chávez regained power, the next move in his playbook would be to round up members of the opposition. This was exactly why Maddox had wanted Sonia out of the country and why, when she refused to go, he had insisted that Rose come protect her.

Even though Sonia wasn't a direct participant in the coup, she was a paid CIA asset. If Brull were to find out that she was also Maddox's lover, he would personally torture her just to get to Maddox.

Near Puerto Ayacucho, Venezuela

The training camp was cleared of hostiles. All twenty-one targets were killed, including the unit's high-value target, Abdullah Zlitini. The Delta Force team took the compound with a lot of noise, firepower and speed.

The terrorists didn't know what hit them until it was too late. They didn't have time to put up much of a fight. None of the members of the Delta Force unit were injured. Now Maddox and the rest of the Delta team scoured the camp, gathering a treasure trove of intelligence.

Videotapes, documents, and loose papers were all shoved into metal ammo boxes to be analyzed later offsite. The compound was in shambles, the terrorists were killed, valuable intelligence data was collected, and no Delta team members were injured.

It was a hell of a successful raid, Maddox thought to himself as he reveled in the aftermath.

While the strike team collected intelligence, the sniper team continued to watch the perimeter around the now-smoldering campground, and Palokangas and Ramos began dropping a final round of C-4 packages throughout the entire camp as well as around the landing strip. When the move-out order came through from Lucas, the unit members jumped onto the waiting MH-6 helicopters for extraction.

As the birds hovered over the camp before starting back toward Colombia, Palokangas detonated the two-dozen C-4 packages left behind, completing the annihilation of the camp.

"Burn, baby, burn!" Ramos screamed as explosions rocked the area and a fireball shot high into the air. The choppers hightailed it back across the river and away from the billowing black smoke. This much firepower would surely be picked up by the Puerto Ayachucho military bases.

"What do you think, Max? They're going to see that now in Ayachucho, no?" a grinning Ramos asked.

Maddox watched the smoldering fire engulf the structures before turning back to Ramos and replying, "Hell, I think they'll see it from Caracas."

CHAPTER TWENTY-FIVE

REVERSAL OF FORTUNE

Caracas, Venezuela

BILL ANDERSON WAS ON THE SECURE LINE WITH THE situation room in Langley. Dick Philips, Executive Director of the CIA Max Hoban, Deputy Director Ben Rouget, and Director Van Loon, along with a smattering of CIA administrative higher-ups, were on the other end.

"I'm seeing a reversal of fortune here, Home Base," Anderson briefed the Langley brass. "We've lost a major asset, the bear." The dream of seeing Henry Calderon become the new director general of the DISIP had died on the Vera Cruz highway in Caracas.

"Condor, how are you handicapping this thing now?" Director Van Loon asked the SOG commander.

"Failure is certain, sir," Anderson responded solemnly.

"Fantastic," Hoban blurted out sarcastically. "As I predicted, this is blowing up in our faces. We should have gone the diplomatic route, reporting the training camp to the UN for sanctions, instead of this thuggery" he continued, seething.

"Settle down, Max. It's done," Van Loon ordered.

"I would like to remind everyone that our primary mission here was Operation Puma, which has been an overwhelming success," Dick Philips said. "The unit has made it back to the forward base camp in Colombia. The *terrorist* training camp has been destroyed."

After a brief pause and pointed stare at Hoban, Philips continued. "Abdullah Zlitini has been terminated, along with twenty other terrorists, and we have a treasure trove of intelligence our analysts are chomping at the bit to get their hands on. Caracas was just the possible icing on the cake, but win or lose there, our main objective has been accomplished," he affirmed.

"If Chávez survives this and remains in power, he's going to tie a tin can around our necks, blaming us for this whole mess," Hoban seethed.

"*If* he survives, that was going to happen regardless of our current involvement. Even if we had stayed on the sidelines sitting on our hands, letting the UN pussyfoot around, we would have still been blamed. That was inevitable," Dick Philips shot back, obviously annoyed with Hoban.

Before Hoban could retort, Van Loon put an end to the debate. "Gentlemen, it's a done deal," he said in a firm voice while staring down his executive director. "I loathe Monday-morning quarterbacking; it accomplishes nothing, so can the what-if shit."

"Yes, sir," Hoban said in a mocking way.

Deputy Director Ben Rouget seethed as he stared Hoban down over his disrespect toward the DI.

"Condor, stand fast while we regroup. Let's touch base in two hours," Rouget instructed Anderson and then disconnected the line.

"Gentlemen, we're expected at the White House shortly," Director Van Loon warned. "What's our next move?"

"We need to get the hell out of there, Director," Hoban insisted.

"Dick?" Van Loon asked Philips, much to Hoban's consternation.

"Well, sir, I think we have a fantastic opportunity to take out Little Napoleon down there," Dick said, referring to Chávez by his codename. "We have SOG on the ground, why not give them the last push?"

"Are you insane?" Hoban protested.

The Langley Room erupted in lively discussion. Unfortunately for Philips, it was him against everyone else, and he knew what was coming. The operation in Caracas was going to be terminated.

CHAPTER TWENTY-SIX

LITTLE NAPOLEON LIVES

Near Causarito, Colombia

THE CELEBRATION at Operation Puma base camp was short-lived, only lasting until Ruben Guzman turned on the television to General Dos Santos's press conference. The number of pro-Chávez protestors on the street had swelled to tens of thousands of people, and they were demanding the reinstatement of Chávez as president. The opposition had been beaten, killed or scared off into hiding.

Everyone in the barracks knew what was about to happen. After forty-eight hours in power, the opposition had been greatly weakened, and the Chávez forces were prepping for a knockout punch. Maddox's secured sat phone began ringing, and he bolted outside of the barracks to pick it up.

"Polar," Maddox answered.

"I have the Duke and am patching him through; hold on," Troy Sennight's said. "Go ahead, Duke."

"Polar, are you there?" Dick Philips asked, over two thousand miles away in Washington, DC.

"Yes, sir," Maddox responded.

"Son, you boys did a phenomenal job tonight. I thank you. Hell, I know this sounds cheesy, but our nation thanks you!" Philips told him.

"Thank you, but it doesn't look like things are going well elsewhere," Maddox said.

"No. Looks like Little Napoleon will survive this," Philips agreed. "I'm headed to the big house; I'm certain that they're going to pull the plug. You need to square yourself away down there ASAP."

Maddox was silent for a few seconds, trying to control his anger. "Yes. Thanks for the heads up; I'll be en route shortly," he managed to get out without railing against the bullshit politics of the situation. He knew Philips felt the same way, so there was no need to preach to the choir.

"Godspeed, son," Philips said before disconnecting the line.

Maddox looked around and then pulled a second sat phone from his LBE. This one was a direct link to Tom Rose. Sennight had secured and set up the phone without asking questions why Maddox wanted another sat phone for personal use only. That was why Maddox liked Sennight so much.

"Hello, mate," Rose answered. Maddox updated him, and they discussed the situation in Caracas. Sonia had finally managed to fall asleep, and Maddox told Rose not to wake her.

"I'm heading back to Caracas shortly. Be ready to execute Plan B if necessary. I'll call you when I'm mid-air," Maddox told him and hung up.

He proceeded to remove his LBE vest and black jungle boots and ditch his unmarked military fatigues so he could take a quick shower in the camp's makeshift stall. Since the shower was hooked up to a cistern built to capture and store rainwater, the water was cold; it felt fantastic as it dropped his body temperature and cooled his skin, which had been cooking in the humid Amazon jungle. Maddox's mind was now in Caracas, more specifically, on Sonia.

After showering, Maddox slipped on a black Under Armour T-shirt, blue jeans, and a black Patagonia River Master Mesh vest, and then he laced up his Timberland Fusion Waterproof boots. It was practical gear that allowed him to look like he had been out hiking and fishing on the Orinoco River, not killing terrorists.

He packed most of his weapons in the hidden compartment of his fishing tackle box and slipped his SIG Sauer into a black waistband holster clipped to his side under his vest.

Before Maddox departed, Bill Anderson called him. He told him that Henry Calderon was dead, that the redshirts had squashed the anti-Chávez demonstrations, and that Dos Santos had secured the airwaves and was now spreading his pro-Chávez propaganda as well as enticing the poor to take to the streets to support their benefactor and president, Hugo Chávez.

He also told him it had been hours since anyone had heard from Interim President Espinoza or Francisco Chacon. It was believed they were still in the Miraflores Presidential Palace, but Anderson didn't have any other contacts inside Miraflores, so he had no way of knowing whether that was true.

Anderson did know that Metropolitan Police Commander Ramiro Navarro and his men had tried to quell the redshirts, but once Navarro was killed, his officers had scattered, surrendering the streets of Caracas to the redshirts; some had even re-pledged their support to Chávez.

Lastly, Anderson informed Maddox that he had not heard from the other council members and, under orders from DC, he had pulled his men back to the embassy. They reported that Brull had consolidated his power over the secret police with General Dos Santos acting as the spokesperson for the Chávez government. Brull had also begun rounding up suspected coup participants.

Maddox went to say his goodbyes to the fine men of Delta Force as they got ready to fly back to the US Army base in Panama for a debriefing and then head back home to Fort Bragg.

"We better get a weekend pussy pass in Panama," Ramos demanded and adjusted his crotch.

"Classy, Hermes," Maddox responded.

"What?" Hermes replied with a smile.

Maddox left the barracks and jumped onto the passenger seat of Ruben Guzman's Toyota Tundra. They drove off, heading back to Causarito so that Maddox could take the ferry back to Puerto Ayachucho and then pilot the Cessna back to Caracas.

Just two hours after the choppers had hovered over the bombed-out former Libyan terrorist training camp, Maddox flew himself back to Caracas.

CHAPTER TWENTY-SEVEN

JAQUEMATE

As DAYLIGHT BROKE OVER THE MIRAFLORES PRESIDENTIAL Palace, the residents of the hillside barrios poured down to the front steps of the presidential palace, demanding Chávez be reinstated as president, and General Dos Santos knew it was now time for jaquemate, *checkmate.*

Dos Santos called the head of the presidential guard, who were still loyal to Chávez but unsure if they should strike back since the junta had Chávez under their control, and told General Pablo Salinas to regain control of Miraflores using the hidden underground tunnels.

At noon, the presidential guard stormed Miraflores from the inside while Dos Santos assaulted from the outside. A brief but fierce and bloody battle broke out as the coup troops tried to hold the line, but the double-pronged attack was too much.

Francisco Chacon and his entourage quickly exited the presidential palace and boarded a private jet he'd had waiting just in case. By the time the Dos Santos-Salinas assault was in full effect, Chacon's private plane was airborne and en route to his home in Switzerland.

Coup leader and the lead military planner Colonel Maximo Coronado were killed inside the presidential palace, along with sixteen of his loyal troops. The remaining troops surrendered to General Dos Santos. Inside the presidential office, soldiers of the presidential guard loyal to Chávez entered the office from a secret entryway of one of the many hidden tunnels.

Interim President Espinoza was arrested, ending his presidency after just fifty-two hours. Moments later, a beaming General Dos Santos held a press conference on the steps of the presidential palace; he declared the coup to be over and restored Chávez to the presidency as the crowd erupted into cheers.

Navy Captain Juan Castillo had no choice but to surrender and release Chávez from his jail cell in the Turimo Naval Base. Two days after the Council had successfully overthrown him, Chávez was back in power, and he was pissed.

Maddox was in mid-air when his company sat phone rang.

"It's Marathon Man," Mary Dent said, identifying herself.

"What's going on?" Maddox asked, knowing it wasn't good news.

"The local operation has failed. Mission terminated," Mary informed him.

"Roger that. I'll be there in two hours," Maddox said and disconnected the call before yelling out, "Fuck, fuck, fuck!" in the empty plane and slamming the control yoke with his fists. After composing himself, he picked up his private sat phone and dialed Tom Rose.

"Hello, mate," Rose answered on the second ring.

"Redman, is it safe?" Maddox asked.

"Yes, mate, but it's not looking good over here; you're heading back?"

"Is that Pete?" Sonia asked in a worried voice as she entered the kitchen and hovered over Rose. He nodded his head yes.

Thank God he's okay, Sonia thought as a wave of relief shot through her body.

Rose passed the sat phone to her. "Honey, I'm fine," Maddox said. "I'll be there soon. We can't talk on the phone, but please do as Tom says. I'll see you very soon."

"Okay," was all she could say in her fragile state of mind. She had slept only a handful of hours during last three days, worried about Maddox, worried about her own safety, and worried about the state of affairs in Venezuela. She was too tired to insist he give her more information, and she was just happy to hear his voice again and find out he was heading back to her.

"I love you," Maddox said and then disconnected the line.

Sonia could feel the tears welling up in her eyes as she handed the phone back to Rose, and she bolted to the living room.

Rotten timing to tell me he loves for the first time, she thought angrily, but then the words sank in. *I love you.* She had been pretty sure Maddox loved her, but he had never said the magic words before and neither had she. While she had fallen in love with him long ago, she knew that saying those words first tended to send men running to the hills, so she had held her peace.

But she had still longed to hear those three little words from him, and now he had finally said them. Even though he'd done so over a secure satellite phone connection instead of in person, she didn't care; he had said them.

The bad thoughts concerning her relationship with Maddox that had crept in during the chaos of the situation dissipated. She realized she would just have to accept that being in love with a CIA agent would mean having to put up with secrets and other strange situations that normal couples didn't face.

While Caracas may have been in turmoil, the small metropolitan airport on its outskirts was not. Maddox landed there and taxied to the secret CIA hangar at around 7:00 a.m.

Mary Dent and Jack Duffy were waiting for him. They watched Maddox exit the plane and look around the relatively peaceful and quiet airport in confusion.

"You should see the Maiquetia," Duffy told him, referencing Simon Bolívar International Airport—the largest in Venezuela. "It's a freaking nightmare over there. Everyone's trying to get on the last plane out of this shit storm."

The ride from the airport to the US Embassy in the white, bulletproof GMC van was surprisingly quiet. Aside from Maddox letting the other two agents know that Operation Puma had been a success, conversation was minimal. They came across a few Toyota pickup trucks packed with the rebels and heading off to battle, but once they passed by, the quiet returned.

"All the action is near Miraflores and the barrios," Dent explained to Maddox.

As the van pulled up to the embassy entrance, A US Marine in full combat fatigues, his finger on the trigger of his M16, stopped them to check their credentials, then quickly waved them in. During calmer times, the embassy guard detail performed its job in blue dress uniforms, but now they were outfitted in their utility combat uniforms, ready for battle.

At 7:30 a.m., the embassy was busier than usual. With the conflict outside now in its third day, there was a lot to do for the American citizens hunkered down in Venezuela during the crises. Maddox, Dent, and Duffy took the private CIA elevator to their floor. They began to head toward the situation room, but Maddox had to make a stop first.

"I have to piss," he informed Duffy and Dent as he detoured to the bathroom.

"Jesus, Pete, you can tell you've been bivouacking with Special Forces," Dent said smiling.

"Yeah, Pete, TMI," Duffy said laughing.

Maddox had relieved a little of the tension with his bathroom announcement, though he hadn't been trying to.

"I'll meet up with you guys in the sit room," Maddox said, waving off their smart-ass comments with a smile. *I guess I still have the field personality going,* Maddox thought, *which is a good thing right now.*

BACK IN THE SITUATION ROOM, Director Van Loon, Max Hoban, and Dick Philips had been patched through from Langley. The DI spoke first.

"Pete, first, I want to thank you for the great job you did taking out that camp. I just got off the line with the Delta Force squad commander; he praised your professionalism and contribution." Van Loon paused to allow for a quick round of applause. "But the situation in Caracas has escalated out of control."

"Sir, I still think we can help them topple this regime," Maddox said.

"Goddamn it, Maddox, this *regime* is a democratically elected government, a fact you seem to continue to forget" Hoban railed, leaning too close to the microphone and causing a reverberating distortion that made Maddox and the others to cringe.

Jesus, even two thousand miles away this guy is still murder on my ears, Maddox thought.

"We're not here to debate, so both of you stand down," an irritated Van Loon instructed. "We're well past that stage. We do nothing. All operations are terminated. You're all under lockdown at the embassy for seventy-two hours or until this is over."

"They're going to slaughter our assets, sir," a dejected Maddox warned.

"Our main objective, the destruction of the camp, has been successful; anything else is out of our control and no longer our business. This directive is coming right from the top, damn it. I'm sorry, Pete, but it's over. Mission terminated," Van Loon said firmly.

"Our sources are clear. Interim President Espinoza is under arrest, Council president Frank Chacon has fled the country in his private jet with his family, Colonel Carmona is dead, and Deputy Defense Minister Julio Wilson is under arrest. Captain Navarro is also dead. We're done," Ben Rouget advised.

The coup had indeed failed.

"That's it. Okay, everyone, stay safe; hunker down until it's safe to travel," Van Loon warned, and then the line was disconnected.

Maddox, Ron Bateman, and Bill Anderson went to Maddox's office after the debriefing. The orders had been clear, but Maddox was too worried about Sonia to stand down.

"I have to go," Maddox said as Anderson and Bateman tried to convince him to stay put. Maddox felt a wave of agitation wash over him, like a caged rat that has just been dumped into a bucket of water.

"Pete, if you go out there, you'll be flushing your career down the toilet," Bateman warned him.

"I can't just leave her out there, Ron."

"Who? What the hell is going on?" a confused Anderson asked.

"An asset," Bateman responded with disdain.

"Listen to Ron, Pete; you can't go out there," Anderson pleaded. "Assets know the stakes when they sign up to play this game. We all do."

Maddox knew he was right, but he couldn't abandon Sonia. Before he'd come along, she'd been a relatively successful and perfectly safe real estate agent, but now he'd ruined her business and put her life in jeopardy; plus, he loved her. All other embassy personnel significant others were safe in the embassy with their loved ones, but he had left her out there in the thick of things, and now that the coup had fallen apart, her situation would only become more dangerous.

Lost in thought, Maddox remained silent.

"Surely you've lost assets before; it's the cost of doing business," Anderson said matter-of-factly.

"She's not just an asset to him; she's *the* asset," Bateman explained condescendingly.

"Jesus Christ," Anderson said, realizing the quandary Maddox was in at the moment. "This is personal?" he asked, already knowing the answer.

Maddox stared off toward the hallway. "My career is probably over anyway once word about the Caracas operation gets out. I'm the one supposed to be left holding the bag, remember?" Maddox looked at Anderson. "And I'm fine with that," he continued before Anderson had a chance to respond, "but Sonia doesn't deserve any of this shit."

"Not after your success in the jungle earlier today; you'll be promoted to Langley," Bateman said with a tinge of jealousy, not knowing that being tied down to a Langley job wasn't exactly a reward for Maddox.

———

It was a strange sight to Sonia, walking into the living room and seeing Tom Rose sitting comfortably in her leather chair with an MP-5 submachine gun across his lap. Rose had perched his laptop computer on the armrest of the chair and was looking at something online when he glanced up at her. "How are you holding up, mate?" he asked.

"I'm fine, Tom. I still don't know why you need to be my bodyguard."

"He's just being careful. There is chaos on the streets of Caracas right now. Pete can't be here with you, so that's why I'm here."

"Well, I think it's silly, but thank you, Tom. I'm going to bed."

"Have a good night, mate," Rose said.

"Are you going to stay up all night again?" Sonia asked.

The past two early mornings when she had come down to the kitchen, she'd found Rose sitting there working on his laptop, his MP-5 within arm's reach, and she had heard him periodically checking around outside during the past two nights.

"Don't worry, I just need two to three hours a night, and I'm good to go," he explained with a smile.

"This is so silly," Sonia said again as she headed to her bedroom. "Goodnight, Tom."

CHAPTER TWENTY-EIGHT

BRULL'S CHAIR

DEEP UNDERGROUND IN THE CATACOMBS OF THE Helicoide building, Johnny Chacon, one of the Council's leaders and brother of the now exiled council president, Francisco Chacon, sat on a concrete chair in complete darkness, deep underneath the Helicoide headquarters of the DISIP.

A thick black hood covered his head, and he had been stripped naked. Both wrists were handcuffed to metal loops attached to Johan Brull's custom-built interrogation chair.

Chacon tried to calm his breathing so he could listen, but that was hard to do knowing he was in the hands of a monster.

The room was quiet, and Chacon assumed nobody was there, but it was a moot point since not only were his hands handcuffed to the concrete chair, his legs were chained to the concrete floor as well.

After what felt like hours, he heard the room's steel door open. A blast of fluorescent light hit him as the black hood was yanked from his head, taking a chunk of his hair with it. The sudden burst of light forced his eyes to clamp almost completely shut as they tried to adjust.

After a few seconds, he could see three men in front of him. He only recognized Brull, who smiled right at him. Sweat dripped from Chacon's forehead and neck but he shivered.

Brull lit a cigarillo, and, in Spanish, once again asked Chacon, "Where is the traitor whore of the CIA gringo?"

"I don't know, I swear," Chacon pleaded.

Brull calmly walked behind Chacon, saying nothing. Chacon couldn't turn to see what the Sadist of Caracas had in store for him, but he braced himself for more pain.

Suddenly, the steel cell door opened again, and two men entered carrying a medium-sized vat used to haul industrial chemicals and other liquids. The container was covered, hiding its contents, but Chacon knew it was going to be bad. *Here we go*, he thought as tears began to trickle down his cheeks.

The two men put the vat directly in front of Chacon and walked out of the cell, closing the door behind them. The two plain-clothed men remained in the room, and Brull still stood behind Chacon.

After a few seconds, one of the men removed the lid from the vat, and a cloud of steam rose into the air. Brull walked back around to the front of the chair so he could be face to face with Chacon.

"You will talk, traitor," he said as he put on thick black gloves. He then dipped a bucket into the vat and mockingly reassured Chacon, "Don't worry, it's only water."

Brull poured the boiling hot water over Chacon's head. Chacon instantly began to scream; he felt his skin peeling off his naked body as the scalding water washed down his head and down to his chest, back, thighs, and genitals. Before Chacon could muster any thought other than pain, Brull poured a second bucket over his head.

Brull then tossed the bucket aside and headed for the door. The two men covered the vat of boiling water, grabbed a side each, and then walked out of the cell, following Brull.

Chacon passed out from the pain as the cell door clanked shut.

Johnny Chacon didn't know how much time had passed when he regained consciousness. Someone was kicking his still-shackled feet and yelling, "Despiertate, traidor!" *Wake up, traitor!*

Chacon's body was now covered in seeping, oozing wounds, and strands of flesh dangled loosely from his arms and chest. His face, however, had taken the brunt of the scalding from the boiling water.

Chacon was in and out of consciousness for almost two days. No medical treatment, no food, no water. He just sat handcuffed to the concrete chair, with his badly burned body in pain.

The only contact was when one of Brull's men would kick his feet with a shout of "Despiertate!" whenever he would pass out.

It had been hours since the boiling water had been poured over his head, and he had had no food or sleep. Brull returned and leaned down until he was face to face with him once again.

"You ready to talk now and go to the hospital, or do we need to continue with the unpleasantness?" Brull asked with a daft smile.

CHAPTER TWENTY-NINE

PERSONA NON GRATA

Caracas, Venezuela

THE TENSION SIMMERED INSIDE THE U.S. EMBASSY. RON Bateman didn't say anything as Maddox quickly left his office.

Maddox was making his way across the CIA floor when the secure sat phone he used for CIA business began to ring.

"Yes," Maddox answered as he walked down the hallway.

"Señor Maddox, como estas?"

Maddox couldn't quite place the familiar voice, but by the tone, he knew it wasn't a friend.

"Who is this?" Maddox asked.

"You're hurting my feelings, Mr. Maddox. It's Johan Brull."

"What do you want, Johan?" Maddox asked curtly.

"I'm so sorry things haven't worked out with your little coup; we're still here, in case you haven't been outside of your precious gringo imperialist embassy walls," Brull cackled.

"Cut the shit, Brull. What do you want?" Maddox demanded.

"I want to stick you in one of my tumbas," Brull hissed,

referring to the secret prison for political enemies that lay hidden beneath El Helicoide—the tombs. "But alas, it's not meant to be," he continued mockingly.

"You can try it," Maddox challenged.

"I could snatch you this very second if I had the okay," Brull yelled into the phone, angered by Maddox's challenge.

Maddox was pleased at getting a rise out of Brull, even though it was easy to push his buttons. He was surprised, however, when Brull regained his composure and even apologized for losing his temper. He then continued in a calm voice, "Actually, I can't, Mr. Maddox. You see, I have strict orders; I'm sure you can relate. You're going to be the face of the coup, gringo; it has been ordered. So, unfortunately I won't get to have fun with you, but you'll soon be expelled from Venezuela, persona non grata," Brull hissed. "Go ahead and check CNN in the morning for your picture; your spy career is gone," Brull said with a laugh and then he went silent.

"You do whatever you have to do, pendejo," Maddox said, breaking the silence.

"Oh, I will. I can't touch you, but your mamacita, the traitor, pobrecita, I'm going to make her squeal like the stuck whore pig that she is," Brull seethed, sending chills up Maddox's spine.

Maddox's mind was racing. *Shit. He can't know about Sonia. Henry was killed before Brull could get his hands on him. How could he know?*

Brull had succeed in rattling him, but Maddox was damn sure not going to show it, so he responded in a bored tone, "Brull, I have no idea what you're talking about. You do whatever you feel you need to do. Now fuck off, malparido," and then hung up.

His body shook in anger at Brull and fear for Sonia. The walls of the embassy began to close in on him, to crush him, making it difficult to breathe. There were people all around, and Maddox was trying to appear relaxed and calm, but inside he was dying. He felt like his world was collapsing around him. His worst and only fear—that Brull would find out about Sonia —had been realized.

Maddox's mind went a mile a minute. Brull could have been bluffing to screw with him, but the threat was too direct. The sadist must have tortured the information out of someone, or perhaps he had uncovered one of the CIA safe houses and followed the paper trail back to Bolívar Realty. But it was too soon for that. Brull must have gotten to someone in Calderon's inner circle.

Maddox second-guessed hanging up on Brull. *I should have fished for more information.* But he had known doing that would have validated that Brull was on the right track. It had been best just to cut him off. Perhaps Brull's was only trying to draw him out of the embassy.

Maddox didn't have the time to determine the validity of the threat. He had to go get her, especially now that Brull could be on her scent. Maddox tucked away the official CIA sat phone, whipped out the private one, and dialed Tom Rose.

"Hello, mate," Rose answered on the second ring.

"Redman, we have a problem. They might know about her. You need to move her. I'll meet you there," Maddox instructed. Rose could hear the worry in Maddox's voice.

"Roger that," Rose and disconnected the line.

It only took Maddox a few minutes to get ready. He strapped on a black flak vest over his black Under Armour, dry fit t-shirt, racked a magazine to his SIG pistol, and chambered a round before shoving the gun into the leg holster strapped around his thigh. He then prepped his Walther PPK .380 and put it in his pocket. Finally, he grabbed an HK MP5A3 submachine gun, slung it tight over his chest, and walked out of his office, heading toward the exit stairs.

"Pete, Jesus Christ, it looks like you're going to battle," a concerned Mary Dent said, catching Maddox by surprise when she happened on him in the hallway.

"I have to take care of something personal. Caracas is still volatile; I'm not going out there unarmed." Maddox tried to explain his appearance like it made perfect sense.

"But we're supposed to stay put, *all of us*," Dent firmly reminded him. "And FYI, it's hairy out there, but you're going to standout in a crowd there, Rambo."

"I know. Listen, you stay put. I have to go." Maddox maneuvered past Dent, leaving her protesting in the hallway as he walked away.

"All of us, Pete. That means you too. Where are you going, Pete... Pete!" Maddox could hear Mary yelling as he double-timed down the hallway. Dent was left alone in the hallway as Maddox disappeared into the stairwell.

———

MADDOX MADE his way down the stairs to the parking lot. A warm breeze greeted him as he stepped outside and headed for his motorcycle.

Caracas was still in chaos. The government troops were clearing the last of the coup troops from the streets, but it was not a peaceful process. And while the redshirts may have turned the fighting over to Venezuelan military, they were still milling around the streets: some shooting their guns into the air in celebration and others taking the opportunity to loot local businesses.

Maddox hoped that in this celebratory chaos and cleanup, one man on a motorcycle with a submachine gun slung across his chest wouldn't attract as much attention as Dent thought. And even if he were noticed, his bike would allow him more speed than troops on foot and better maneuverability than those in vehicles. Maddox jumped on the Ducati and headed for the Jose Felix Ribas barrio. Hopefully Elvis would be home.

CHAPTER THIRTY

WORST-CASE SCENARIO

Caracas, Venezuela

SONIA WAS SITTING ON HER COUCH, FLIPPING THROUGH channels on her plasma TV when she heard Rose walk into the living room.

"There is nothing about Venezuela on CNN or Fox," Sonia said in disbelief.

"Sonia, we have to go right now," Rose said.

Sonia turned to look at him and froze. He was holding the emergency kit he had prepared for her the previous week— a backpack with enough clothing and supplies to last a few days on the run. He also now wore a flak jacket and a fully stocked LBE belt harness over his black fatigues, and his MP-5 slung was across his back.

"What the hell is going on, Tom?" she asked, the fear clear her voice.

"Sonia, there is no time to talk right now. We need to leave. Here, let me put this on you." Rose slipped a black flak jacket on her.

Although Rose had explained the worst-case scenario to Sonia, including showing her the bulletproof vest she would have to wear, her heart still felt like it was about to beat out of her chest when she realized the worst-case scenario was happening right now.

Before she could protest or ask questions, Rose was hustling her outside and into Maddox's armored Jeep Grand Cherokee. Once inside the vehicle, Rose finally spoke again. "We need to move to a safe house; I don't have the details, but we need to go there right now."

Rose pulled out of her garage and onto the street of the gated community. The guards recognized the Grand Cherokee and had the gate already opened by the time the Jeep approached it. Instead of smiling and waving to the guards like usual, Sonia just looked down in fear.

The neighborhood was eerily quiet. It was 8:00 p.m. and pitch dark. No one dared leave the relative security of their houses. Gunfire could be heard breaking out in the distance. Rose drove from the nice streets and homes of Prados del Este toward the shantytown slums of the Jose Felix Ribas barrio.

"Why are we going there, Tom? The barrios are dangerous enough on a normal day, and they're crawling with the most loyal of Chávez supporters; are you two crazy?" Sonia asked, the concern evident in her voice.

"It's the last place they'll look. We have a friend there, so we'll be safe while we wait to rendezvous with Pete."

"Peter will be there?" Sonia said, perking up for the first time in days.

"Yes," Rose said smiling, "you kids in love."

Sonia managed to crack a smile even though she was terrified inside, and the idea of going to the crime-infested barrios wasn't exactly soothing her fears, but she was happy at the prospect of seeing Maddox again for the first time in ten days.

CHAPTER THIRTY-ONE

ELVIS'S RANCH

Caracas, Venezuela

MADDOX WOVE THE DUCATI IN AND OUT OF TRAFFIC. Maddox had been riding motorcycles since he was a teenager; he had broken his arms on a dirt bike once, but even with both arms in casts, he couldn't wait to get back to riding.

Those skills had come in handy when he joined the Army Ranger motorcycle reconnaissance team, but even his Ranger-issued motorcycle hadn't come close to the precision and speed of his souped-up Ducati.

The closer he got to the barrios, the worse the traffic became. An orgy of cars and people flooded the streets, but Maddox was able to maneuver through the throngs of people, burning vehicles, and pickup trucks packed with hammered redshirts celebrating their victory and Chávez's reinstatement.

Maddox was making great time and thought he would probably get to Elvis's rancho before Rose and Sonia. A few shots rang out as he rode, but Maddox wasn't sure if they were meant for him. Maybe there was a firefight nearby or drunken redshirts popping off celebratory shots into the air.

Maddox exited the Autopista Fajardo onto Avenida Sur Altamira, almost losing control of the motorcycle in the Avenida La Castellana turnabout; the bike wobbled, but he quickly regained control, twisting the grip throttle and revving the engine as he sped onto Jose Felix Ribas Street.

Elvis's gang had placed a barricade at the start of the street, but it was no match for Maddox and his Ducati; he twisted the grip as he approached and whizzed through a narrow opening between a car and two burning barrels at over sixty miles per hour.

Once he had breached the barricade, Maddox slowed down. He glanced back, but no one was shooting or following. Elvis must have let them know to let the crazy gringo on the fast motorcycle through. Or, perhaps they were still scrambling to react over how easily Maddox got past their supposed high security parameter that consisted of trash barrels with their insides set ablaze.

Maddox came to a stop at the bottom of the barrio steps. He revved the engine a few times and twisted the grip of the motorcycle, then rode the Ducati up the steep, uneven concrete stairs leading to Elvis's rancho. The stairs were hard enough to tackle on foot, much less a machine, but Maddox managed to quickly maneuver the motorcycle up the steep steps, his entire body shaking from the bike's wild vibrations. The few people he encountered on the stairs froze when they heard a horn blaring and engine revving but then dove out of the way upon seeing a man with a weapon slung across his chest riding a motorcycle up the stairs toward them.

In a matter of minutes, Maddox had cleared the steps and come to a sliding stop right in front of Elvis's rancho. The barrio leader was already waiting for him outside, sitting in a lawn chair on his porch and cradling a shotgun. His gold teeth flashing as he grinned and got up to greet Maddox.

"Verga, pana," he breathed as he checked out the Ducati, "now that's the way to go up those fucking stairs. Holy shit, you scared the shit outta mi gente down below." He held up his walkie-talkie. "But I knew it was you. That's a cool moto pana," he said while continuing to stare at the Ducati.

"Elvis, thanks for your help, brother," Maddox said, extending his hand to the gangster. "Are they here?" he asked hopefully as he peeked inside the house.

"No, a car can't move fast like that beautiful moto of yours," Elvis replied, looking back at the Ducati again.

Maddox smiled and entered Elvis's rancho. Three gang-bangers sat inside. They were young but their faces were hardened, and they wore blue bandanas to represent their colors. Venezuelan gangbangers had learned how to dress, talk, and act like gangsters from watching American movies like *Colors* and *New Jack City*, so they looked like they came straight out of central casting, but they were the real deal and deadly.

Maddox nodded hello to the gangbangers. They were armed with dirty looking Tek-9s that would probably jam as soon as they were fired. Apparently their gangster movies didn't put much emphasis on the importance of keeping a weapon clean. Elvis headed to the bottles of booze on the kitchen table.

"Quieres un palo?" Elvis asked Maddox as he held up a bottle of Scotch whisky.

"No gracias," Maddox said, waving the bottle away. He appreciated his host's hospitality, but the last thing he needed in his body right now was alcohol, no matter how much he felt like taking a pull from the bottle of twelve-year-old blended whisky.

"No problem," Elvis said. "The enemy of my enemy is my

friend." He smiled, poured whisky into a glass, and downed it in two gulps. Elvis let out a quick snort and his body shook a little as the Scotch made its way down his throat to warm his belly.

"I really liked that chamo," Elvis said as he poured himself another drink. "Henry was a good dude, for a fucking cop."

"Yes, he was," Maddox said. He hadn't really had time to think about Henry Calderon's death until that moment. "You know what, Elvis? Fuck it; pour me a drink in Henry's honor," Maddox said with a smile.

"All right, Jefe, now you're talking." Elvis whipped out another glass and poured Maddox a drink.

"To Henry," Maddox said as he lifted his glass.

"To Henry," Elvis repeated, doing the same.

The two men downed their drinks and clanked the empty glasses together. The stiff drink felt good, but Maddox still turned down a second one. Of course, that didn't stop Elvis from downing yet another glass of whisky, his third in the last few minutes.

Maddox chuckled as he removed the sat phone from his flak jacket and punched in the number to reach Tom Rose.

"Hey, mate, I have an ETA of less than ten minutes," Rose said, not bother with a greeting.

"Okay, I'm here; I'll be waiting for you guys," Maddox replied and hung up the phone. He put that one back into his flak pocket and then quickly flipped open his official company cell phone to see if he'd received any calls. *None. Perfect,* Maddox thought. *That's one less thing to deal with right now.*

Nine minutes later, the inside of Elvis' rancho was lit up by the headlights of an approaching vehicle. Both Maddox and Elvis grabbed their weapons just in case, Maddox his HK MP5 submachine gun and Elvis his sawed-off shotgun. Elvis's men did the same with their Tek-9s.

It more than likely was one of Elvis' men since the barricade was still blocking access to the ranch. Elvis looked down, recognized the beat-up Toyota pickup truck, and confirmed to Maddox that those were his men. Two of the young gangbangers held rickety rifles and sat next to a blue tarp in the bed of the pickup. When the vehicle came to a stop, they jumped off and grabbed the tarp, revealing Rose and Sonia hiding beneath it.

"Muchas gracias, caballeros," Rose said to the young men in his heavily accented but passable Spanish.

The group headed up the stairs and as soon as they entered the rancho, Maddox smiled in relief and made a beeline for Sonia, only to be intercepted by a mischievously grinning Rose. "So nice to see you too, mate," he said as he embraced Maddox.

"Get the fuck away from me," Maddox said, giving Rose a friendly shove and resuming his path to Sonia. Rose, Elvis, and his gangbangers broke out into laughter.

The moment of levity was cut short when Elvis's walkie-talkie crackled to life; the message from one of his men at the barricade was urgent and ominous: "They're coming."

A split second later, one of Elvis' spotters on top of the rancho's roof shouted a warning about three approaching white SUV's. Maddox barely had time to react, grabbing on to Sonia as all hell broke loose down below and the barricade radio went dead.

"Shit, it's the internal police! They just opened fire at the barricade!" the spotter yelled as he grabbed his Glock and shimmied down from the roof to the front of the ranch.

"Mierda!" Elvis screamed, tossing the now useless radio aside. "It's the DISIP, they're coming," he warned as he and his men scrambled to arm themselves.

"Goddamn it, how did they know we would be here?"

Maddox shouted, upset that the safe house had been compromised less than thirty minutes after his arrival.

"Go, go!" Elvis yelled at Maddox and pointed to the sliding door leading out to the backyard. Maddox, Rose, and Sonia scrambled out into the small backyard and headed toward the fence gate, which led out to a street alley. As lights from the quickly-approaching SUV's shone onto Elvis's rancho, Maddox heard him say, "Eat shit, motherfuckers," followed by a burst of gunfire. Elvis dove back inside the house as bullets whizzed all around. His gangbangers began randomly spraying bullets from their Tek-9s as the well-trained DISIP agents began their assault.

Maddox held Sonia's hand as they ran down the alley; Rose covered them from behind. They could hear the gunfight raging at the front of Elvis's rancho as the three of them spilled out from the alley onto the street, Calle Ocho. Maddox pulled Sonia along as they struggled to run down the pockmarked road, through the people milling around the streets and sidewalks celebrating Chávez's return to power.

A group of thugs noticed the three foreigners running down Eighth Street and one yelled, "Alto!" *Stop!* but the group scattered when both Maddox and Rose pointed their MP-5 submachine guns in their direction. Maddox was glad the men just ran; the last thing they needed right now was to get into a gun battle with citizens. He grabbed Sonia by the hand again and yelled to Rose, "This way!" as he bolted down the steep stairs of the barrio. His pace was so quick at times that Sonia screamed out in fear; tumbling down the crumbling asphalt stairs was not a pleasant prospect.

They made it down the stairs and onto Avenida Central— the main thoroughfare in and out of the barrio—in record time. The streets were thick with people celebrating around barrels set on fire.

Maddox and Rose scanned the crowd and tried to blend into it, but that was a tall order for three people dressed in black fatigues, with black flak jackets, and submachine guns. Maddox and Rose flanked Sonia, their very visible weapons keeping the mob at bay.

"This one," Maddox said pointing to a 1975 Chevy Impala four-door hardtop sedan. The old gas-guzzler with its faded green paint job was perfect. Its thick heavy steel frame and big block V8 were the closest they could come to a civilian tank, plus old cars like the Impala were easy to hotwire. Rose smiled, said, "What a beaut," and whipped out his car theft kit from his LBE belt. Maddox had Sonia scoot down next to the driver's side back door, and he stood guard while Rose shattered the driver's side window with a silver window punch and unlocked the car.

"Get in and stay down, babe," Maddox told Sonia, feeling bad about shoving her into the backseat of a car they were stealing.

By the time both Sonia and Maddox were settled in the backseat, Rose had already hot-wired the old car. He was beginning to pull out when they once again heard someone scream, "Alto!"

Maddox looked up to find it wasn't a group of young gangster wannabes this time; there were three Venezuelan DISIP paramilitary troops running toward them.

Rose hurled a flashbang grenade at the men; the metal canister clinked as it hit the ground and rolled toward them. The three DISIP agents stopped in their tracks at the sound and then tried to scatter. When the grenade detonated a moment later, the dark of night gave way to a brilliant flash of light followed by an ear-piercing blast. The intended targets fell to their knees disoriented, blinded, and deafened. The effects of the grenade were only be temporary, but they would give Rose, Maddox, and Sonia the head start they desperately needed.

"Go, go, go!" Maddox shouted as Rose grabbed the steering wheel and shoved the car into gear.

Rose floored the gas pedal, and the big car fishtailed as he peeled out, but he almost immediately had it back under control as they drove off. One of the dazed soldiers blindly opened fire but did not even come close to striking the car as it sped away.

Rose headed west and out of the barrio. He descended the narrow streets that wound through the hillside slums at break-neck speed, slamming the rear end of the big car against a couple walls without stopping; each collision jarred them inside the seatbelt-less car. "Sorry about that. Hold on tight, lads!" Rose would yell with each smash.

They were nearing the bottom of the hillside when they saw the lights of an approaching SUV coming closer and closer.

"Shit!" Maddox said.

"We won't be able to outrun them in this piece of shit," Rose said.

Rose slammed on the brakes, sending Sonia onto the car floor. "Fuck!" Rose yelled at the throng of people milling around on the street. He had no choice but to slow down as he began maneuvering the Impala through the crowded streets of Avenida Central.

There were people everywhere. Celebrating. Drinking. Looting. Partying. Fighting. Finally, weaving from one side of the street to the other, Rose was able to steer clear of the crowds, and the road opened up in front of them. Rose floored the accelerator, pushing the Impala beyond its ability; it began to vibrate as it sped away from the oncoming SUV.

"It's just one truck," Maddox said relieved as he stared out the back windshield. *We can take out just one truck*, he thought.

He turned around with his MP5 and lowered the window. "Stay down, Sonia," he said as he shoved her onto the floor-boards. Before he could even fire a shot, Maddox cried out, "Oh, Jesus!" and grimaced at what he was seeing.

Unlike Rose who had driven around the crowd of people clogging the street, Brull's men in the SUV plowed right through them. Bodies flew through the air and tumbled onto the streets with bone crushing force.

"What's going on?" Rose asked.

"What's happening?" Sonia cried out as she tried to sit up, but Maddox held her down.

"Stay down, please, honey," Maddox begged before answering both her and Rose's question. "They're just driving straight through the people, plowing through everyone like they're nothing more than piles of leaves!"

"We won't be able to outrun them, then," Rose said, gripping the steering wheel tighter.

"Stay down, honey, and don't get out of the car," Maddox instructed Sonia, who was now crying. He removed the safety from his MP5 submachine gun.

"We'll have to face them, Tom," Maddox said.

"Right," Rose replied and swerved the car sideways, bringing it to a sudden stop. Maddox and Rose jumped out of the car, aiming their weapons at the speeding SUV. As the vehicle plowed through the last group of people, someone in the crowd threw a brick through the windshield, hitting the driver who then lost control.

The SUV swerved crazily to the right and then veered sharply back to the left as the driver overcorrected in an attempt to regain control; he failed. The vehicle spun out of control and flipped on its side, sliding about twenty feet before coming to a stop against the sidewalk. Like David and Goliath, a lone stone brick had brought down the large vehicle and its heavily armed men. The crowd went wild and cheered as they mobbed the wrecked SUV like a crowd of L.A. Laker fans celebrating an NBA championship.

Maddox and Rose watched the scene in shock. They saw a flash of muzzle fire from inside the SUV and then heard two or three shots, but the crippled SUV and its injured passengers were no match for the angry mob out for the blood of the men who had just plowed through their friends and family.

"Street justice," Rose said, still aiming his weapon toward the chaos.

"We're so fucking lucky," Maddox said. "Let's get out of here."

Despite Maddox's pleas for her to stay down, Sonia had watched the events unfold from the back seat of the car.

Are those men dead?" she asked when Rose and Maddox jumped back in the car.

"Appears so," Maddox answered as they sped away.

"What about Elvis?"

Maddox didn't say anything knowing Elvis was dead.

"The bloke was a good man for a crook," Rose chimed in. "Elvis has left the building for good..." Rose trailed off, realizing he wasn't being respectful of Elvis's dying while trying to help them.

CHAPTER THIRTY-TWO

8675309

Caracas, Venezuela

The Prados Del Este Freeway was eerily calm compared to the chaos of the barrio streets, and the stolen Impala was holding up very well. There were a couple of bullet holes and the side paneling was beat to shit from the car bouncing off the walls of the narrow streets, but they had made it out alive.

Tom Rose's adrenaline was still pumping, and he let out a celebratory yell. "Yeah, fuck yeah, that was a close one, mates!" He banged the steering wheel of their stolen vehicle with his fists.

Maddox ignored his friend and turned to Sonia. "Are you all right?" His question was met with silence, and she continued to stare out of the car window as she had been doing for the last ten minutes.

"Sonia, are you hurt? Are you all right?" He grabbed her shoulders in an attempt to snap her out of her trance-like state.

"Don't touch me!" she shrieked. "You've ruined my life." She buried her face in her hands and burst into tears.

Maddox slouched back into his seat, feeling like he had been kicked in the chest by a mule. Her recoiling from his touch was more painful than anything Brull had in store for him.

He couldn't think of anything to say or anything to do to comfort her. She was right. He had ruined her life. He had recruited her as an asset. He had trained her on how to find safe houses for the agency. He had taken her to dangerous locations on missions, and now they were on the run.

Had the coup been successful, they would probably be back at her place making love. But it had failed. Now she was a traitor to the state and wanted by Johan Brull. She had refused to leave her beloved Venezuela before, but now there would be no choice. She had to leave—leave her house, her real estate business, her friends, and her life as she knew it without delay.

I have ruined her life, Maddox despaired. There was a part of him that had naively hoped Sonia wouldn't care about the horrible events unfolding around her since they were in love, but when the person you love has turned you into a desperado fugitive and has torn your whole life apart in an instant, well, love might not be enough. Especially as they were speeding down the Carretera Petare roadway towards the Autopista Petare highway at 3:00 a.m. in a stolen Chevy Impala.

Then he mentally shook himself and focused on the issue at hand. He needed to get her out of the country at all costs, even if that meant she would hate him and he would never see her again.

Rose glanced at the couple in the rearview mirror; he thought about saying something to defend his friend and hopefully make Sonia feel better, but decided to hold his tongue. He couldn't even say, "Hey, at least we're alive," since their long-term plans for staying that way were still a bit up in the air. One thing was clear: They needed to get out of the country. Brull would not take their escaping the clutches of his men lightly.

Maddox and Rose had hatched their worst-case scenario plan the day after the Brit first arrived in Caracas. Even though both of them had been confident they wouldn't actually need to make use of such a scenario, professionals always planned for the worst—a good thing since their confidence hadn't mattered and it was now time to implement the worst-case scenario plan. They needed to get to their rendezvous destination with Ruben Guzman.

Colonel Ruben Guzman was a good friend to Maddox and Rose. In appreciation for the work Maddox had done in the Amazonian jungle and in San Cristobal, he had agreed to smuggle Maddox and Sonia into Colombia if necessary.

In a few hours, Chávez would assure the country he was still in power and place all the blame for the failed coup on the CIA, which meant Maddox would be exposed, labeled persona non grata, and immediately expelled from the country.

Maddox had already disobeyed the direct order from Langley to stay put at the embassy, so he was watching his CIA career being flushed down the toilet, but he didn't care about that. He had to get Sonia out of Venezuela. Even if she never wanted to see him again, he would at least be able to live with himself knowing that she was alive and safe.

Maddox sent Guzman the pre-arranged text to his cell phone: 8675309, Jenny's number. Maddox loved that Tommy Tutone song, and making it the code for the worst-case scenario had seemed funny at the time since he'd thought the plan probably wouldn't be needed. But here he was sending the text, and the Tommy Tutone inside joke didn't seem as funny now.

In less than a minute, Maddox got a text back from

Guzman: "I got your number." The worst-case scenario plan was now operational.

Guzman was taking a huge risk. Maddox was considered a rogue agent since he disobeyed a direct order to stand down and hold tight at the embassy. But they wouldn't expect Guzman to put his neck on the line like this, so the plan could work.

They were to meet up with Guzman in an hour, near the entrance of the small terrarium located within the huge Parque del Este, Caracas's own version of Central Park. Maddox felt it an appropriate meeting place since the terrarium had on display dozens of snakes and other reptiles and the men they were running from were cold-blooded.

Under the cover of another couple hours of darkness, Guzman would take Maddox and Sonia to a safe house, where they would regroup and change clothes, and then sneak them into Bogotá.

Once safely out of Venezuela, Maddox and Sonia would become Guillermo and Maria Mendoza. They would then take a Taca commercial flight to the Juan Santa Maria International airport in San Jose, Costa Rica. Maddox already had the needed documents: forged passports and Costa Rican cédula ID cards.

Since Maddox was now in direct violation of the CIA's orders, he was on his own, so Tom Rose had rented a safe house near the San Jose airport in the Cariari neighborhood. By the time they arrived there, Maddox and Sonia would be exhausted, so after getting some sleep, Maddox would drive down to his small beach house in Junta.

Ten years ago, Maddox had bought a nice piece of land within walking distance of the beach. A couple years later, he had built a small house there. It was nothing fancy, basically a little cabina where he could get away from it all; he couldn't think of a better place to go and hide for a while, but first they had to get out of Venezuela.

At the meet up location with Guzman, Rose would part ways with Maddox and Sonia. He had done a terrific job of protecting Sonia, but now the situation was too hot for him, and there was nothing he could really do for them from this point on. He would leave the rendezvous point and double-time the three miles from the park to the British Embassy in the La Castellana neighborhood. Once there, he could secure a flight back to the UK.

Rose and Maddox decided there was safety in numbers, so instead of taking the surface streets from the barrios to the park, they drove down the more heavily traveled Carretera Petare-Santa Lucia. The car blended in well with the traffic, but if any of the Chávistas on the streets took a close look and recognized them, they would have to shoot their way through since they were not going to stop for anyone. Luckily, it didn't come to that, and the Petare road was quieter than they expected as they headed east, exiting on the Avenida Boyaca and onto Avenida Sucre straight into the park.

They arrived unchallenged by Brull's men and having avoided the many checkpoints manned by Chávista militants, so they were able to quietly slip into the park at 4:20 a.m. Rose shut off the headlights as he drove the Impala into the parking lot, where they would ditch it.

Even though Sonia hadn't said another word to him during the drive, Maddox needed to communicate with her in order to keep her safe. He turned toward her and spoke firmly. "We're ditching this car and meeting up with Guzman. It's about a one-mile walk east of the zoo. Stay in the middle of us. Be quiet, don't say a word, and stay alert."

"I need to check your gear," Maddox said as he began to tug at her flak jacket. "Do you understand?"

"Yes," Sonia said softly. The tone of her response sounded as if she might be beginning to come around, as if she might feel guilty about how she had treated Maddox, but he knew there wasn't time to delve into that now. He wasn't issuing out orders to her because he was mad—he was trying to get her out of Venezuela alive. Now they were going to be out in the open, clichéd sitting ducks for Brull.

Fortunately, Maddox and Rose were certain they hadn't been followed. Elvis and his gangsters must have taken out the lead car back in the barrio, and they had seen with their own eyes the mob serving street justice to the occupants of the second car. They didn't know what became of the third SVU, but it wasn't in sight.

Even if Brull sent reinforcements, it would be a while before they were dispatched. With the coup crackdown, the tombs would be full of political prisoners for him to have fun with, so he would be busy, but he still wouldn't pass up the chance to see Maddox suffer.

Maddox imagined Brull's commander, Dos Santos, was giddily waiting to splash Maddox's face on television. He would grant an exclusive interview to CNN so he could out the CIA station chief and declare to the world, "Here is the gringo behind the coup." They would never acknowledge the coup was planned locally, and to ensure that Chávez's version of the events of the past seventy-two hours would stand and become part of the history they were writing, the coup leaders were to be rounded up and killed.

Rose, Sonia, and Maddox abandoned the stolen car and took off on foot through the park. Electricity was touch and go throughout the city and, luckily for the trio, the lights were out in the area, so the entire park was covered in a blanket of darkness. The place was quiet and deserted, but they heard gunshots off in the distance. Either there were still pockets of resistance out there or the Chávistas were still firing their weapons into the air in celebration.

They jogged single file toward the terrarium; Maddox led the way, Rose brought up the rear, and Sonia was in the middle. Rose and Maddox had their MP5 SD submachine guns with their silencers attached to the barrels at chest level, scanning the park with their trigger fingers resting alongside the weapons' stocks. The triggers were set to three-round bursts. Even though the MP5s had silencers, only around forty percent of the sound would be suppressed, so even with a silencer, a full automatic would be noisy. A three-round burst would be perfect to drop anyone who challenged them but not make too much noise or garner the attention of others that could be nearby.

They made it to the rendezvous spot at 4:47 a.m. Guzman was waiting behind some trees on the south side of the terrarium.

"Goddamn, it's good to see you, Ruben," Maddox said as he embraced Guzman.

"Nice to you see you, my friend," Guzman replied. He was wearing civilian clothes—a nice, black long-sleeved dress shirt tucked into a pair of Banana Republic khakis.

"Tom, nice to see you too," Guzman said as he embraced Rose. Then Guzman turned to Sonia, took her hand, and spoke to her in calm, smooth Spanish. "Don't you worry, Sonia. We're going to get you out of the country safely." Switching back to English, he addressed all three of them, "Come now, we have to go. I have a car," and turned toward the pathway leading to the main road. "It's not safe here."

They headed toward a parking lot right on the Avenida Sucre. As the group emerged from the darkened park, a black Nissan Pathfinder drove toward them. Maddox and Rose raised their MP5s, but Guzman waved them off. "It's okay. He's one of my men."

The Pathfinder quickly pulled into the parking lot. "Get in; we need to go," Guzman said, still retaining the calm and reassuring voice he had used with Sonia. He opened the passenger side back door, revealing the empty seats. Rose got in first, and then Maddox escorted Sonia in second so she would be between the two of them.

Guzman climbed into the front passenger seat. The driver looked about thirty-five, was olive-skinned, and had black hair and a thick black mustache; he too wore civilian clothes. The driver had said nothing as the group piled in, and he did not acknowledge them as he put the SUV into drive.

"Vamonos," Guzman told him, and the driver promptly pulled out of the parking lot onto the Avenida Sucre. Maddox could tell he was heading onto the Autopista Francisco Fajardo.

"Is everything in place?" Maddox asked Guzman.

"Yes, we got a room at the Hotel Centro Lido. We'll be there in a few minutes," he replied.

The Centro Lido was a luxury hotel near the Olympic Stadium. It was located down the street from the Colombian Embassy and less than two miles from the British Embassy.

"Well, my friend, Little Napoleon is fully back in charge, stronger than ever now," Guzman said, unable to hide his disappointment.

"Where is Frank Chacon?" Maddox asked.

"He's now in exile; fled to Switzerland," Guzman replied.

In less than ten minutes, they exited the freeway onto the Avenida Libertador. "Liberator Avenue," Maddox said, amused at the irony.

"Appropriate, no?" Guzman asked with a smile as his driver pulled into the hotel.

———

THERE WAS nothing Sonia wanted more right then than to take a long, hot shower. She was pleased that the hotel had strong water pressure, and she let the warm water wash the dirt, sweat, grime, and fear of the last two days from her body.

Tom Rose sat at the room's desk with his laptop, planning his exit to London in a few hours. The TV was tuned to CNN, and the talking heads were discussing Chávez's victory and the United States' role in the whole situation.

In the adjoining room next door, Guzman and his driver acted as lookouts and were ready to provide backup if needed. The rooms were on the third floor, next to the emergency exit and facing Avenida Tamanaco. A well-placed bribe by Guzman had allowed them to access both the building and their floor via service entrances, and as far as the hotel personnel were concerned, the guests were journalists who, along with their security detail, were in Caracas to cover the coup for the BBC.

It appeared that the group had successfully thrown Brull off their tracks, but they knew it was just a temporary reprieve. They would spend only two hours in the hotel before heading out. Guzman would drive Maddox and Sonia to the airport to catch the 12:05 p.m. flight to Bogotá. Guzman had prepared Colombian diplomatic papers for them, so they'd appear to be just two more Colombian diplomats leaving Venezuela during these uncertain times. It was a beautiful cover as long as they could avoid Brull's men.

Maddox used the downtime to head to the lobby and check in with the embassy and Dick Philips. He had missed several of their calls during the last twenty-four hours, but he didn't want to make any calls with Sonia in the room. Maddox took out his secure cell phone and dialed Philips's direct line.

The time difference between Caracas and Langley was just thirty minutes ahead, so it was 7 a.m. in Langley when Maddox began punching in the number for Dick Philips on his phone. Philips picked up on the second ring.

"Are you on a secure line?" Dick asked without saying hello.

"Yes," Maddox replied sheepishly, like a child who knew he was in trouble with his father.

"I don't know how you fucked up this bad," Philips said in a calm but stern manner. Philips rarely cursed, so Maddox had an idea of just how angry he was.

"I couldn't leave her here," Maddox told him. There was nothing more he could do, or even attempt to do in order to salvage his career at this point.

"The asset?"

"Yes, sir," Maddox confirmed.

"Are you in the country?" Dick asked.

"Yes, but not for long. I'll be going dark for a few weeks, Dick."

"Hoban has tied a tin can to your tail; this will give him more ammo to bury you. Just come in. Go to the embassy; it's over."

"I can't do that, not until I know she's safe."

"I can't protect you then," Philips said, sounding more despondent than angry.

"I know. Are you all right?" Maddox had been worried about throwing his long-time mentor under the bus.

"You don't have to worry about me, son," Dick answered, sounding a bit better.

"Come in, Pete. Just go to the embassy. Bring the asset; it's all right. That way you'll just be expelled."

"I can't protect her through the official channels," Maddox

said. "I'm sorry, Dick. I never meant to hurt the team, to hurt you."

"You're not hurting me; Operation Puma was a stellar success. The events in Caracas are the problem, and that has nothing to do with you, so you haven't hurt me. Hoban is going to let us twist in the wind no matter what; I just don't want you there solo," Dick explained, sounding like a worried parent.

"Thanks, Dick, but I can't come in yet. I'll be in touch."

"Be safe. Call me in forty-eight hours, for my sake," Dick pleaded.

Maddox was silent for a few seconds before saying, "Okay. Thanks, Dick." Then he hung up.

Maddox knew Philips was being sincere. Max Hoban was playing a chess game from the safety of his Langley office. He was going to seize this moment to politically terminate Maddox, but that was just a bonus; Hoban's true goal was to burn Philips, and he had him squarely in his crosshairs.

The little fuck must be shaking in his boots with excitement, Maddox thought.

Next up was a quick call to Mary Dent. Maddox knew that if he called his second-in-command, Ron Bateman, he would just get the party line, but he could rely on Mary to speak freely and frankly with him. She picked up on the fourth ring.

"Condor?" Mary asked.

"69789," Maddox replied with his secure code.

"Jesus Christ, you're alive," a relieved Mary Dent responded.

"Nice to hear your voice, too," Maddox said with a chuckle.

"The shit has hit the fan here. You've been compromised by the DISIP; they're officially expelling you, persona non grata, at a news conference at 3:00 p.m.," she told him.

That was actually good news for Maddox. He would be in Bogotá by that time, so they should be able to blend in at the airport and board their flight before his face was plastered all over the news.

"So I've heard," Maddox replied.

"Ron's been appointed interim SC; they've labeled you as having gone rogue."

"I know I fucked up, but I couldn't leave her behind," Maddox explained without regret.

"Holy shit, I knew you were pussy-whipped, but not that bad," Mary said, her Boston accent growing even stronger due to her agitation.

"Sorry, Mary. I know you had feelings for me," Maddox teased.

"Yeah, I'm wet for you," Mary replied sarcastically. "Well, at least you jest in bad times." She sounded relived that Maddox was taking the demise of his career so well.

"Just tell the team to hang in there, and I'm fine. I can't tell you anything else," Maddox explained.

"I know. That's why I haven't even bothered asking where the hell you are. Take care of yourself, Pete. It was an honor serving with you," Mary said.

"Right back at you," Maddox replied as he ended the call.

As unpleasant as those calls had been, he was terrified that the conversation waiting for him in the hotel room upstairs would be so much worse.

Sonia came out of the bathroom feeling revived. Her hair was still wet, brushed back, and she wore a white robe, courtesy of the hotel. Rose was sitting on the edge of the bed, still in the same blue jeans and black T-shirt but minus the flak jacket. His MP5 submachine gun was within arm's reach and his eyes were glued to the television. The celebrity journalists on CNN were still dissecting the failed coup and America's possible role in it. They didn't have a clue or any new information and just kept repeating the same analysis in different ways so they could milk it for few more hours. None of the media outlets had said anything about the terrorist camp being taken out, so that was good news for Langley.

"How you feeling, mate?" Rose asked Sonia.

"I'm feeling better now," she replied. "Where's Peter?"

"He's making some calls. I know you're mad at our lad, but he's just trying to protect you," Rose said, no longer able to hold his tongue.

"I know, Tom. I was just scared and angry that life as I knew it changed in the blink of an eye," Sonia explained, her voice tinged with guilt.

"But you still have your life. You need to listen to him; if you stay here, they will arrest you, or worse if they discover who you are," Rose warned ominously.

"His job, it's just . . ." Sonia searched for the right words, but Rose didn't let her finish.

"His job is finished, so you won't have to deal with it anymore," Rose said.

"What do you mean?"

"Just listen to him until you're out of the country," Rose said, not answering her question. Three knocks sounded on the door; Maddox was back. Rose grabbed his MP5 and looked through the peephole to double-check before opening the door. Maddox quickly stepped in, and Rose closed the door behind him.

CHAPTER THIRTY-THREE

CRISIS CONTROL MODE

CIA Headquarters. Langley, Virginia

Back at Langley, the agency was in crisis control mode. While Maddox, Bill Anderson, and the others were out in the field waging their missions, the failed coup had splintered the Langley camp into two groups: those supporting Dick Philips—who was trying to salvage Maddox's career and ensure he didn't lose any of his people on the ground—and those supporting CIA Executive Director Max Hoban—who was seizing the opportunity of the failed coup to wage a political war against Philips, SOG, and direct covert action by the agency.

The success of Operation Puma was the team's only saving grace at the moment, but the failed coup would be problematic even though the CIA's role in the actual military action was minimal. But Maddox going AWOL had given Hoban the ammunition needed to win his battle against Dick Philips.

Ron Bateman had become acting station chief in Venezuela and the entire CIA team was hunkered down at the embassy.

Anderson and his SOG team had left the country, as ordered, in a military transport plane. The SOG team was upset about leaving the Venezuelan coup fighters on their own, but there was nothing they could do; as soon as the coup had appeared on the brink of failure, they were ordered to leave Caracas. The opposition fighters became political collateral.

Bateman didn't have good news for Philips, confirming that Maddox had gone off script in his effort to rescue an asset with whom he was romantically involved. Philips knew this already; Maddox had told him what he was planning. Philips was certain that if anyone was able to pull off what Maddox was attempting, it was Pete Maddox, but it would cost him his career. Maddox had failed to report his relationship with a foreign national as required by CIA regulations. Although that alone wouldn't have cost him his career, disobeying an order to stay at the embassy and not become involved in any direct action in Caracas would end it.

Dick Philips was in his office as he recalled the conversation he had with Maddox eighteen hours before. But Bateman hadn't finished delivering the bad news to Dick Philips. In a few hours at 11:00 a.m., Alberto Santana, the Minister of the Interior, would hold a press conference to announce that the CIA was behind the coup and that the mastermind, CIA Station Chief Peter Maddox, was being expelled from the country, persona non grata. Bateman's source was a newspaper journalist for *Últimas Noticias*, the largest national newspaper in Venezuela, which was pro-Chávez. They had Maddox's photograph, which was being published in just a few hours.

Philips would be unable to sit on this information any longer once Bateman reported it through the official channels, cutting ties with Maddox. He would now be on the run and on his own.

Max Hoban and Derek Hall, the CIA Liaison to Congress,

summoned Philips to Director Van Loon's office for a meeting. Philips knew the meeting wouldn't be a good one, especially since Maddox had confirmed he wouldn't return to Langley until the asset was secure outside of Venezuela. He was now officially AWOL, and Max Hoban had his scapegoat all wrapped up in a pretty bow.

Director Van Loon didn't mince words. "Goddamn it, Dick, what the hell is going on with your boy down there?"

"He's AWOL, Director; my last communication was forty-eight hours ago. I ordered him to the embassy, but he's gone solo to take care of a personal matter."

"You're shitting me. A personal matter?" Van Loon seethed.

"It's a woman, an asset with whom he has a personal relationship, and he is trying to protect her from the current roundup of local coup supporters," Philips explained.

"This asset, is she in government?" Van Loon asked.

"No, sir, she's a civilian."

Hall spoke then. "Dick, we have a serious problem here. The Venezuelans are releasing Maddox's picture in a few hours. The chairman of the House Committee on Intelligence Affairs is aware of this and will be calling for an investigation once this is public."

"And it's not going to help if your station chief, who is about to be expelled persona non grata, isn't around to answer these questions," Hoban seethed. "This rogue agent of yours has put us in an even worse spot." Hoban sat back in his chair, happy to have slammed Philips's back against the wall and tightened the noose around the neck of Maddox's career.

"Maddox will be back, he will take responsibility, and he will answer your questions. He'll be back," Dick reassured without a trace of hesitation or doubt in his voice.

"How can you be certain?" Hall asked.

"He's one of my best men. Once he secures the asset, he will return and face the music. I guarantee it," Dick replied.

"You really want to claim this rogue agent as one of your best men?" Hoban taunted Philips.

Before Philips could respond, Van Loon interceded, "I won't have the boy disparaged, Max. He's done a hell of a lot for the agency, including making Operation Puma a success, which the president is extremely happy with."

Hoban crossed his arms like a scolded child trying not to throw a tantrum.

"But the fact is, he has put us in world of shit," Van Loon continued, now addressing Philips.

"He'll have to fall on his sword for this, Dick," Hoban spoke up again.

This time DI Van Loon nodded in agreement.

"Maddox knows the rules of the game," Philips said with a blank stare.

"Are you sure?" Van Loon asked, making full eye contact with Philips.

Philips returned the eye contact and said, "Yes, sir."

With that, Philips was dismissed, leaving Van Loon, Hoban, and Hall to deal with damage control. Hoban was at his best, unleashing a political battle to bury his internal CIA enemies.

The room was silent as the three remaining men sat at the conference room table. Finally, Hoban spoke up.

"Maddox is finished with the agency; we could actually use him going AWOL to put the whole thing on him—just a rogue agent acting on his own to overthrow Chávez."

"Derek, will Congress buy it?" Van Loon asked.

"Operation Puma was a huge success, so that helps; it's not a stretch to say Maddox wanted to go a little further with a complete regime change. SOG is out, and it was clean, so the only one being expelled is Maddox," Hall replied. He then sat quietly, as if choosing his next words carefully.

"If the Venezuelans are going to pin this on Maddox, I say we play along," Hoban interjected.

"Damn it," Van Loon breathed as he threw his glasses on the table. He knew this was the way to play the situation, but he didn't like the move.

Hoban sat with his chest puffed out. He managed to not crack a smile, but he was enjoying his apparent victory. And now, he was ready for the double kill.

"Dick Philips can't survive this either," he argued. "If he stays, then the press will say there is no way a rogue agent could pull this off on his own." Hoban let his words sink in before continuing and shoving the proverbial knife deeper into Philips's back. "Someone at Langley has to pay the price as well."

Director Van Loon was silent as he contemplated the options. Van Loon's silence was music to Hoban's ears. He was finally going to be able to force Dick Philips out of the agency in humiliation.

CHAPTER THIRTY-FOUR

ALBERTO AND MARIA BLANCO

Caracas, Venezuela

THE DOOR ADJOINING THE TWO HOTEL ROOMS WAS OPEN, and it was time for a final meeting before Sonia and Maddox made their escape from Venezuela. Guzman had thoughtfully provided food and sodas, but aside from Tom Rose, no one was really in the mood to eat.

"Come on, mate; you need to get some food in your belly," Rose said to Sonia as he handed her a cheese and ham arepa. She took it and began to pick at it.

"Pete, here are your papers," Guzman said, handing Maddox a manila envelope.

Maddox unwound the envelope's red string and pulled out a pair of passports and ID cards.

"Congratulations, you're now a Colombian," Guzman said with a smile. "Those are two Colombian passports under the name of Alberto and Maria Blanco. The ID cards are your diplomat papers. You're a Colombian diplomat who is leaving the country with your beautiful wife, Maria," Guzman said as he smiled at Sonia and slid the two passports on the table over to Maddox. "Diplomats from all over the world have been fleeing the country, so those diplomat ID cards should get you right on that flight."

"Thank you, Ruben, you're a good friend," Maddox said as he shook his hand.

"Well, don't thank me yet. They should get you through airport security, but if you're arrested, we will have to turn our backs on you. The official press release will say you procured those documents on your own, illegally," Guzman warned.

"Of course, without question," Maddox confirmed.

Maddox couldn't help but reflect on the events of the last seventy-two hours: The Venezuelan government had decided to expel him from the country, Colombia had stated it would turn its back on him if he were caught with their fake documents, and his own government had decided to hang him out to dry as a rogue agent. *Three countries in three days,* Maddox thought, *that must be a record.*

He turned to Tom Rose who had showered and ditched his flak jacket, dirty jeans, and T-shirt. He was now wearing a green Under Armour polo shirt with yellow stripes and a blue Under Armour logo resting on the left-hand side of his chest. The shirt was a slim fit exposing his barrel chest, broad shoulders, and hulking biceps. Rose clipped his holstered 9mm P226 to his belt behind his back and slipped on his sports coat. He was leaving all his other weapons behind with Colonel Guzman.

"You squared away, Tom?" Maddox asked.

"I'm set, mate; no worries. My friend with MI6 is picking me up at 0900 a couple clicks from here. He's made all the arrangements already. I'm getting a free ride home on a C-17 that's leaving at 1300 hours."

"We need to leave now," Guzman interrupted.

Maddox turned to Rose and gave him a firm handshake and a warm embrace. "Thank you for everything, Tom."

"No worries, mate. Make sure you keep your head low getting out of town."

"You got it." Maddox promised.

Rose then turned to Sonia, opened his arms, and gave her a gentle squeeze when she stepped into them.

"He loves you, mate, don't forget that," Rose whispered into her ear.

"I know; it will be okay," she whispered back to him before stepping away.

"You take care of our boy out there," Rose laughed as he pointed at Maddox.

"Thank you, Tom, for taking care of me. I know I was a bitch at times," Sonia said.

"Hey, now, don't say that. You acted like a pro with all that is going on. Now take care, you hear me?" He stared into her eyes. "And listen to our mate until you're out of here, okay?"

"I will," she said nodding.

"After that, don't listen to a damn word he has to say," Rose told her and then burst out laughing.

"We'll get together in a few months. Reminisce and share a pint." With that, Tom Rose exited the room.

Maddox was also leaving his submachine gun and more powerful firepower with the colonel. The safety blanket provided by the night shadows had long been burned off by the warm Venezuelan sun. So close to the equator, it was already 80 degrees at 7:00 a.m.

He also felt rejuvenated after his shower and two large coffees with milk. He had ditched his dirty and sweaty clothing from the last two days and donned a white dress shirt, his Ludlow two-button jacket, and a pair of Italian wool pants ordered from the JC Crew website the previous year—semi-casual business attire that a Colombian diplomat might wear to travel.

He had also completely disassembled his P226 SIG Sauer and concealed the pieces in a specially-made toiletry bag that could circumvent the more stringent baggage checking policies of the post-9/11 travel world.

Maddox racked a six-round magazine into his Walther PPK pocket pistol, chambered an extra round, and clipped the weapon to his belt. He would have seven rounds ready should Brull's men catch up with them on the way to the airport, but then he would have to ditch the PPK before reaching their destination. He hated the thought of losing a good gun, to say nothing of being unarmed, but it couldn't be helped. Though Maddox was trained in hand-to-hand combat, that would be of little use against a group of heavily-armed Venezuelan soldiers. *One step at a time*, he reminded himself.

Guzman's driver and bodyguard put all the weapons and gear into a large black duffel bag and carried it back into the adjoining room while Guzman, Maddox, and Sonia said their goodbyes.

"You're always welcome in Colombia should you need to lay low," Guzman said to Sonia before he stepped into his room and shut and locked the door.

Now that it was just him and Sonia on the run, Maddox had to make things right.

"Are you all right?" Maddox he asked, trying to look into her downcast eyes. "I'm sorry I put you in this mess."

Sonia looked up and met his gaze, and tears started to trickle down her cheeks. Before Maddox could say or do anything else, she threw her arms around him and buried her face into his chest.

"I'm so sorry, I've been awful to you," Sonia sobbed. "Can you ever forgive me?"

"There is nothing to forgive. I just hope you can forgive me for what I've done to you," Maddox said as he held her in his arms.

"I agreed to help you and the CIA, you paid me, and you warned me about getting involved with you romantically. I made the decisions on my own. I had no right to be angry with you, and now you've risked your life and ruined your career to save me. I'm so sorry," she cried.

"I can't live without you, baby, so none of that matters to me anyway," he said softly into her hair.

They kissed and held each other for the next few minutes. There was nothing Maddox wanted more than to fall into bed with her, but that had to wait. They needed to leave for the airport now if they wanted to escape.

It took Sonia a couple minutes to redo her makeup and fix her mascara; the tears had made a mess of her face. After making her repairs, she took one last look at herself in the mirror. Her stylish blue jeans, form-fitting long-sleeved top, long leopard-print scarf, and tan Prada were casual but elegant. Her hair worn loose and a few pieces of tasteful silver jewelry completed the look. She was terrified about going to the airport and using a fake Colombian passport, but at least she would look good doing it.

She stepped out of the bathroom and slowly spun in front of Maddox before asking him, "How do I look?"

"You look like a beautiful Colombian diplomat's wife," Maddox he replied smiling.

Sonia smiled back.

"Are you ready?" he asked.

"Ready," she said with more confidence than she felt and

then exhaled loudly, trying to expel the fear she was feeling along with her breath.

Maddox and Sonia took the stairs down to the hotel's covered parking lot.

"Stay close to me," he told her, and then they dashed through the parking lot hand in hand. Maddox's eyes scanned the entire empty parking lot. He needed a car but had to be careful. There was a yearlong waiting list to buy a new car in Caracas, which fueled a lucrative used car market—sometimes a used one ended up costing even more than a new one—so there was always a guard watching parked cars. Car owners usually slipped the guards an extra few bolívars while asking them to "me lo cuida," *Watch it for me*. But life in Caracas still hadn't normalized; the lot was empty.

Maddox had already surveyed the parking lot earlier that morning and knew where the two security cameras were. Avoiding them wouldn't be a problem for a black ops-trained spook, but it wasn't himself he was worried about. If anyone were to track him to the Lido and think of pulling the security video, he would be long gone by that point; still, he didn't want to leave a clear image of Sonia. Maddox instructed her to walk with her head down and her large Gucci sunglasses always on, Hollywood celebrity style.

He searched the lot for the red Toyota 4Runner he had seen earlier in the morning and was relieved when he spotted it. "Follow me," Maddox said, and they made a beeline for the car. "We're taking this car," he told her when they reached it.

Maddox walked her to the passenger side door then made his way to the driver's side, scanning the entire parking a lot a few more times. He took out his car kit from his suit pocket and was inside unlocking the passenger side door for Sonia in twenty seconds.

"Get in," he told her, and she jumped inside and closed the door.

"Holy shit, you're stealing this car?" Sonia asked.

Tom Rose had stolen the Impala the previous night as they blasted their way out of the barrio, but seeing the man she loved pick a lock and dive underneath the steering wheel of the car was still a bit stunning.

"We need wheels. Please, honey, just give me a minute." It was Maddox's nice way of asking her to shut up as he fumbled with the car's wiring.

It didn't even take him a minute to bring the engine to life. Cumbia music suddenly exploded into the silence of the car, making both Maddox and Sonia jump. He quickly switched it off and turned his head toward her. "Damn. Guess they like it loud," he said smiling and then proceeded to drive calmly out of the Hotel Centro Lido parking lot.

"Let me know if you see a car or person watching or following us for the next few blocks," Maddox told Sonia as he headed east on Avenida Tamanaco, toward the Prados del Este Highway.

Traffic on the freeway was surprisingly light for 8:30 a.m., but then most Venezuelans were probably staying home until normalcy returned to post-coup Caracas. It was a thirty-minute drive to the airport, and Maddox drove only a few miles over the speed limit. Luckily, they didn't encounter any military or police roadblocks.

Twenty-five minutes later, they exited onto Avenida Aeropuerto and could see Simon Bolívar airport only a few hundred feet away. They were almost there. Sonia's heart was about to beat out of her chest. Her hands were sweaty, and she felt like she was about to pee in her pants as they approached the airport.

Maddox knew this would be difficult for her, so he had only

allowed her to drink half a cup of coffee and one glass of water that morning. "Trust me, honey, you don't need caffeine freaking you out, and if you have too much liquid in you, you might not be able to control it if you get scared or nervous," he had warned her back in the hotel room.

CHAPTER THIRTY-FIVE

MIDNIGHT EXPRESS

Simon Bolivar International Airport. Caracas, Venezuela

As the red Toyota 4Runner approached the airport, Sonia and Maddox could see that the departure and arrival lanes were jammed with cars. It appeared just as many people were leaving Caracas as were returning now that Chávez was back in power. The long-term parking lot for the international terminal, however, was wide open. Maddox was easily able to drive in and pull his ticket. *Hopefully, the owner won't be stuck with the parking bill once this stolen car is found abandoned here,* Maddox thought.

He pulled into the first available parking space and, after a quick check to see how Sonia was holding up, they walked toward the international terminal. Maddox spotted a group of trash cans close to the curb near the entrance. As they approached them, he looked around and then removed the small backup pistol from his belt. He took out the firing pin and ejected the magazine, then dumped the pistol in one can, the magazine in another, and tossed the firing pin down a street drain. He was now weaponless.

Maddox and Sonia walked into the terminal just like any other traveling couple. They headed through the long sheltered walkway leading from the third floor of the parking lot into the terminal. There were very few other people in the skywalk, but it was mayhem inside the terminal, loud with the chatter, cries, and screams of people in various stages of travel. The chaos inside the airport worried Maddox. Could they have canceled all flights?

Sonia was doing her best to act normal, but inside she was terrified. She felt like a drug smuggler.

"Pete, I have to go to the bathroom," she pleaded.

"Sure, honey. Let's walk to the flight info monitor over here; there is a bathroom right next to it."

She felt like the guy in *Midnight Express*. Her heart was beating a million times per second and, even though her liquid intake was minimal as Maddox had suggested, she felt like she was going to piss in her pants, she was so nervous.

Maddox had to ensure Sonia was okay. For him, this type of operation was old hat. He'd been trained to escape from a lot worse situations than this, and he'd lost count of how many fake passports, documents, and identities he'd used during his career. But for Sonia, a civilian, this was a terrifying ordeal. She wouldn't feel calm until she was on Colombian soil. Even that felt a little too close for comfort.

As Sonia used the facilities and regained her composure, Maddox checked the departures:

Avianca 69 Flight Status: Departure: 12:05 p.m.... Current Status: ONTIME

A wave of relief flooded through him; the flight hadn't been canceled or delayed. However, it was only 9:00 a.m., and a lot could happen in three hours. Maddox looked around the crowded airport; everything appeared fine, and they blended in well with all the other harried travelers.

He pulled out the only cell phone he had kept, the secure one he used to communicate with Tom Rose—the others were too easy to track. Rose had indicated to Maddox that he would text him with any updates, so he fired up the Treo 180g GSM smartphone. There were two text messages. The first text message was just one word:

> Hereford

Maddox smiled; the text was good news. Tom Rose had made it to the UK Embassy and was en route to Hereford, a quaint English town on the River Wye. The British SAS was based out of nearby Credenhill, which would be easy enough for Rose to get to.

Another text came through:

> No update

There weren't any new developments, and no news was good news since it reassured Maddox that Brull had no idea where they were. Now they just needed to get on that flight to Bogotá.

Sonia emerged from the bathroom looking refreshed. She had touched up her makeup and brushed her hair; she looked more put together.

"Did you make it to the bathroom on time?" Maddox asked with a smile.

"Yes," she said with a roll of her eyes and friendly hip bump.

For a moment, Maddox felt at ease; he let himself forget that the Sadist of Caracas probably had his minions out looking for them all over the city. For just a moment, Maddox pretended it was over.

He quickly returned to reality, powered off the Palm Treo, and put it back into his messenger bag. Then he grabbed Sonia by the hand and headed for the security gate. Now was the perfect time to go through since she seemed a bit more relaxed.

———

UNFORTUNATELY, queuing up in the security line unnerved Sonia again. She felt her heart begin to beat out of her chest once more, the sharp pain in her stomach returned, and she again felt the urge to urinate. *How could that be?* She thought. *I just peed.*

The fear and the nerves wrought havoc on her insides. Still, she was determined to keep up appearances and plastered a smile her face. She also tried to ignore her increasingly sweaty hands—a circumstance which normally would have embarrassed her into letting go of her boyfriend's hand, but there was nothing normal about this situation or her CIA agent boyfriend whom she had seen shoot his way out of a barrio, steal a car, and perhaps even plan a failed coup.

Her other hand, however, had nothing to hold on to, so she began fidgeting with her face and hair: touching her nose or her ear, rubbing her brow, and continuously tucking her hair behind her ears. When she became too fidgety, Maddox would gently squeeze her hand and smile at her; it would calm her down for a few minutes, but then she would begin to fidget again.

———

THEY SPENT an hour in the long security before finally reaching the customs official checking for passports and boarding tickets. The terrorist attacks of 9/11 were just seven months removed, so airport tension was still palpable and security was heightened—even in Venezuela—and the coup attempt had made things even worse.

How ironic, Maddox thought, *I just took out a Libyan terrorist camp on Venezuelan soil just a few days ago, and now they're checking my papers.*

Maddox and Sonia were assuredly on the wanted list, but he doubted Brull and his secret police would send out a traditional APB. In between hand squeezes to calm Sonia, he watched the line and the customs officer—a young man of about twenty-five. Perfect. The officer couldn't have much experience.

Maddox was holding a business-class ticket, but had chosen to remain in the longer line. This allowed him to scope the area better, and he liked the security in numbers. When it was finally their turn, he was relieved to see Sonia turn on the charm.

She greeted the customs officer warmly with a big smile and—in Spanish—expressed how bad she felt about the poor hard-working guard having to deal with so many travelers today. The guard smiled sheepishly as he handed back her Colombian passport.

Maddox greeted the young customs officer in Spanish and with a perfect Colombian accent. He handed over his Colombian passport, diplomat ID, and boarding pass from Avianca Flight 69. The officer glanced at the passport, shot a quick look at Maddox, then turned back to Sonia with a shy grin and waved them through. They had cleared airport security.

Maddox and Sonia walked into the passenger-only section of the airport and headed to the Avianca VIP Lounge, access complements of their business-class tickets. Once inside, they quietly hugged in relief over making it through the first stage of their escape and then allowed themselves to relax a little. Each had some orange juice, a bagel with cream cheese, and coffee.

"A Pabellón criollo sure sounds good right now," Maddox said as he smiled at Sonia. It was the national dish of Venezuela; just about every country in Latin America has their version of this traditional dish consisting of some kind of meat – shredded beef in Venezuela – rice and beans, and fried plantain slices, topped with a fried egg. Maddox thought about that meal as he ate his stale bagel.

After a thirty-minute wait in the VIP Lounge, it was time to actually board the airplane. En route to their gate, Maddox made a stop at the La Casa De Las Arepas and purchased ham and cheese arepas for the flight. Although Sonia's stomach was still in knots, she felt better seeing Maddox relaxed enough to buy food to eat during their escape. *That has to be a good sign*, she thought.

The boarding went off without a hitch, but Maddox had dragged plenty of targets right off airplanes, so he knew they wouldn't be in the clear until they landed in Bogotá.

Avianca's business-class section on the Airbus A330 was quite nice: The cloth blue seats boasted ample, pillowy headrests and there were only two seats per row, guaranteeing he and Sonia would not have to deal with any nosey passengers potentially overhearing their conversation. There was also plenty of legroom, and the seat backs in front of them each had a large monitor filled with plenty of in-flight entertainment options. Water bottles and headsets were waiting for them as they sat down.

The flight attendant asked if she could get them anything. They both ordered a Diet Coke and settled in. Sonia was seated on the window side, Maddox the aisle, where he assessed every passenger who entered the cabin.

After a thirty minute boarding process, the captain's voice cracked through the overhead speakers. He greeted and welcoming the passengers, and then encouraged them to relax and enjoy the hour-and-fifty-minute flight from Caracas to Bogotá. Within a few minutes of the captain signing off, the plane began taxiing down the runway.

The Simon Bolívar International Airport was in the city of Maiquetia, seaside to the Caribbean with the mountain range of the El Avila National Park in the background. The airplane taxied down the runway and took flight, briefly flying over the Caribbean Sea before making a sharp turn over the mountains surrounding Caracas and heading south toward Bogotá.

Sonia felt a huge weight lift from her shoulders as the airplane took flight. When it settled into its cruising altitude several minutes later, she looked over at Maddox, grabbed his hand, and kissed it. She gave him smile and then turned to look out the window, saying goodbye to her beloved Venezuela down below. It was a bittersweet moment.

—————

BACK AT THE US EMBASSY, Troy Sennight had patched a live feed from the Caracas television station Venevisión, which had begun reporting on Chávez's ranting and rambling press conference in which he accused the United States of planning and carrying out the coup against him. The television flickered images of reporter Silvia Cabrera as she informed viewers of the president's accusations against the United States government and the CIA.

Dick Philips, who was fluent in Spanish, was intently watching the local Caracas news when suddenly Pete

Maddox's picture flashed on the television screen as Silvia Cabrera continued her report:

"DISIP General Director Antonio Dos Santos has confirmed the expulsion of the CIA station chief of Venezuela, Peter Maddox, also known as Rick Castro. We reached the American Embassy, but they had no comment. The CIA would neither confirm nor deny that Peter Maddox is an employee. General Dos Santos has indicated that the CIA has acted on the expulsion demand, and the DISIP believes Mr. Maddox is no longer in Venezuela."

The news report then moved on to other developments related to Chávez's regaining power. Philips sank into his seat.

"Sir, that's the report making the rounds here," Ron Bateman's voice said over the speakerphone. "His picture is also all over this morning's newspapers."

Philips remained silent for a few moments.

"Thank you for the update, Ron. Keep me posted on any developments or if you locate Pete." He could hear Bateman confirming the order when he disconnected the call. Dick walked over to his office couch and sat down, contemplating his next move.

CHAPTER THIRTY-SIX

AVIANCA

Avianca Flight 69

THE EXHAUSTION OF THE LAST FEW DAYS QUICKLY overtook Maddox and Sonia, and soon after the plane hit cruising altitude, they both fell asleep. Maddox slept for almost an hour and awoke to find they had missed the flight breakfast. Luckily, he had the ham and cheese arepas that he had purchased in the airport terminal.

It was now time to get ready for the next phase. He opened up his messenger bag and pulled out his laptop, a Troy Sennight custom job that was untraceable. It was wired with a highly secure Bluetooth device, and Sennight had ensured that whenever the machine was fired up, it went through so many proxy servers and IP addresses that it would be impossible to trace if used in thirty-minute increments.

Sennight had been working with Bluetooth technology since Ericsson first released it as a wireless alternative to RS-232 standard modem connections. Wireless provided a blanket of security and anonymity that Sennight embraced and perfected. The connection was so secure that the cockpit would have no idea the laptop was piggybacking on their system. The screen was also covered with a military-grade, anti-glare privacy coating which allowed no one except the person sitting directly in front of the laptop to discern what was being displayed.

Maddox fired up the laptop and began to check if Brull had indeed exposed him. It was a strange feeling for a clandestine CIA officer to see himself in the news—his face, his real name, and his alias all available for public consumption. He had always been so careful about being photographed, but apparently not careful enough. The fact they had a photograph of him to print hurt his pride more than anything in the accompanying article.

That he was being blamed for the failed coup was irrelevant. The CIA didn't confirm or deny shit anyway, but having your cover blown was a career-ending occurrence.

Soon his whole life story would be played out on the news. Maddox shuddered at the thought of journalists swarming through his life. They would dig through his collegiate and military records looking for dirt, latching on like leeches to his service as an army interrogator and his time with the 75th Ranger Regiment. The Ranger angle would give Brull more fodder for painting him as some sort of Special Forces mastermind behind the failed coup.

In the movies, CIA agents had no past, but in real life, they had records, and it was called a record for a reason. It was a piece of evidence about the past that had been recorded to withstand the passing of time. The agency wouldn't confirm or deny his existence, but the attention guaranteed his CIA career was over, even if he had obeyed orders and left Sonia in Brull's sadistic hands while he sat safe at the US Embassy. Not that he doubted his choice; a part of him was sad for letting down Dick

Philips and throwing his career away, but as he saw his picture staring back at him on the laptop monitor, it was a moot point.

At the twenty-eight minute mark, Maddox powered off his laptop. He then tapped CTRL and the L, M, and K keys, wiping the laptop's hard drive. Next, he pressed the ZNMQ keys and then the space bar, which detached the laptop keyboard to reveal a hidden compartment invisible to airport screening machines; inside were several passports, driver's licenses, and other fake documents.

He checked on the items they would need once in Colombia, including the two dark blue Costa Rican passports.

Maddox had secured a fake Costa Rican passport two years ago, so he had gone back to his contact at the Costa Rican embassy in Caracas three months before to get one for Sonia, just in case.

Maddox had wired two thousand dollars to his contact's bank account and provided him with two passport pictures of Sonia. Four days later, he had received a Costa Rican passport and a cédula national ID card with Sonia's picture under the name of Yolanda Ramirez Quesada.

Maddox put the documents back into the hidden compartment, pressed the space bar twice, and tapped the Q and the 4 keys. The compartment locked back into place. They would be landing in Bogotá in forty minutes, so Maddox closed his eyes for a quick nap.

Bogotá, Colombia

Maddox and Sonia spent the night at the Sheraton Bogotá, which was just a few miles from the El Dorado International Airport. They showered and had dinner, and she learned that they had airline tickets from Lacsa, the Costa Rican-based airline, for the next morning. Maddox handed her a new Costa Rican passport and cédula.

It appeared that changing papers and identities was as normal as changing socks for Maddox. Sonia just stared at her new identity. She was now Yolanda Ramirez Quesada, and she had the papers to prove it.

Sonia was beginning to find the adventure thrilling. Unlike in Caracas, no one was shooting at them here, so it felt more like a fun game to her, even though her nerves were still shot about having to travel again with a fake passport.

That evening, they ate at a quaint restaurant on Calle 82 in Bogotá. It was actually a romantic dinner, and it took her mind off the reality of this trip. However, reality interrupted her fantasy of just being on vacation with her boyfriend on several occasions, like when they stopped at the Salitre Plaza Mall on Avenida El Dorado, and Maddox purchased what he called "disposable cell phones."

They were cheap, pre-paid cell phones: two Nokia 1616's —a blue one for him, a red for her. These were ugly, bare-bones cell phones which, as a fashionable Caracas girl, she would normally never be seen using in public, but all that mattered at the moment was that they were pre-paid with 500 minutes of talk time each and couldn't be tracked.

MADDOX THEN ASKED Sonia to wait as he went to another mobile phone kiosk inside the Salitre Plaza Mall, where he purchased a third pre-paid phone.

"Okay, honey, let's go to dinner," a smiling Maddox said, like it was normal to buy three cell phones and travel with fake passports.

CHAPTER THIRTY-SEVEN

SANCTUARY

Playa Barrigona, Costa Rica

MADDOX SAT IN THE SUN IN PLAYA BARRIGONA, COSTA Rica, a small, somewhat isolated beach about a mile from his get-away-from-it-all beach house.

He had purchased the land his house sat on several years ago when the son of a local farmer split up his recently deceased father's acreage and put the pieces up for sale. Maddox had bought three lots to avoid having close neighbors.

The land sat back about half a mile from the main road and about thirty feet from a small but beautiful beach usually only frequented by locals. The closest big beach towns were Playa Nosara fifteen miles west and Playa Samara about three miles east.

Although Samara and Nosara were popular with tourists, the other smaller beaches in between the two towns were not. They were small beaches with hard-to-access roads that kept them a bit isolated and quiet; just as Maddox liked it.

The last few days had been an excellent opportunity for

him and Sonia to rekindle their romance. She knew they were hiding out and keeping a low profile, but the escape had been a success, and now they were just enjoying being together without fearing that Brull was around the corner.

Headlines concerning the coup had faded rather quickly from the news. The war in Afghanistan was entering its sixth month, and there were rumors that the US might invade Iraq. A failed little forty-eight-hour coup in Venezuela wasn't big enough news to hold the attention of the major networks for long.

Maddox's expulsion from Venezuela had breathed a few more days' life into the story, but since the CIA wouldn't confirm or deny he worked for them and Chávez was sounding even crazier and more paranoid than before, the national US news outlets had lost interest in that angle as well. This was all good news for Maddox even though he was still in a world of shit with the CIA, the White House, and Congress, but those were all internal issues and not making the news—and neither was Operation Puma.

The White House still had that trump card in its pocket. The complete destruction of a Libyan terrorist camp on Venezuelan soil was something Chávez didn't want out, so he backed off on specifics and didn't make any demands on the UN or OAS to investigate his accusations against the CIA getting up to shenanigans near Puerto Ayacucho.

News of the camp would be bad news for the Chávez government. Public knowledge of the US attack on Venezuelan soil coordinated to coincide with the coup in Caracas would also be bad news since it would basically prove the US government knew about the coup and could lead to more inquiries. It was best for both sides to keep that nugget of information from the public, so a small cold war broke out between the two countries. Chávez kept his battle verbal and light, more showman-ship than anything else.

The only public casualty for the United States was Peter Maddox.

Maddox had dropped Sonia off in Samara and then driven his red Jeep to the desolate Playa Barrigona. He sat on the beach, pulled out his secured and clean satellite phone, and called Dick Philips's direct line.

"How are you, Pete?" Philips asked.

"I'm doing well, sir," Maddox replied.

"You need to come in, son." Philips sounded dejected.

"I know, and I'll be there in a few days. I promise," Maddox answered.

"The political heat has died down, but Hoban wants our heads," Dick explained.

"I'm not worried about Hoban," Maddox responded with annoyance. "My days with the company ended the second my picture hit CNN."

Philips didn't say anything for a few seconds. "You have to come in, Pete," he simply repeated.

"I will see you in a few days, Dick," Maddox said and then killed the connection.

CHAPTER THIRTY-EIGHT

OUT OF THE SHADOWS

One Month Later. Washington DC

MADDOX FROZE LIKE A DEER IN HEADLIGHTS AT THE throng of reporters camped out front of the Capitol building. Since his return to the US, he had found being out of the shadows both difficult and annoying, especially since he was almost constantly surrounded by the press. He took a deep breath and was swarmed as he began walking toward the steps. Cameras and microphones filled his vision, and the sound of many reporters asking the same questions at the same time nearly deafened him.

"Mr. Maddox, did you plan the Venezuelan coup against Hugo Chávez?"

"Mr. Maddox, were you the CIA station chief in Venezuela?"

"Mr. Maddox, did you try to kill Hugo Chávez?"

"Mr. Maddox, will you take the Fifth?"

Maddox said nothing, responding to all the questions with

silence and stoicism and keeping a normal pace as he walked up to the Capitol in his Calvin Klein striped navy suit.

What a shitty way to ruin a beautiful DC summer day, he thought.

Privately, Maddox's thoughts were racing. *That fucking Hoban, he must have tipped off the press about my arrival to testify in front of Congress.* His pride took a hit when he thought about how much Johan Brull would enjoy watching this on CNN.

Sonia was glued to the television back at Maddox's Arlington condo in Arlington, waiting to see if he would be mentioned on the news, when suddenly the CNN anchor interrupted the current segment to go live to their DC affiliate, who was reporting on the scene:

"Peter Maddox, the reputed CIA station chief in Venezuela who was expelled from that country for life, has just arrived to testify in front of Congress about his and the CIA's role in the April coup attempt against Chávez."

For a moment, she was actually excited to see her boyfriend on TV, especially as he looked so handsome in the suit she had picked out for him at Macy's, but her excitement quickly turned to anger as the swarm of media surrounded Maddox, asking him stupid questions they knew he couldn't and wouldn't answer. It was like they just wanted to humiliate him.

As Maddox steadily ascended the Capitol steps and disappeared inside, the cameras turned onto the reporters, who basically reported that nothing had happened and there was no news.

"Fucking idiots!" Sonia screamed at the TV.

Maddox was going in front of the US House Permanent Select Committee on Intelligence, the committee in charge of overseeing the intelligence community in the United States, including the CIA.

The committee chairman was Dan King, a seven-term Republican congressman from Texas. The ranking member for the Democratic minority was Nancy Adler, a six-term congresswoman from California.

Max Hoban had pushed Congresswoman Adler to make the hearing public, but sanity had prevailed and, due to the classified information that would be discussed, Chairman King had ordered the hearing closed to the public and to the press.

The hearings would last for over a month. All of the Venezuelan CIA operatives had been ordered to testify: Ron Bateman, Mary Dent, Troy Sennight, and Jack Duffy would all be there. So would Max Hoban and CIA director Doug Van Loon, but the congressional representatives really wanted to hear from Pete Maddox and Dick Philips.

Bill Anderson's name never came up, and Maddox doubted the committee even knew of the SOG commander's existence. He felt a bit of jealousy at Anderson's ability to remain a ghost. The last thing Maddox heard about Bill Anderson was that he was quite busy in Afghanistan and Iraq.

The buzz inside was palpable as Maddox was one of the first CIA station chiefs to have ever been publicly exposed and then kicked out of the country while working in an official capacity. It seemed like everyone wanted to see what the disgraced spy had to say. His lawyer, Ted Trumbo, flanked him.

Maddox's hearing was contentious and short. It began with Chairman King saying, "Mr. Maddox, I want to remind you that you are under oath," pausing for effect, and then asking "Did you plan the Venezuelan coup?"

"No, sir," Maddox answered.

And that was the end of Maddox's directly answering any questions.

"Were you aware that a coup was being planned?" Chairman King asked.

"On counsel's advice, I invoke my right under the Fifth Amendment not to answer on the grounds I may incriminate myself." Maddox stared back at the committee members.

"Did you ever meet with any of the coup leaders?" Democratic Representative Andrew Burns from Oregon asked.

Maddox leaned toward the microphone in front of him and once again stated, "On counsel's advice, I invoke my right under the Fifth Amendment not to answer on the grounds I may incriminate myself."

The questions kept coming.

"Did you or anyone in the CIA provide any type of support to coup leaders?" Democratic Rep. Diana Adamczyk from Illinois asked.

Maddox's response was the same.

The dance continued for over an hour, the members of the committee peppering Maddox with questions and Maddox pleading the Fifth over and over again.

It was not in Maddox's nature to back down from tough questions, to not be a straight shooter and speak his mind, but he had decided to take his attorney's advice and take the Fifth. The silver lining was that this decision seemed to infuriate the congressmen on the committee; Maddox enjoyed pissing off politicians who tried to Monday morning quarterback operations.

His CIA career was over. Even if Hoban didn't get his way and he wasn't fired, Maddox would be dumped at an analyst desk somewhere in Langley and then he would resign anyway, so he didn't feel there were any points to be scored by talking to the committee. They would need to find their own rope with which to hang Maddox; he sure as hell wasn't going to help.

"Mr. Maddox, why are you hiding behind the Fifth?" an exasperated Ted Ames, a Republican from Nebraska, asked.

But by taking the Fifth, he would not just obfuscate what he perceived to be a Max Hoban-led witch hunt, he would also protect his mentor's thirty-two-year CIA career.

CHAPTER THIRTY-NINE

MACALLAN NEAT

McLean, Virginia

MADDOX ARRIVED AT DICK PHILIPS'S HOME AT 7:00 P.M. sharp. Philips was a stickler for being on time. Philips's house was at the end of a sleepy cul de sac on Spring Hill Road in McLean, Virginia, a short four miles from CIA headquarters. His home had all the appeal of an English countryside cottage. Dick's wife, Marianne, had recently renovated the four-bedroom, four-bath home, and it now boasted beautiful home of hardwood floors, wood columns, granite countertops, and new stainless steel kitchen appliances. Maddox hadn't seen the house since Marianne had completed the renovation of the house she and Philips had bought in 1979.

After a nice dinner, Maddox and Philips retired to his study to enjoy some Scotch. Maddox figured his mentor wanted to talk about something big when he broke out one of his finest bottles, a twenty-five-year-old Macallan single malt. *Elvis would have liked this Scotch*, Maddox thought as he remembered the drink he'd shared with the barrio leader in honor of Henry Calderon.

Philips preferred his Scotch neat, and Maddox took his on the rocks but with just a couple of cubes. The two men settled into plush leather chairs next to the fireplace with their glasses. It was a hot summer day so the fireplace was dormant. The entire ambiance felt right out of *Town & Country*, which was exactly the way Dick Philips liked to relax. All that was missing was a pipe or cigar, but neither of them smoked.

"Pete, I wanted to make sure you heard this directly from me before Monday morning," Dick began, as he glanced down at his glass of Scotch. "I've agreed to retire, effective immediately."

"Those bastards," Maddox seethed.

"In exchange, they'll stop the witch hunt inside my team and, even more importantly, for SOG."

Before Maddox could protest, Philips continued, "I'm not being all gracious here, son; in exchange for my immediate retirement, they'll allow me to do it honorably and with my pension intact. Had I fought them and failed, I would have lost my pension, my thirty-two years of service would have been for naught, and Hoban would have gone after the entire Venezuela station and possibly even SOG."

"Your honor would have been intact regardless of what that asshole Hoban did," Maddox said.

"Thanks, son, I appreciate that, and on principle you're right; I've never done anything to dishonor the agency or our country. But on paper, had I been fired or been indicted by Congress, my thirty-two years would have vanished, as would my pension." Philips took a drink of his Scotch.

"I'm sixty years old, too late to start over from scratch, especially with Sandy a sophomore at Georgetown. And . . ." Philips took a sip from his Scotch, "I guess I'm just too tired to even try to fight them, so I took the easy way out." Philips looked down in shame, but Maddox thought he had nothing to be ashamed of.

Philips took another sip and continued, "I tried to protect you, son, but Hoban wants to spill the blood of one of us on the congressional committee's altar." Philips was unable to look at Maddox again.

"It's okay, Dick. You warned me about this possible outcome, and I signed up for it; I also left you with little recourse when I disobeyed orders so I could rescue Sonia." Maddox leaned forward on his leather chair and patted Philips's knee to let him know he didn't blame him and held no grudges.

Philips was moved, but it still didn't make the situation tolerable for him. Maddox was his best agent; he was one of the few remaining CIA operatives who could straddle the fence between the black ops and regular agency worlds. Letting Maddox twist in the congressional wind left Philips with a pit in his stomach about

"I wish I could tell you what's going to happen to you, but obviously they're keeping me in the dark," Dick shared. "I asked that they keep you, told them that a reprimand would be enough."

"Thanks, Dick, but even if I weren't fired, Hoban would ensure that I'd be tied to an analyst's desk monitoring Nicaraguan election results. I couldn't handle that," Maddox said with a smile as he took a sip from his drink.

"I figured as much, but I wanted to at least give you that choice. With them forcing me out, however, Hoban won't rest until you're out of the agency for good, and I'm afraid he's going to blacklist you as an independent contractor as well," Philips warned him.

"Well, I don't know what's next for me, but working for one

of the asshole cowboy freelance agencies out there wasn't too high on my list anyway," Maddox said, stirring his glass so that the ice cubes rattled around, cooling down the Scotch. "But I still have some loose ends I need to take care of, so I can use the time on the bench for that," Maddox smiled.

For the rest of their visit, Dick and Maddox—two soon-to-be former CIA spies—focused on enjoying their Scotch and each other's company.

CHAPTER FORTY

LOOSE ENDS

Cayo Santa María, Cuba

FOR JOHAN BRULL, IT HAD BEEN A FANTASTIC SIX MONTHS. The coup had failed, Chávez was back in power, having only been ousted for forty-eight hours, and Brull had emerged as one of the big heroes of the battle against the coup.

He had remained loyal to Chávez and led his men against the rebels. He had waged a brutal campaign and rounded up most of the coup participants—from the leaders, to the military planners, to the actual fighter. All were beaten, some were tortured, and the bulk of them were killed, their bodies disappearing into his three large kilns deep inside El Helicoide. The constant smoke billowing from the compound after the coup was the only hint of the nefarious deeds going on inside.

For show, some of the well-known names had been tried and found guilty of treason. They were sentenced to between nine and thirty years, depending on their connections, and shoved into one of Venezuela's notoriously violent prisons, where Brull could easily kill them whenever he pleased.

Although a few of the coup leaders had been able to flee into exile, Brull wasn't worried; he had open cases on each one of them, and though it might take months or even years, his assassins would get them eventually.

Brull's crowning glory that had earned him the most accolades from higher up the chain of command, however, had been embarrassing the CIA. He had publicly exposed their station chief and had him expelled persona non grata, banned from ever returning to Venezuela.

It had taken several days, but Johnny Chacon had eventually told everything he knew about Henry Calderon, the Council, the gringo Rick Castro—who he assumed was CIA—and the real estate broker who helped secure safe houses.

Confirmation that Rick Castro was Peter Maddox came from Johnny Chacon identifying him via a photograph.

Although Brull had wanted to put Maddox in his interrogation chair, just for fun, and then shove him into one of the burning kilns, Dos Santos had showed him that they could get benefit more from exposing the gringo spy and humiliating the CIA.

Hanging the coup around Maddox's neck had given Chávez a lifetime of fodder against the CIA. It was beautiful, Brull thought. He was amazed at how politically astute Dos Santos was and how much he had to learn from his mentor.

Brull would be able to learn even more from his mentor, having recently been appointed deputy director of the DISIP. He was now the number two at the intelligence agency and heir apparent to General Antonio Dos Santos.

Life for Brull was good. He smiled as he lay on one of the plush lawn chairs around the beautiful pool of the Barceló Beach & Colonial Resort in Cayo Santa María, Cuba. For all his hard work, he had been awarded a fat promotion and an all-expenses-paid trip to one of the most luxurious resorts in the Caribbean. Communist Cuba knew how to run luxury resorts.

Cayo Santa María was an island located north of Cuba in the Jardines del Rey archipelago, and although life on the main island for the average Cuban was rough, in the luxury beach resorts dotting the island, Europeans, Canadians, and Latin Americans enjoyed the pampered life. There was no larger contrast than the streets of Havana and the beaches of Santa María—the same Communist nation but two completely different worlds.

For Brull, who had grown up dirt-poor in the Venezuelan countryside, life just couldn't get much better than this: vacationing at one of the best resorts in the Caribbean, all expenses paid, with a beautiful, young Venezuelan model as his companion.

A posh resort like this was too incredible to bring his wife to (and bringing the six children wasn't even a thought), so Brull had told her this was an official government business trip, and that wasn't entirely untrue. Brull did stop in Havana on his way to Cayo Santa María for a fifteen-minute photo op with Fidel Castro, one of his heroes. Castro had been delighted with Brull's embarrassing the CIA and exposing one of its top agents in public, so he had been eager to meet Brull and ensure he received VIP treatment at the resort.

It only took a glance at the odd couple frolicking poolside to figure out why a beautiful woman in a skimpy bikini would be doting on this short, fat man with an acne-scarred face, bushy black mustache, and hard-not-to-stare-at unibrow.

Brull was only five six—and that was while wearing man heels. He had all his shoes and boots custom-made to make him look taller. He was wearing a Panama Jack hat, a white Guayabera shirt, and a blue speedo bathing suit, which revealed much more than anyone wanted to see.

Brull's mistress was a five ten, blonde beauty from Mari-acbo, Venezuela. She was wearing a Rio-type thong bikini that made the men stare and the wives glare. Her large breasts were a gift from Brull, who had sent her to the top plastic surgeon in Caracas.

Johan Brull beamed as he sipped on banana daiquiris with his beautiful girlfriend.

In the evenings, Brull and his mistress liked hit one of the resort's two twenty-four-hour bars for Cristal champagne, margaritas, rum shots, and dancing. That evening, Brull showed his class by wearing his favorite clubbing shirt, a bright blue affair with a giant print that would make Ed Hardy blush: a huge rooster stood front and center, and the face of a beautiful woman rested in the foreground; dollar bills floated around them both. On the right-hand side of the image, in huge white letters, were the words, "Los Gallos Me Dan Dinero . . . Las Mujeres Me Lo Quitan," *The Roosters Give Me Money . . . the Women Take It Away*. It was an ode to his favorite pastimes, cockfighting and beautiful women—specifically gold diggers. Brull didn't care they were only after his money as long as they would give him what he wanted at night.

Brull had started trying out dogfighting recently, but it didn't hold a candle to the excitement of a cockfight, where two beautiful, large, majestic birds with razor blades taped to their claws were tossed into a ring to shred each other to pieces.

Betting bolívars—or dollars for very exclusive cockfights—only added to the excitement as the surviving rooster would produce a windfall of cash that Brull would then spend on his mistresses.

Not that Brull needed the money from cockfights to fuel his mistresses or his party life; he had his hands in the pockets of the major drug lords and the barrio kingpins. He also got a taste of every bribe collected by his secret police force. Everyone kicked up to Brull to avoid disappearing into one of his kilns.

In addition to the money-making options his job provided for him, Brull had a deal with his brother-in-law as well. Tomas Matos was a prominent Caracas businessman who always won the bids for construction work—even if his wasn't the lowest bid. No one wanted Brull to open a file on them, a powerful business advantage Matos was happy to make use of; he was also more than happy to give his brother-in-law a nice cut. The money Brull made from cockfighting was just for fun.

That evening, Brull hit the nightclub with his obnoxious shirt, white pants, and matching white shoes. He had slicked back his black hair with globs of Vitalis Hair Tonic, which gave it a high sheen and strong antiseptic smell, and doused himself in cologne; people around him recoiled from the smell.

His mistress, Vicki Nuñez, either had no sense of smell or the allure of power and money had made her immune to the stench as she rubbed up against him and stuck her tongue in his mouth. She wore a super short miniskirt and low-cut shirt that allowed everyone to see the plunging cleavage of her fake breasts. Her huge hoop earrings, gold and silver bracelets, and a gold anklet displayed the spoils of a kept woman.

At around 1:30 a.m., Brull was too drunk to go on, a coked-up Vicki wanted to keep partying. She put her tongue in his ear and begged him to let her stay while she partied with her new friends, a young couple from Peru. *It's the drawback of having a twenty-four-year-old girlfriend who loves to party*, Brull thought. He was too drunk to fuck anyway, so he left the bar and headed to his VIP suite, leaving his girl to party on through the night.

———

IN THE VIP suite across the hall from Brull's, Maddox saw his chance. He had arrived at the resort three days before Brull and began setting up surveillance: bugging the popular restaurants and clubs, the base of the umbrella stands in Brull's exclusive poolside cabana, and Brull's own suite. The deputy director of the DISIP and head of the secret police had no clue he was being watched.

The work Brull had put in to get this all-expenses-paid VIP treatment came with a price.

Former Council Chairman Frank Chacon, the billionaire oilman from Caracas who had fled to Switzerland, was bankrolling this freelance operation. Brull had tortured Johnny Chacon to death with scalding hot water, and now Frank wanted vengeance.

Maddox was more practical about these types of things, but he saw Brull as a continued threat to Sonia. Working for the first time as a freelancer, Maddox was amazed how much easier it was to run an operation when he could tap into the vast resources he needed, when money, budgets, and politics were no longer an issue.

Chacon had offered Maddox fifty thousand dollars plus all expenses to take Brull out. Even though he was in exile, Chacon still had a lot of friends in Venezuela, and even those who weren't friends had still been happy to sell him information about Brull. When Maddox had learned the details of Brull's sun-soaked vacation to Cuba, he'd known this was his chance.

He'd been happy to scrap the more risky plan of sneaking into Caracas to get to Brull. Getting in and out of Caracas wouldn't have been a problem for Maddox, but getting close to Brull would have been quite a challenge, so this trip was a gift that had landed in Maddox's lap.

Maddox was looking at the three windows he had open on

his MacBook Pro so he could watch Brull poolside, in his favorite club, and in his room. Watching the beautiful Vicki Nuñez put in an Oscar-worthy performance as she climbed on top of that fat pig and moaned and groaned was something he could have lived without seeing, but he recorded it anyway. It didn't help that Brull liked to pop the blue pill, so poor Vicki had to work hard to live the lifestyle of mistress to one of the most powerful men in Venezuela.

That type of video could come in handy. But he wasn't there to blackmail Brull. He was there to terminate him.

As soon as the drunken Brull stumbled out of the club alone, Maddox sprang into action. He could have taken Brull out his first night, but not without also taking out young Vicki.

Frank Chacon may not have cared about collateral damage, but Maddox did. Vicki was a bimbo, but she didn't deserve to die for being Brull's bimbo. Maddox had started to believe he would have no choice since Brull demanded his trophy girl hang around him all the time, but tonight she had stayed at the bar drinking, flirting, dancing, and doing more coke with her new friends.

Maddox grabbed a box of fishing line and quickly exited his room, then used his copy of Brull's key card to gain entrance to his suite. Once inside the darkened room, Maddox removed his thick, black leather gloves and tore off enough of the line to get the job done. He then tied a knot at the center of the fishing line, put his gloves back on, and wrapped the fishing line around his hands several times. Leaning on the wall beside the door, he waited.

It took the plastered Brull ten minutes to make it to his room and another three to swipe the card correctly. Maddox remained with his back to the wall, not moving an inch, the entire time.

The door to the room finally flung open, briefly concealing

Maddox behind it, and Brull stumbled inside. He hit the light switch next to the door, illuminating the darkened room as he staggered forward, letting the door close behind him.

As the door clicked shut, Brull continued toward the bathroom, staring at the ground and oblivious to the now fully-exposed intruder. Maddox lunged at him from behind and wrapped the fishing line tightly around Brull's neck, perfectly centering the knot right over his larynx.

Startled, Brull popped his head up and saw Maddox in the mirror in front of him, but it was too late to do anything. He could feel the fishing-line garrote tightening around his throat, and all he could muster was a barely audible "Nooo!" before Maddox shoved him face first into the ground while continuing to put unbearable pressure on Brull's windpipe.

The fishing line cut into Brull's neck, which began to seep blood. Maddox shoved his right foot into the man's back and used it to add more pressure. The handmade garrote pulled Brull's head back toward Maddox.

Brull could do nothing aside from feebly kick a few times as he struggled for air. His limbs began to turn blue as the knot on the fishing line crushed his larynx, strangling the life out of the sadist of El Helicoide.

When he felt like the job was done, Maddox stopped applying pressure and jumped off Brull's back as he shoved the fishing line in his pocket. He quickly double-checked that Brull was dead; he was. Maddox then slowly opened the door and stuck his head out. The corridor was silent and empty. The other guests continued to sleep, undisturbed and unaware of the silent assassination that had just occurred. Maddox pocketed his surveillance cameras, took off his gloves, then exited Brull's room and quickly entered his own across the hall.

Maddox took off his clothes and put them, the bloody fishing line, and his gloves into a white cloth laundry bag. He then put on a new T-shirt and khaki cargo shorts and broke down his equipment and belongings before grabbing the white bag and leaving his room.

He headed to the beach fire pits, where the bonfires usually went on until dawn. While there were several people still hanging around, the crowds had thinned to just a few lovers and groups of friends, and—at 2:00 a.m.—they were all too drunk to notice Maddox walk up to one of the raging bonfires and toss the laundry bag into it.

———

BY THE TIME a drunk and coked-out Vicki began screaming at finding her dead sugar daddy on the floor, Maddox was gone. He had packed his gear into a large scuba bag, loaded it onto his Canadian-registered sailboat, and quickly slipped out of the Cayo Santa María marina for the thirty-hour trip to Matthew Town, Bahamas, where his Caravan Cessna waited to fly him back to the United States.

Alone with his thoughts on the thirty-hour sailboat trip, Maddox felt conflicted. He could justify the hit. Sure, the revenge aspect was nice—Brull had killed several of his Venezuelan friends and ruined his CIA career by outing him as a spy—but what had sealed Brull's fate was his trying to kill Sonia.

As long as Brull was alive, Sonia would be in danger. Normally a low-level asset like Sonia wouldn't have popped up on anyone's radar, but once Brull had tortured the truth out of Johnny Chacon—that she was also Maddox's girlfriend—she became the asset Brull wanted in custody most.

It had been confirmed that she wasn't an official target of the DISIP, but more of a pet project for Brull. That alone was enough to justify the hit in Maddox's mind, but when Frank

Chacon had come calling and Maddox took money for the hit, he had crossed a line and was now a hired assassin, regardless of his justification.

Sure, Maddox had taken out targets before, but it had always been on Uncle Sam's behalf and on the government payroll. He couldn't sugarcoat what he had now become. But so what? The CIA had fired him, and this was what he did best. Protecting Sonia and taking out a piece of garbage like Johan Brull for almost as much as he made in an entire year was just gravy. He was out of a job now, so he might as well freelance.

CHAPTER FORTY-ONE

INDICTED

Arlington, Virginia

MADDOX WAS STILL IN BED WHEN HE HEARD SONIA cursing in the condo's kitchen.

"Babe?" a barely awake Maddox called out.

Sonia entered their bedroom going on about "those assholes" and holding the morning edition of the *Washington Post*.

The sight of her wearing nothing but his Minnesota Twins T-shirt woke him up more than her cursing.

She dropped onto the bed next to Maddox, who was now sitting up, and laid the newspaper on the bed in front of him so he could read the headline:

Former CIA Station Chief in Venezuela Indicted on Four Counts.

Underneath was a picture of Maddox's entering the Capitol building to appear in front of the House Permanent Select Committee on Intelligence. The article was short, too short to really be an article. It was more of an announcement:

Colin Ng, Washington Post | November 25, 2002

WASHINGTON, DC - Peter Maddox, the Central Intelligence Agency station chief in Venezuela, who operated under the pseudonym Rick Castro, was indicted on four counts of obstruction and lying to Congress.

Mr. Maddox appeared before the US House Permanent Select Committee on Intelligence, chaired by Texas Republican Dan King. Due to the highly classified nature of the inquiry, the committee hearing was closed to the public. The committee has been looking into any role the United States, and particularly the CIA, had in the failed coup d'état against Hugo Chávez in Venezuela this past April.

Sources speaking on the condition of anonymity, due to the classified nature of the hearing, indicated that Mr. Maddox refused to answer questions and continuously invoked his right to take the Fifth Amendment against self-incrimination.

The indictment marks the first time that a CIA station chief has been charged with crimes allegedly carried out during his duties as a CIA operative. Mr. Maddox was expelled from Venezuela in late April by the Chávez administration and has been given a lifetime ban from returning to Venezuela.

We were unable to locate Mr. Maddox for comment. His attorney, Ted Trumbo, refused to comment aside from saying his client is "a real American hero."

Maddox chuckled at the truth behind the article. "Anonymous sources my ass," Maddox laughed, knowing that it was Max Hoban, or more likely his top aide since he would be too chicken shit to be the actual source of an agency leak.

"Unable to locate," meant they hadn't even tried to contact him directly. They just went to his attorney, but it made the journalist look better, like he was really covering all the bases.

"I can't believe they're doing this to you," Sonia said, her anger fading into sadness.

"Honey, we've talked about this. Ted warned that this was a possibility. They want a scapegoat, and it's me." Maddox put his arms around her.

Ted Trumbo had already informed him that an indictment was certain, that he was already working on his defense, and not to worry. But until it was official, Maddox hadn't seen the need to tell Sonia, just in case the indictment fell through. The newspaper confirmed it had not fallen through, and Sonia began to cry.

"It's my fault; I ruined your career and now you might go to jail," a teary-eyed Sonia said.

"Hey, babe, we've covered this too. You are zero to blame for anything that has happened. Zero."

"I don't know what I'll do if you go to jail," she said.

"I'm not going to jail, don't you worry about that," Maddox replied, laughing.

"I still feel bad," Sonia said.

Smiling, Maddox said, "If it makes you feel better, we can call it even since I ruined your life in Venezuela.

"You're such an ass," Sonia said, playfully elbowing him.

"Hey now, that's assault," he said as his hands wandered up inside her T-shirt.

"You're so bad; you just read that you're being indicted and you want to have sex?"

"Come on, baby, I might go to jail . . ." Maddox said, laughing.

"You're such an asshole," she said.

As they lay down together, the phone began ringing.

"Don't answer that," he said as they continued kissing in bed.

CHAPTER FORTY-TWO

INSPECTOR GENERAL

Langley, Virginia

MADDOX HAD BEEN ON SUSPENSION SINCE HE RESURFACED from Costa Rica and in limbo while the Congressional hearings had gone on, but now that he was under indictment, he was summoned to meet with Max Hoban at Langley.

The meeting was on a different floor from the Western Hemisphere desk, which was a good thing; he was too embarrassed by all the recent events to want to see any of his coworkers.

Maddox entered the conference room for the meeting. It was a room he'd never been inside during all his years with the agency, but it looked just like any one of the other conference rooms littered throughout the building, bland and awash in the phosphorescent glow of buzzing overhead lights. The lights actually remind him of a bug zapper. *And I'm a bug,* he thought.

The large table in the middle of the room could easily sit

ten to fifteen people, but there were only four chairs. On one side of the table sat Max Hoban, front and center. His deputy, Phil Hughes, flanked his right side. Maddox didn't know the dirty blond, mustachioed, forty something Hughes well enough to determine if he was an asshole like his boss. Sometime people couldn't choose who they worked for.

Maddox didn't recognize the man flanking Hoban's left. He was rather tall and gangly looking, with black hair and eyes; his pale skin indicated he didn't get out much, and Maddox put his age at around fifty.

The final chair at the table was directly across from Hoban, Hughes, and the mystery man. It was empty, waiting for Maddox. Two other men stood by the door. Maddox didn't recognize them either, but they were young, fit, and they wore military high-and-tight haircuts. Enforcers, probably recently recruited to the CIA Security Forces from the army or the marines.

The reason for the meeting was clear to Maddox. The CIA was cutting him loose. The two goons were there in case he flipped out. You just never knew how someone who had been fired would react, and that was at a normal corporate-type job. Maddox was a former Ranger trained in black ops, and Hoban knew Maddox hated him as much as he hated Maddox.

"Everyone's so serious," Maddox said as he stood behind the empty chair and took a look around the room.

"Please take a seat, Mr. Maddox," Phil Hughes said as he waved at the empty chair.

Maddox pulled the chair out and sat. He took a quick glance at the two goons behind him. They had moved from standing by the door to hovering right behind him.

"Let me guess; I'm fired," Maddox said.

Hoban had a black file on the table in front of him.

"Mr. Maddox, I believe you know my deputy, Phil Hughes," Hoban said, pointing to him.

"I do," Maddox replied.

"This is Matthias Kill; he's the special assistant to the inspector general," Hoban said, now pointing to the mystery man.

Maddox recognized the name immediately. Anyone with a last name like Kill who worked in the Office of Inspector General—the OIG, the CIA's equivalent to an internal affairs department—was impossible to forget.

Matthias Kill had worked for the Philadelphia PD for twenty-five years, the last ten years as an internal affairs detective. Then he had joined the CIA and was directly placed into the OIG; he had been there for the last five years, going after the CIA's own men and women. Kill's presence only further confirmed the purpose of this meeting: Maddox was being booted out.

Inspector Kill didn't say a word after being introduced, just gave a Maddox a quick glance of acknowledgment.

"Who are the two goons behind me?" Maddox asked, pointing at the guards.

"Jesus Christ, Maddox, don't start with your shit," Hoban barked.

Inspector Kill gently tapped Hoban's arm, silencing him before calmly replying, "They're OIG Special Agents, Mr. Maddox."

"So I'm being fired?" Maddox asked as he sat back in his chair, getting comfortable. He wasn't going to give Hoban the pleasure of seeing him riled up.

Hoban opened up the black file in front of him. "You're finished, Maddox," he said as he pulled out a single piece of paper and shoved it across the table. "This is your dismissal letter; you're being terminated from the agency for disobeying orders while in the field, going AWOL for six days, and for conduct unbecoming a CIA officer."

Maddox looked down at the letter with the official seal of the Office of the Inspector General. It was signed by the IG and Executive Director Max Hoban. A third signature line stood blank, but printed underneath was his own name

"I'm not signing shit without my lawyer," Maddox said as he shoved the paper back across the table to Hoban.

"Cut the shit, Maddox; you're done," Hoban said. "This just confirms that you've received this letter and that you've been notified of your termination, effective immediately. You'll get thirty days' severance pay."

"That's generous," Maddox said sarcastically.

Hoban's face began to flush and he threw the letter back at Maddox.

"You fucking ingrate. It was my recommendation you not get shit, but DI Van Loon insisted you get thirty days' severance for the supposedly good work you've done as a cowboy for the agency." Hoban seethed, his face now bright red.

Maddox smiled coyly. He had gotten under Hoban's skin again. It was petty, but he enjoyed making him fume.

"Don't expect a thank-you card, asshole," Maddox said, looking right into Hoban's pale blue eyes. "And I'm not signing shit without my lawyer." Maddox shoved the letter back to Hoban.

"Gentlemen," Inspector Kill interrupted, "that's enough." He grabbed the letter and the black file in front of Hoban and slid them over to the spot in front of him. He then put the letter back into the folder.

"That's fine, Mr. Maddox. I'll get this to your lawyer. Ted Trumbo, correct?"

"That's right," Maddox answered. "Are we done here?"

Maddox glanced over at Hoban and gave him another amused smile.

"Mr. Maddox, the OIG is working closely with the DA who has indicted you," Kill said. "We're investigating, and if you cooperate, we can make sure you don't do any time. We might even get them to drop the charges. We know Mr. Richard Philips and elements of SOG were active during or aware of the coup. If you're willing to cooperate, we can make these charges go away." Kill smiled.

"Not interested in OIG deals, but that piece of shit knew," Maddox said, pointing to Hoban.

"Bullshit!" Hoban screamed.

"Mr. Hoban, please," Kill said, and then continued addressing Maddox. "We know you weren't a rogue agent acting alone; we know your superiors knew, and that's who we want. You were just following orders, right?"

"I'm not saying shit, and I'm not interested in any deal. You can all go fuck yourselves."

Maddox glanced over at the two guards behind him. "That goes for your two goons as well." Maddox was grinning again.

"So be it," Inspector Kill said as he quickly picked up the folder, tapped it once against the table, and put it back down, indicating the meeting was over. "If you want to go to prison, so be it."

Then he addressed the two men standing behind Maddox, "Special Agent Brown, Special Agent White, please escort Mr. Maddox to his car," and waved his hands at them dismissively before turning his attention back toward Maddox.

"We will get to the bottom of any malfeasance within the CIA. The days of overthrowing foreign governments are long over, Mr. Maddox."

Hoban leered at him from across the conference table.

"We're rooting you all out, Maddox. People like you and Dick Philips. Cowboys." Bitterness dripped from his words.

"I'm sure Al-Qaeda will be cheering you on," Maddox said as he got up from his chair.

He motioned toward the two guards with his head and said, "Let's go, boys; walk me out." Then he headed out the door with the two agents in tow.

EPILOGUE

THE SMELL OF CHOCOLATE CHIP COOKIES PERMEATED THE
air of Maddox's condo.

"Are those for me?" he asked with a smile, already knowing
the answer.

"Mmm, no; they're for the open house," Sonia replied
furrowing her brow.

"But if you leave in the next ten minutes, you can have one
for the road." She smiled as she held out a hot cookie out of
Maddox's reach.

"Deal," Maddox smiled back.

Though the proverb "hope springs eternal" was rather
cheesy, Maddox couldn't help think just that. The cold winter
of Northern Virginia was fading into memory as another beautiful spring day melted the snow and warmed weary, cold
winter bones.

Sonia Collins, former Venezuelan real estate broker and
owner of Bolívar Realty, had been licensed as a realtor by the

Commonwealth of Virginia and joined the Kenwood Hayes Realty Group as a real estate agent, covering the most populous region of Northern Virginia and the Washington DC Metropolitan Area.

Luckily, Maddox had wired her money out of Venezuela right before the coup of last year. After months of limbo and living off their savings in Maddox's Arlington condo, the stress of the past year had worn them down.

Being hunted down by the head of the Venezuelan Secret Police, Johan Brull, and escaping Caracas with fake passports. Hiding out in Costa Rica. Then watching the man she loved go on trial for obstruction and lying to Congress. Then getting fired by the CIA. It was a miracle that their relationship had survived it all, but it had.

Sonia was beginning to feel excited about being able to get back to work, and real estate beckoned. She had missed working in the real estate business.

Around the end of October or early November, Sonia didn't recall the exact date; Maddox had given her the all clear to contact her friends in Caracas. Her first call had been to her friend Graciela Kohl.

Graciela had begun crying upon hearing Sonia's voice on the other end of the phone. She had seen Maddox on the news, so she knew he was in the CIA and that he had been arrested. She had feared the worst had happened to Sonia since her boyfriend was the spy accused of masterminding the coup.

Graciela had tried to continue running Bolívar Realty along with the other agents, Jerry Low and Eddy Rocamora. Unable to afford the expensive lease, they had moved into a much smaller, less posh office space. Then, Jerry Low decided to take control of Bolívar Realty and forced Graciela and Eddy out. Jerry had continued to run Bolívar Realty, but without the lucrative embassy business, the CIA bankroll, and the Sonia

Collins flare for the realty business, the company was just a shell of its former glory days. Eventually, Jerry couldn't even afford the cheaper office space, so he had shut it down and moved to Thailand, where the cost of living was cheaper and it was safer and more welcoming toward American expats.

Graciela and Eddy had joined Century 21's Caracas office, but it wasn't the same for Graciela without her friend. A few months later, she quit and began to work for a public relations agency. Eddy had continued on with Century 21 and was doing quite well.

Even though Sonia was happy to be moving on with her professional life, her personal had been in tatters while the indictments were hanging over Maddox. The two of them had begun to talk about long-terms plans, including marriage, but Maddox's legal problems had made thinking too far ahead difficult.

Special Assistant Inspector General Matthias Kill, and Executive Director Max Hoban had teamed up with Assistant District Attorney Roy Carr to make an example of the disgraced former CIA station chief of Venezuela.

Fortunately Maddox's attorney, Ted Trumbo, had proved to be not just an excellent attorney but a true friend; he mounted a vigorous defense for his client and plead not guilty on all four charges against him.

Dick Philips had warned Maddox that the politicians wanted blood, and that was exactly how it had played out, as for months, the legal maneuvering made its way through the court system, which was as slow as a DMV line.

Maddox didn't see his mentor after the evening they drank very expensive Scotch in Philips's den. It had been best that they not communicate while Maddox was under indictment, but at least, with his forced retirement, Philips was left alone and received his full pension.

Trumbo had put forward a motion to declassify CIA data as he mounted his defense for Maddox, something that the CIA refused to do, so Trumbo sued to get access to CIA data. While the lawsuit had dragged on, Maddox and Sonia's lives continued to be in limbo.

Finally, after months of legal back and forth, Attorney General Brenda Witt refused to declassify the information the defense sought, and Judge John Root dismissed all charges against Peter Maddox. Just like that, the legal battle was over.

Ted Trumbo and his wife Ellie had taken Sonia and Maddox out for a celebratory dinner and night on the town. It felt like a huge weight had been lifted from their shoulders as they enjoyed the night out, worry free for the first time in a long time. Maddox just wished he could have seen Max Hoban and Inspector Kill's faces at the news that they couldn't touch him in a court of law.

It wasn't total vindication for Maddox, though. The court didn't say he was innocent, just that they couldn't proceed due to the defense not having access to classified materials. The CIA firing still stood, and Maddox had no desire to fight that. He wanted to move forward. So, for now, he was unemployed.

It was heart wrenching for Sonia to see Maddox publically ousted in disgrace, and the economic impact was very costly as well. Maddox's pension was gone, along with his main source of income and healthcare benefits. His thirty days' severance pay had been used up months before, and now there were legal fees to deal with.

Just like in Venezuela, he was now persona non grata within the CIA. The White House washed its hands of him and continued to paint him as a rogue agent who acted alone in Venezuela to overthrow Chávez. Word of the Libyan terrorist training camp on Venezuelan soil never became public, and that was fine with Maddox.

Freed from the legal yoke around their necks, Sonia and Maddox grew tired of life in the Washington DC metropolitan area. He used to love the view of the DC skyline from his ninth-floor living room balcony, but soon it just reminded him of the political bullshit going on down there.

Sonia, who was accustomed to living a lot closer to the equator, was happy to have survived a Northern Virginia winter but wasn't keen on living through a second one. With Maddox's legal troubles over, they decided to move to Florida so Sonia could be closer to her mom and sister.

Before they could move, however, Sonia had to sell Maddox's condo. It was realtor Sonia Collins's fourth active listing. The condo was in a trendy condominium location in the popular Courthouse neighborhood in the heart of the Rosslyn-Ballston corridor of Arlington.

The Court House Metro rail station was just two blocks away and coffee shops, shopping, and restaurants were all nearby. The condo listing description boasted about the premium finishes and appliances and the breathtaking views of the river and the capital city.

Maddox explored his employment options. Former employees of the CIA usually ended up making a lot more money as independent contractors for the CIA, but Max Hoban had ensured Maddox would never work as a contractor for the agency. Tom Rose said he could keep him busy as a contractor with the British security firm Rose had worked for since retiring. It was steady work baby-sitting journalists and corporate types traveling to hot spots abroad. Ruben Guzman also had freelance work for Maddox in Colombia, and then there were the even higher paying gigs from very rich men like Frank Chacon who wanted enemies like Johan Brull killed.

Taking out Brull had been one thing, but taking on contract killings solely for the money was another. Maddox wasn't sure that was something he could do again, even though Chacon had more scores to settle. It was definitely something he could not discuss with Sonia, but no matter what lay ahead, at least they were together.

Sonia smiled and gave him a hot chocolate chip cookie; she got up on her toes and kissed him gently on the lips before kicking him out of the condo for the upcoming open house.

Maddox smiled as he stepped outside, chewing on the cookie. His future was uncertain, but he had Sonia in his life, and that's all that mattered.

A NOTE FROM THE AUTHOR

Thank you for taking the time to read THE ASSET.

Your review on Amazon would greatly help increase its visibility to other potential readers.

Visit my website at www.AlanPetersen.com to connect with me and stay updated on my work. Thank you!

ABOUT THE AUTHOR

Alan Petersen, a native of Costa Rica, was raised in a culturally diverse environment with an American father and a Costa Rican mother. This multicultural background influences his writing as he explores the themes of cultural identity in his novels.

Alan now resides in San Francisco with his wife and furry friends, and frequently travels to visit his family in Costa Rica.

When he is not writing, Alan can be found hosting his podcast, MEET THE THRILLER AUTHOR, where he interviews prominent mystery and thriller writers.

Connect with Alan on his website, www.AlanPetersen.com, and follow his journey on social media.

facebook.com/AlanPetersenBooks

twitter.com/AlanPetersen

instagram.com/AuthorAlanPetersen

amazon.com/author/AlanPetersen

bookbub.com/authors/alan-petersen

ALSO BY ALAN PETERSEN

The Pete Maddox Series:

The Asset

She's Gone

Odd Jobs

The Elijah Shaw Series:

Gringo Gulch

The Past Never Dies

Always There

www.ingramcontent.com/pod-product-compliance
Lightning Source LLC
Chambersburg PA
CBHW060907250626
47159CB00008B/2900